THE SLIDE

AARON RYAN

Award-winning author of the bestselling post-apocalyptic alien invasion 6-book saga *Dissonance*, the Christian dystopian fiction saga *The End,* the sci-fi thriller *Forecast, God is Not Santa, The Christian Kids Values, Identity & Affirmation Picture Book Series* and many more.

Published in 2025, Edition 1.

Paperback ISBN # 9781965372067 · Hardcover ISBN # 9781965372074
eBook ISBN # 9781965372081

Edited by CM LLC. Published independently.

Cover art by Aaron Ryan & CM LLC

This is a work of fiction. Any similarities to persons living or dead, or actual events is purely coincidental.

For Sweeps, Bren & AJ:
my true loves.

Thank you for keeping me from sliding.

Chapters

"A person often meets his destiny on the road he took to avoid it."

-Jean de La Fontaine

"Men are not prisoners of fate, but only prisoners of their own minds."

-Franklin D. Roosevelt

"If you can't change your fate, change your attitude."

-Amy Tan

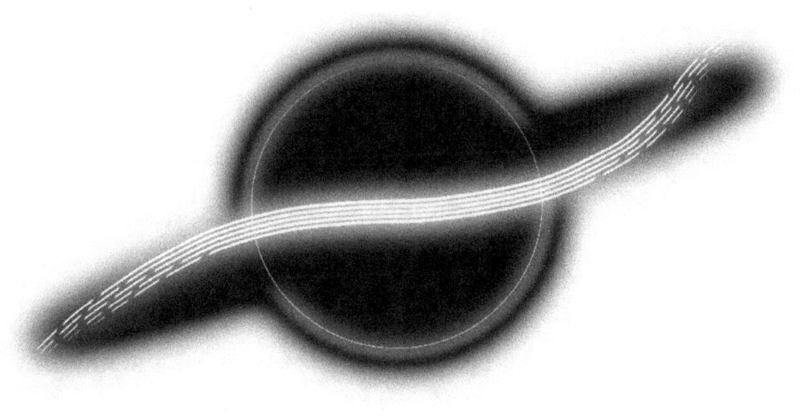

Note on AI

We live in an age of AI. Every day, more and more services spring up promising revolutionary and innovative results using artificial intelligence. The authoring industry is not immune to this.

I want every one of my readers to know that not once did I employ, nor will I *ever* employ, the use of AI to sculpt any part of any of my stories. Those who know me know that I am staunchly and adamantly opposed to such cheats.

I'm very proud to be a verified human. The ability to create is a gift that I was endowed by my Creator, and I will never forfeit that nor set it aside to propagate something synthetic and imitative.

Everything you've read by me in this novel, and in my other works, is 100% entirely created by me, the genuine article. I'm a verified human, and always will be.

To my fellow authors, I urge you to preserve the sacred gift of human creation and never stoop to such lows. Always cherish this gift you've been given. If you encounter writer's block, take a break. Don't cop out. Don't take the road more traveled by. Don't cheat. Toe the line for all of us, and keep creation – *true* unadulterated creation – alive.

Long live humanity.

Sincerely,

Aaron Ryan,
Verified Human

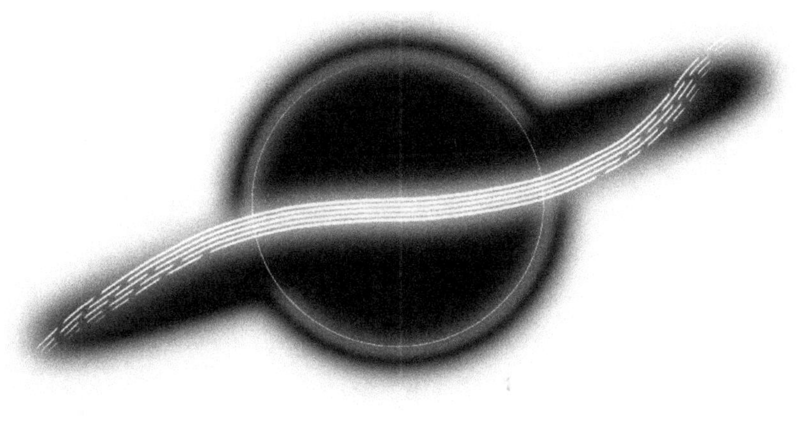

PART ONE:
THE LAST DAYS

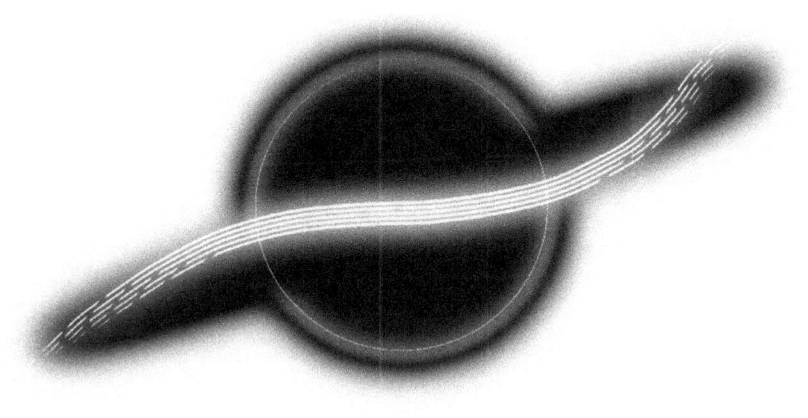

1 | Incoming

November 6th, 2025

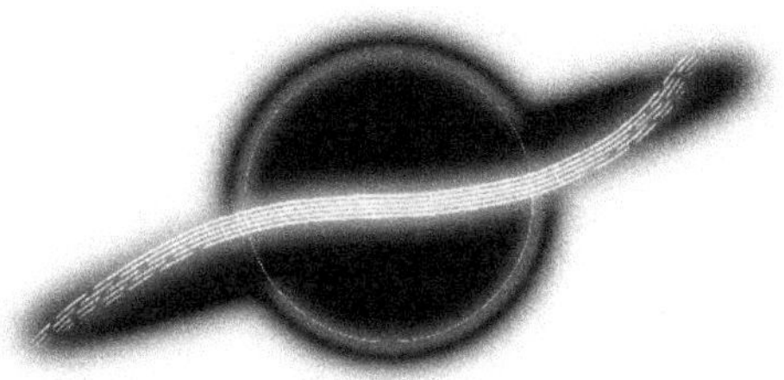

We were reading it right. At least, we wanted to. But it defied belief.

I was now sitting with Dina Jensen in the UW lab.

"And you're sure? Not some kind of…I don't know, transitory anomaly or otherwise?" I asked her, watching the signal crawl across the screen.

"I'm sure, Dane," she replied. "DSCOVR thought it was something in flux between two overlapping stars, but they're sure now. Everything else is already catalogued. Its mass would suggest a limitation of orbital or suborbital speeds, but it's above average velocity for the category. Over one-tenth the speed of light. Averaging twenty-one point three."

I just stared at it, my mouth agape. "*Damn.* That sucker's huge. DSN has it at thirty-seven times the mass of

Sagittarius A." I bit my knuckles as I watched. "Call Isaac right away and have him get down here to run reciprocal."

"Yep," Dina replied. She punched up numbers into her keypad as I whirled around to telemetry. "Are we sure it's *not* Sgr A, not some kind of echoed con-?"

"No!" I snapped. "It is *not* Sagittarius. Confirmed. No way the Milky Way's one got bloated that big, that fast, and Sgr A has been stationary for years. Still next to Sagittarius and Scorpius, five point six degrees south of the ecliptic," I verified. "It's *not* Sgr A."

Sure enough, it was traveling, and traveling *fast*. Twenty-one thousand three hundred miles per second. *Over one-tenth the speed of light,* I mused slowly, with horror. Powerful jets of particles trailed behind it that were even *at* the speed of light. "Look at the trail. This thing is no blip, as Isaac suspected. This is an ELE maker," I muttered. Dina heard me. She knew all too well what an Extinction Level Event was, and had researched them for years.

"Yes, it is," she breathed coldly, and then jerked back to her com. Her voice was stern. "Isaac, it's Dina. I'm with Dane. Get down to E3 right away. *Yes,* right away. Need you on recip." Technically, the two of them were contemporaries, and neither was subordinate to the other; both reported to me. Dina, however, was ready to whip him into shape.

Dina Jensen was 24 years old and all manner of gentility: focused and purposeful. African-American and pleasantly conversational with everyone, she was always nice to be around, and a pleasure to partner with.

Isaac, on the other hand, was about as quiet and stoic as you could get. Born to Israeli parents who had emigrated to the United States in 1998, he was her polar opposite: reserved and analytical, studious and standoffish.

"Mother of all that's holy," I breathed one more time, and my flesh crawled. "Look how fast it's spitting out the trail!"

Dina then slid her chair up close to mine, squinting at the screen. Our faces glowed blue. "It's not TON 618," she said calmly, trying to compose herself, I guess. "That's forty billion times the mass of our sun! That's a relief, I think? I mean, if the satellites were glitchy and the VLA arrays were misinterpreting something up close as far away, TON 618 is thirty to forty times our whole solar system in diameter, it would swallow us completely already. Gravitational waves only catch 'em sometimes…"

"There's no way we could have missed this-"

"I mean, with its makeup it could be Phoenix A or Arp 220, IC 1459, Messier 77-" she kept going. "Neither LIGO nor Virgo had it, nothing within IMBH range… no on RIFT-"

"Nothing on proximity alert from DSN, nothing from Harvard and Smithsonian, ESA never said anything-" I whispered next to her, checking other readouts, squinting, and feeling my knuckles flex. We were totally talking over ourselves, not hearing each other.

"Doesn't fit the description of a quasar," Dina continued, studying with me, "not a hypercompact; that thing is seriously big, Currier."

"Yes, it is."

Isaac strode in briskly, donning his specs. "What's up?" His voice wasn't nonchalant, but it wasn't primed for alarm. Not yet. He yawned into the darkness of the room, our faces awash with monitor light. "The one I found?"

I turned to him, pointing at the screen. "Yep. Take a look at your blip, Isaac," I said, somewhat accusingly. "Still think that's a passerby?"

He bent over the bank of monitors, and it didn't take long for his mouth to drop. "HLX-1?" I shook my head. "Messier? Not Sagittari-"

"No, it's *not* Sagittarius," I insisted. "Good lord, people. Look at its size! That's a supermassive, yes, but it's on steroids. It's a super-*super*-massive. And look how fast it's going!" I slid out of the way, running my hands through my hair and filling my lungs with cramped air. "Get on recip, please, Isaac."

"Roger, on it." He squinted and leaned in further, then his head cocked and his eyes went wide. "OK, mirroring Dina *now*. Wait - its accelerating? Twenty-one k? There's no way. It must have… merged with another one?"

"Ya *think*?" I asked, with intentional sass, stifling a burp that was trying to make its way out of me. I glanced at my watch. The stupid symposium was going to start in twenty minutes, and attendance was mandatory.

"Cut it out… I didn't know," he said, sitting down and typing into a console. "Yeah, it definitely did. Spiral trails confirm it. Gravitational waves all around it are off the charts. Dina, who's our contact at DSN Tidbinbilla again?"

"St. James," she said with a shrug. "Doubt if he's up right now. It's 2 am in Aussie land."

"Yeah, he'll have a better vantage point with his morning light below the equator," Isaac said. "But that means we won't hear for another three to six hours. The way that thing's cruising…"

"It's cruising, alright," I droned, glaring at the monitors and sighing yet again. I tapped my fingers on the desk impatiently, trying to think. We needed to act.

"Okay, we can't wait," I resolved. "Dina, issue a communique to DSN, whoever it is, the- ya know, those guys at the Deep Space Advanced Radar Capability initiative office," -here I snapped my fingers at her trying to remember- "uh, the NRAO VLAs, and especially Nick at the GEODDS office." Jensen's fingers were flying across her terminal. "Tell them we've got a supermassive on the way, point of intersection unknown, time unknown, potentially ELE, threat level orange. Recommend launching probes right away to confirm," I said, rubbing my hands fiercely against my face and stretching my mouth. A nervous yawn escaped me. Too much staring at screens, and my eyes were tired. "Send that last one up to the Secretary General's office now, please. And get back to DSCOVR and send them confirmation of what we've found. EHT as well. What's right ascension and declination now?"

"Checking," Isaac stuttered slowly, studying his screen. At length, he scribbled down some numbers. "RA ten hours, sixteen minutes, thirty-two seconds. Dec plus thirty-six degrees, twenty-three minutes, thirty seconds."

I tilted my head and squinted. "Not possible. That's close to TON 618! How could it just lurch into view so suddenly and escape monitoring all this time? I don't understand. It's like a bee turning into a friggin' semi-truck."

Farragut shrugged. "Well, they *did* merge." I scowled at him. "Hey, I just read 'em like I see 'em."

I said nothing in reply, and just watched him. A notion passed through my head that was too incredible to believe and too frightening to rule out.

Here I was, a measly 'nothing' scientist at the University of Washington with my undergrads. If those readings were right, we might have just discovered a supermassive black hole that was on its way to our tiny little corner of the universe. On its way to us. And on its way *fast*.

And then, pinging me with an annoying alert that would see me pulled away from what was *truly* urgent, the symposium calendar reminder sounded. All I could do was force out a heavy sigh and request that the gang keep me in the loop and text me with any new developments, just before I scampered off.

Yet, the entire way, my mind couldn't help but draw a parallel from this new development… to the development I called my own. It couldn't be coincidence.

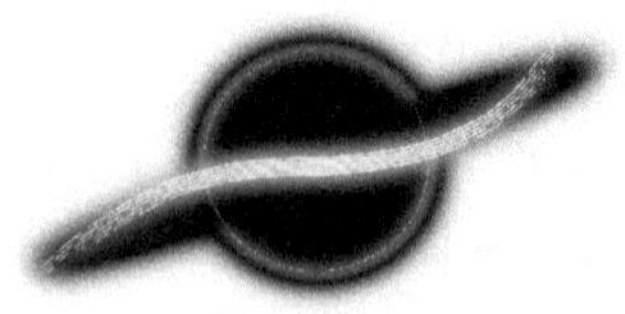

"The best thing about humanity is its technology. And the worst thing about humanity is… wait for it… its technology."

Everyone laughed, and the sound of it resounded throughout Turner Auditorium at UW. This was the beginning of the lecturer's closing statements, and he thought it was downright ingenious and right on the money. "Mankind is always in the pursuit of bigger, better, faster, cleaner. Anything ending with -er," he said.

"But I'd like to remind you," he continued, "of that classic movie from only thirty-four years ago, *Jurassic Park*. In it, one of the protagonists, Dr. Ian Malcolm, cautioned an overly ambitious British billionaire with these words." Everyone leaned in. I didn't. I'd already heard it, and my mind was elsewhere, frankly, hoping that Dina and Isaac were taking care of everything back in the lab.

"*Your scientists were so preoccupied with whether or not they* could *that they didn't stop to think if they* should," the lecturer breathed.

Again, everyone nodded. Frankly, that was the bottom line, right? Hubris. Overextending one's neck. Risky business. Thank goodness I never demonstrate such behavior. I knew my limits. I knew what worked and what didn't, and I knew where my ceiling was.

I already knew that I *could,* and I was convinced that I *should.* It wasn't a question of morality or ambiguity over any kind of ethics or responsibility. It was simply a question of *when.* I had seen Jurassic Park, sure. Gene splicing and dinosaurs. The stuff of fiction. That wasn't my thing.

Interstellar phenomena and physics were my thing. What he was talking about was pop culture from a bygone era intruding upon modern progress, to be sure. Certainly, a notion to consider, of course, for most people.

But I'd already considered it, right? Dinosaurs and people are *not* the same thing. I admittedly rolled my eyes, sitting there, as he droned on and on with silly tripe and scare tactics. I think I may have even noticeably shook my head. He's talking about something sixty-five million years ago, and yet I had just laid eyes upon a potential Extinction Level Event in the making. God only knew how much time we might have left. That thing could intersect with Earth's orbit in five hundred years... or five weeks. We wouldn't know until Tidbinbilla confirmed it in a few hours.

That thing... man, it was on my mind during the entire symposium, and it was irritating to have to sit through knowing that Jensen and Farragut were seeing things that I wasn't. I would only be able to catch up with them once we were let out, but the text updates were coming in hard and fast, and it was difficult to focus.

With every fiber of my being and the fire of a thousand suns, I felt that I'd been given *Courier* for just such a time as this. Coincidence? A scientific impossibility. Nature abhors a vacuum. Checks and balances. The stars had aligned just so as to put this in my mind so as to be ready for whatever that thing was out there that was on its way to us. It was not chance; it was *destiny.* If that thing out there truly *was* a supermassive, then that meant my invention might prove timely beyond words.

But where would we go?

It was November 6th already, and I couldn't believe the year was nearly done. My deadline was coming up quickly, and it would take every ounce of me to fundraise and rally all the support that I could for *Courier 3.1*. I already had the tests to show everyone… now I just needed the chance to perform it on a live human subject, and I already had a volunteer.

Me.

"Hey, Currier," said a sharp voice, wrenching me out of my thoughts. I looked over.

"Yeah?"

"We gonna get something to eat?"

I gawked at her, her head tilted down and her eyebrows up, awaiting my reply. Trapper was always eating. *Always.* I never understood how she could maintain her lithe figure if she was always stuffing her face. Her metabolism was the stuff of fiction. I laughed.

"Sure, Trapper, sure. Just let me grab my things," I said. "I can't stay long though; I've gotta get back to the lab. But I'll go with you to pick it up and I'll scarf it down on my way back."

"Suit yourself," she replied in a drab monotone.

Megan Trapper was three years my junior at UW, but she was a kindred intellect. Very saucy and a quick wit. She's always kept me focused and grounded. After all, I always needed to have a comeback at the ready should she try to one-up me.

"Yo quiero Taco Bell, Señor Dane."

"Fine."

"No sour cream for you, pudgy," she shot my way, glancing at my midsection. Oh! I forgot to mention she was brutally honest, too.

"Watch it, toothpick," I fired back absentmindedly, reading the latest from Dina while collecting my books and unconsciously sucking in my gut. For an undergrad, Megan Trapper was brazen beyond her tender age of twenty-seven.

"Oooh, *toothpick*," she jousted. "Clever. That one's new."

"Yeah well, you undergrads are getting a little too big for your britches. We have to keep you in your place. And I already used 'stick' twice I think. *Toothpick* will suffice for today." I grinned at her. "Oh, wait, what am I thinking? I can't have tacos," I said, remembering my GI issues.

"Why not?" she screeched in incredulity, gawking at me. "Oh, right. The… *problem.*"

"Yep. Tummy troubles," I said. "Grumbling. Better play it safe and grab some Subway."

She smirked. "*You* play it safe with Subway. I'm grabbing tacos. Catch up with ya later," she said. She leapt over the balcony railing with her backpack firmly affixed over her shoulders, her red hair bouncing clumsily against her nondescript straps. "Toothpick in pursuit of dinner," she offered with a final grunt as she propelled herself over it, sprinting for the exit. I lugged myself over the railing too, panting hard and apologizing to the grad student next to me as he tried to make a clean exit himself. There were grads and undergrads all around in a sea of students, and

Trapper's figure was growing tinier in the distance as I tried to wade through.

Trapper was aptly named. Here I was, trapped, while she was off again. I glanced down at my phone for the latest.

Telemetry confirmed, Dina typed. *It most definitely is a super-supermassive. And Dane? It's headed right for us.*

This just got worse. My stomach grumbled. Here came the burps, and I hadn't even eaten yet.

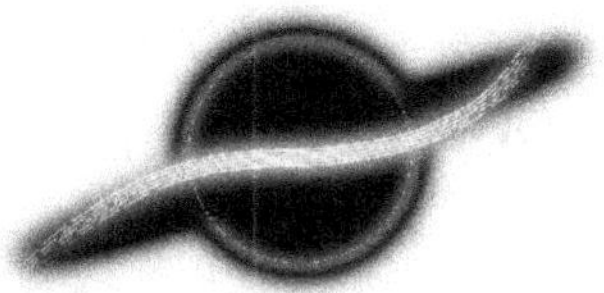

Dinner was over. The Subway was still rumbling in my tummy, and the sulfur burps were coming strong and fast now. It's amazing how fast they come. They're revolting, but that's what you get when your nerves are on fire, you know things people don't, and you've eaten too fast.

I know better than to eat too fast.

I texted Megan that I'd catch up with her tomorrow. I wasn't sure if I meant that. All I knew right now was that I needed to catch up with Isaac and Dina and assess current position. And then I had to get back to my apartment and keep working. Trapper protested firmly, desiring company in her unapologetically demanding tone with multiple exclamation marks.

I ignored her. She knew *Courier* was important and that I had to get back to it. She was the *only* one who knew about it beside myself.

Double-timing the University wasn't my intent. But ever since this passion enveloped me, I've wanted *Courier* more than anything in the world. Only two people knew about it, and I wasn't ready to launch any kind of Kickstarter yet; I just had *so* many high hopes for this thing. Aside from a play on my last name, it would be novel… revolutionary… mind-blowing… *life-altering.*

If *Courier 3.1* was truly capable of what I thought it was, it might be able to do exactly what we all needed, and I would be on the cusp of becoming a millionaire. Or billionaire? *Trillionaire??* Move over Jeff Bezos.

Courier 3.1 could deconstruct your atoms and reassemble them somewhere else. Quantum physics didn't grasp the gravity of teleportation. Not yet. And no one knew what it could do but me and Megan. I hadn't even told Dina and Isaac yet. I wasn't ready.

What I *was* ready for was for these accursed sulfur burps to end. Whatever was going on inside me needed to be deconstructed and reconstructed without the physical affliction and ailments. It was gastrointestinal, that much was certain, but beyond that, no one knew, and it seemed like no doctor *wanted* to put their finger on it.

Even worse than the burps was the acid reflux. The heartburn was terrible and unending.

Doctors weren't unanimous, and I'd had so many second opinions that there were now second opinions piggybacked upon second opinions, to multiple powers of second opinions beyond that.

None of them could uniformly pinpoint if it was lactose intolerance, irritable bowel syndrome, Crohn's, ulcerative colitis, gallstones, or God knows what else. I desperately loathed them for that. Every single doctor's appointment ended in irritation. Knowledge is power, right? They didn't know what it was, so I didn't have any power.

But the one area I *did* have power in? I could show them that I knew more than they did about something else. After all, what else are graduate studies for?

The one thing that I knew definitively was that I was going to be Patient Zero for *Courier 3.1*, and that was that. There was no other logical option. In good conscience, I couldn't send Megan Trapper through. *Courier 3.1* was mine, and it was revolutionary, and it would change everything. I had to go through myself first.

But, in the meanwhile, all of that would just have to wait. The docs said what they said, and all of them were 'fairly' certain that it was what they thought it was.

However, the docs might *not* be reading it right. I think they wanted to. But simply surrendering to their beliefs would be an act of defiance.

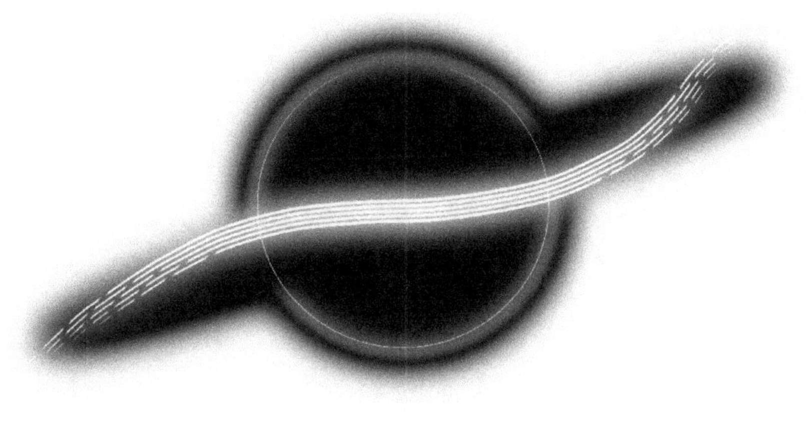

2 | *Outgoing*
November 6th, 2025

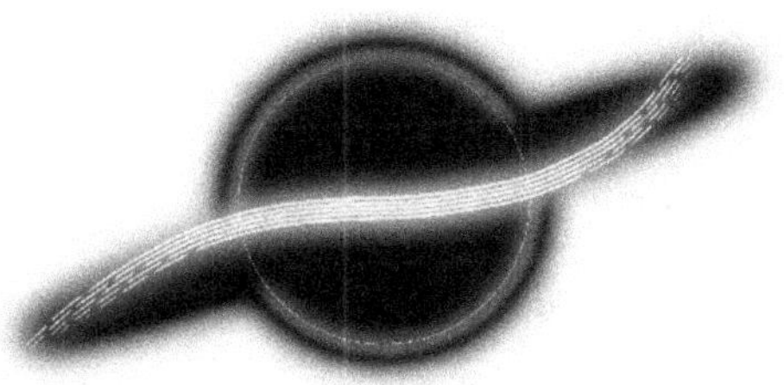

It was high time for a difficult conversation.

AARO head Doctor Ron Sikorsky was a young man stern beyond his years, supremely focused on the All-domain Anomaly Resolution Office's purpose to protect our skies and keep Earth safe. He partnered with planetary defense at the European Space Agency, but they had no love for him. His namesake was bound to the helicopter business as an industry leader, but that didn't mean that he himself was a leader. It was clear our dear Ronnie had his hands full already and didn't want to be bothered with any more – or any *new* – phenomena.

Sorry to ruin your day, Ronnie, I thought, *but there's incoming that you really might want to take a look at before it lands on your head.*

"You've triple-verified telemetry?" he asked Dina.

"Yes, sir, we have," she replied.

He just stared at the screen. "*Shhhit*," he finally groaned. "DOD will have my head now that you've let this get this close to Earth, folks. I hope you're happy."

"Mr. Sikorsky, with all due respect," I began, "this 'thing' just literally appeared two days ago, verified by Mr. Farragut and Ms. Jensen. Look at the speed at which its traveling sir. This isn't a slow-moving traditionally-trackable blip, sir. It's moving at over one-tenth the speed of light. We've confirmed it."

By the look on his face, that defense meant nothing to him. He rubbed his hand through his hair feverishly and then blew out hot steam.

"Alright, keep me apprised. This is not good, folks. Anyone else running reciprocals and checking your readings?"

"Of course, sir," I said. "The typical ones: DSN, the NRAO VLAs, GEODDS, DSCOVR, and EHT," I rattled off, reading Dina's list from earlier that I had requested she update.

"Any idea on point of intersection?"

"Not until we have confirmed with Tidbinbilla in two hours."

"Who's your contact?"

"Henry St. James."

"Someone's gotta wake him. I don't care if he's sleeping. We need answers on this ASAP. Find someone to wake him."

"Roger that, will do," Dina replied.

Sikorsky's mouth closed and he just stared at us somberly through the screen. "This is an ELE, isn't it? Level with me."

I didn't know what to say. The truth would have to suffice. "Yessir, it is. It's bigger than TON 618, and it's growing, sir. We think two of them merged." He remained silent. "Once we get confirmation of its point of intersection, we'll know more then, but it's already drawing too near to us to just glance off. At some point trajectory confirms it'll wander into the Milky Way. That could be weeks or years, we don't know yet. But when that happens…," I trailed off intentionally. My thoughts went once again to *Courier 3.1*, its implications on the black hole, and vice versa.

He nodded grimly. At length he blinked and cleared his head. "Right. Well, get back to me once you've talked to Tidbinbilla."

I nodded back. Sikorsky switched off.

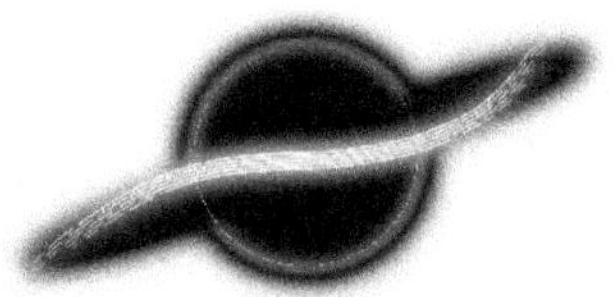

Dina and Isaac were to send me any and all updates. I awaited them eagerly. Sikorsky was not our preferred point of contact for the DOD, but he was all we had right now, and that was the top of our pecking order. He would brief the President soon.

All of our other contacts were buzzing.

So why was I so discontent? If everyone on a need-to-know basis was being brought into the fold, briefed on the potential cataclysm heading our way, why was my stomach grumbling so obstreperously? Shouldn't I be content now that the powers that be were on it? In a matter of time we would have a more definitive confirmation from Tidbinbilla and we'd know more concretely what we were dealing with. There was no sense in worrying.

So why was I worried, gnawing my fingers like a termite through a cedar two-by-four?

My half-eaten Subway sandwich lay beside me on a paper plate, un-gnawed. Paper plates were disposable; recyclable, and less work than doing dishes. I didn't mind the extra expense. Life is a picnic anyway, right?

Might not be in a few weeks, I thought to myself.

I stared ponderously at my glorious invention, downing a sip of water to chase yet another Tums tablet which I had ground into powder.

There they both were. Both chambers.

What was stopping me? Fear? Uncertainty? Didn't I have unquestioned and unqualified belief in *Courier 3.1*? Hadn't it proven itself already?

I looked at Macy. Her paws under her muzzle, those big, black, beautiful eyes stared up at me – that is to say, my *sandwich* – longingly. When she noticed me watching her, that tail began to wag once more.

It was the same tail. It had gone through. Those eyes were the same. That muzzle was the same. Same personality, same longing for human company, same everything. Her harness was five feet behind her draped over the recliner. That was the same too.

I watched her as she continued to wag. She had gone through, and emerged the same. She was biological, animate, and the exact same as she was before going through. She looked, felt, smelled and seemed identical. Even her bad dog breath persisted.

In fact, Macy even seemed improved in some ways. Her graying hairs were gone. Her eyes seemed clearer for a 12-year-old lab-hound-pointer mix. It was almost as if an idealized version of her was interpolated from the source chamber (whom I lovingly called *Nova*), and given form in the target chamber (endearingly dubbed *Ava*), but run through particle reorganization filters that saw fit to selectively remove any degenerative artifacts.

Nova read her, and Ava listened. Nova sent the data, and then Ava assimilated it, reassembling her on the other side, improved, without the gray. Ava could also be used as a relay unit, however, and could further send the signal elsewhere should there be sufficient equipment to receive it. For now, they were tied together, but they didn't need to be; Ava could be positioned halfway around the planet as long as there was sufficient Internet signal; all those 1's and 0's could definitely travel. For the moment, I was compelled to use everything as a LAN configuration to ensure an uninterrupted signal and minimize interference.

So what the heck was stopping me?

The bad breath.

That was it, for sure. I crunched another Tums.

If her bad breath persisted, that was a biological and organic byproduct of canine anatomy that was undesirable. Normal, yes, but still undesirable. Her plaque had not been removed from her teeth. Her left paw still had that strange protrusion. Those had *not* been fixed. So why was she no longer graying and had clearer eyes, but the rest was left uncorrected? Her white beard was now the black of youth.

Some things remained unchanged, and that meant that I would be taking a chance. A chance with my own safety... my own *life.* Could I do it? *Should* I do it? The line from Jurassic Park came back to me once more.

Your scientists were so preoccupied with whether or not they could *that they didn't stop to think if they* should.

I rubbed my face angrily, rolling my eyes. My right knee was bouncing nervously. How many times was I going to do this? To request volunteers and begin screening candidates would let the cat out of the bag, and my secret would be cooked... *and so would I.* My entire future would go up in flames.

No. It had to be *me*, and *only* me.

I stared down at Macy again, my thumbnail now gnawed down to the flesh. She wiggled once more.

"You're alright, aren't you, girl?" I asked her, my eyebrows clenched. "Aren't you? Come here." She instantly rose with ears laid back in happiness as she came to my left side, close to the side table with my Subway on it. Her eyes darted over to it and then back to me. Once more, to the table, and then back to me.

Those eyes of hers are so clear now...

That was it, wasn't it? She was seeing clearly. Was she improved mentally? Were the features that had been improved more internal only, and less aesthetic? Follicular regeneration from the inside out? Ocular nerves repaired and upgraded? Was she smarter even?

She seemed smarter.

I glanced over at Nova, and then slowly over at Ava, subconsciously fetching my sandwich from its plate. Macy's ears went up curiously as she watched my hand. I slowly brought it to her mouth and she took it without hesitation, as my eyes were drawn back to the chambers.

Six feet high and three feet wide, they resembled tiny sound booths, or those older phone booths or talk boxes, but more egglike, and with a DuroLast chrome reflective paneling inside and clean white 3M padding all around. The particle accelerators would be hard to explain to anyone. Cables were suspended parallel to the rear of the chambers in tight conduits mounted with symmetry. The main link conduit conjoined them together in inseparable harmony over a ten foot spread, running from Nova to Ava, and back to Nova for a mirror check once transfers were complete. They worked. They *really* worked, as long as they were kept sterile, dust-free, devoid of confusing particulates and vacuum-sealed. The polyurethane door seals and sweeps ensured a tight airless suction fit. Megan Trapper helped me put them both together.

Good thing I was a neat freak as well. That's why I got Macy; she didn't shed. Nova and Ava would say that they appreciated that, if they had been given AI voices.

The chambers were state of the art, and the UW didn't ask any questions about the requisition orders, nor had they ever sent any kind of auditor to check on the equipment. Keep things practical and don't overblow the budget, and they look the other way. After all, I was in a research lab, and we had funding. They had in this case. Thus, Nova and Ava were born.

It was rudimentary 3D printer firmware at first, and scanners re-coded and adapted to accommodate biological materials beyond the 1's and 0's that the old syntax was built upon. *CourierOS* operated on higher plains than that old stuff, interpreting biological and organic material as truly alive, requiring quantum levels of computation and analysis: higher spheres of thinking. As such, my power bill was astronomical each month. A small price to pay.

Then came the setbacks.

Neither Inky, Pinky, Blinky or Clyde made it. My zebra-tailed finches never knew what hit them, until they were inside out and spliced together inside Ava's receiving dish. That was awful. I couldn't keep birds long enough, and the pet stores were on to me, I feared. Next, Merry and Pippin went through, then, finally, Frodo and Sam.

Same thing. They were all chirpy and contented. They lived a cheerful, happy life on a stick, pecking at seeds one day, and then the next, fused together in an unholy abomination of matted feathers, tissue and intestines, their beaks ground to powder. Neither *Courier 1.0, 1.5, 1.8, 2, 2.6, 2.7, nor 2.9* could figure it out. By *2.7* I was getting close. Sent them through one at a time. But they were stillborn on the other side. They were intact, yes, but frozen in suspended animation: a haunting tribute to a life that was.

That's when I had the breakthrough: *Courier 3.0.* The computer needed to analyze the precise cellular makeup of zebra-tailed finches. Only then would it understand what a zebra-tailed finch was. Same with Macy. I had to sedate her and cut a sample of her tissue – after she went through it was completely healed – and fed it into biometric analysis tubes to get the precise makeup. Then it knew what a lab-hound-pointer was. It understood her hair coloration, her age, her cellular makeup... to a *T.* After that, I was able to simply draw blood and have it scanned in a spectrum analyzer. No more flesh samples. Macy – and I – were brave enough to send her through on 3.1. You should have seen my fingernails; they were gnawed to the bone. I sent two final finches through – Iron Man and Thor – and they made it. They made it! I returned them to the store. No one knew or would even suspect that they were identical facsimiles of their original selves.

So, the question remained: would I be a near-identical facsimile of my original self? Or would I be *me?*

I took another hard look at Macy. Damned if she wasn't absolutely herself. Not just her skin, her hair, her eyes, but *her very soul* – it was her. No doubt.

She wasn't outgoing fodder for the previous *Couriers.* She was here to stay.

There was only one way to find out if I would be here to stay. I had to go through.

Just… once I could eventually get past my own nervousness and fear. Those were standing in the way for one obvious reason: I wanted to live. But if that thing out there was coming to kill us, wasn't I just staving off the inevitable?

I sighed, resigned to wait. I had to get back to the lab anyway. Dina and Isaac were waiting.

I would go through. Just… not yet.

It was time for some definite consternation.

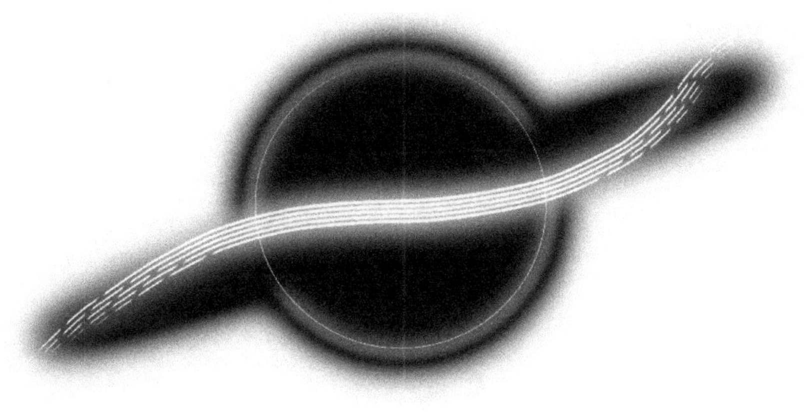

3 | Clarification

November 6th, 2025

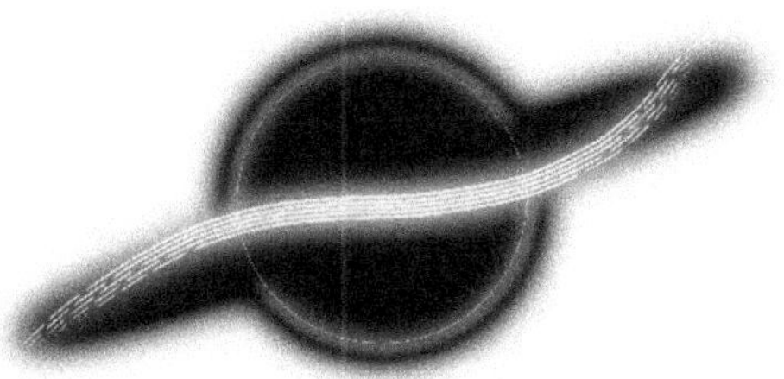

There was no disputing it now.

Redundancy checks were run, and, *unfortunately,* they matched. Henry St. James was reading it exactly as we were, and all doubt was dispelled. "I guess the only thing left to do now is name the bitch," Henry offered sardonically. "That Sheila's a killer and no mistake."

I had not really talked at length with St. James… ever. A heavyset and woolly bedouin who wandered from tech office to tech office, he very clearly filled up his off-hour pints with the strongest alcohol possible. Consequently, his health suffered for it, and his quality of life had deteriorated to filling his chair and staring numbly at screens. Indeed, the glass rim of his obviously full mug could be seen peeking out of the corner of the screen, and his beard glistened.

"You said it," I mumbled in response.

"Look at that light trail," he said with unsuppressed amazement. "She's speeding up too. Incrementally here, of course, but she's on her way."

"Best guess for intercept?" I asked him blandly.

"Us intercepting it or vice versa?" he jested.

I was in no mood for it. "You know what I mean, Henry."

He shook his head. "Well, based on this parabolic course and its current location, we're probably looking at late February, I'd say." He drained his mug noisily as if resigning himself to our inevitable extinction. "It's an ELE bomb, that's for certain."

February. As in only three months from now.

The wind was sucked right out of my sails. I honestly felt a gut punch, and my GI tract grumbled in response as I shook my head. "That's only three months away, Henry. Are you sure?"

Dina was tapping away at a keyboard, analyzing the screen and punching numbers into a predictive algorithm. She sighed and turned to me mournfully, nodding. I glanced at her and Isaac in painful resignation, and then turned back to the screen as I bowed my head.

"As certain of anything as I can be," he shrugged.

"What do you expect will happen at that point, Henry? Best chances of survival?" I asked him without a shred of optimism in my voice.

"Well," he replied, "I mean, they ripped me up out of my beautiful dream-filled sleep, but I'm seeing this clearly, and it's not pretty, Dane, it's really not. I can't see anything surviving this monstrosity. Something that massive has an intense gravity that nothing, not even light can escape it. All that matter, warping spacetime, the event horizon… light bending, modulating orbits of stars, it's going to pull our smaller planets into it, and then split the sun apart I reckon, and then after that, there'll be no place to hide, sure. I think one by one it's bound to pull everything in the bleedin' Milky Way into itself, and we're in for a pretty bumpy roller coaster ride when that happens. Ready your vomit bags." He shrugged again.

I don't know why I wasn't more filled with sadness. Three months was a long time – and it wasn't. Certainly, we'd feel some of the inescapable side-effects long before our planet began to hurtle toward it. In reality, we had probably only *two* months before things started to go sideways.

I just stared at the screen and sighed. "Alright. I need to brief Sikorsky and the AARO on this. DOD wants an update yesterday. Thanks, Henry."

"Sure, mate. She's a Sheila for sure. What do you reckon we call her?"

I motioned to my undergrad. "Well, Isaac discovered her, Henry. I think it's his call."

Isaac shrugged. He opened his mouth as if to say something, and then froze and closed it.

"Isaac?" Dina prodded.

He bowed his head. "I don't wanna name that thing. I'm *not* putting my name on something that's going to destroy our world."

I stared at Dina. He certainly didn't have to. I wouldn't want to name it either. Thankfully, Henry butted in.

"Well, I reckon we call her Norma."

I turned back to him. "Why Norma?"

"My first wife. Terrible woman. Evil to the core. Took me best mates and me dog, Dane. Good riddance." He held his mug up and snorted, drinking.

I could only offer him the feeblest of smiles. I shook my head dismissively. "Alright, Henry. We'll be in touch."

"God speed." He signed off, but not before he reached for his mug yet again.

God speed. The very phrase seemed repulsive. Where was God in this, and… *speed?* We would be going fast enough when the effects of that supermassive hit us.

Norma. I shook my head again. In all likelihood there wouldn't be much happening other than head-shaking over the remaining two to three months.

Earth, and the Milky Way, were about to be ripped apart by a supermassive black hole named Norma. Of course, the scientific community – and history – would come to refer to her differently in time, and she would most likely take on the moniker of *Farragut* due to Isaac's discovery. I wasn't sure how he would take that, having the galaxy's most lethal and mysterious force named after him.

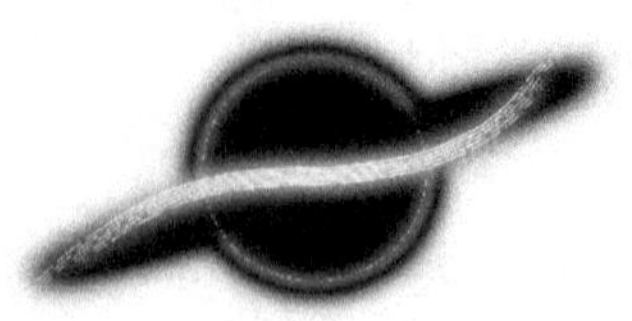

"And he is absolutely certain? Is there *any* way this could be a misread?"

It was late, Sikorsky's face was red, and his hair was disheveled. He was so close to the screen I could see into his pores, not that I wanted to. Secretary of Defense Erick Donze was also on the call. I turned to address him given that Sikorsky was obviously a wreck. Donze was stoic.

"We ran redundancy checks again. Telemetry was already verified, and these things don't lie. Senator, there's *always* a chance that something could alter its trajectory. Gravitational interactions with various cosmic bodies or turbulence within the galactic surface. Something could disrupt its central axis, its rotation, and it could become lopsided. Alternatively, you could have comets… uh… meteors, drifting space debris large enough to disrupt its orbit. There could be a number of things that could divert it, maybe?" I was reaching out, and I knew it. So did he.

"Spare me, Mr. Currier," he growled curtly. "All of these no doubt register a hair's breadth chance of actually happening. Their likelihood sounds infinitesimal based on what you've discovered already. Give me hope built on facts, not on prayers."

I took a deep breath and nodded. "Yessir."

"So, let us deal plainly in facts and not conjecture. That's what the President will want, and that's what the American people deserve."

"Will do, sir," I nodded again.

"Tidbinbilla is projecting late February for collision. And in your estimation we can expect the destructive effects before then?" the SecDef asked.

"Correct."

As if the weight of the realization finally descended upon her, Dina began to quietly cry next to me. I put a hand on her shoulder and squeezed, probably too hard.

"And when that happens, what can we expect?"

I took a deep breath. "Well, sir, it's not going to be pretty. The," -here I paused, trying to conjecture what a total cataclysm like this would be in such epic proportions- "well, the proximity would cause unpredictable gravitational seismic disruptions. Tides would surge, continents would crack, and time itself would seem to warp in localized pockets. The black hole would effectively warp gravity, causing catastrophic quakes and atmospheric collapse. It would be a slow-motion apocalypse as the planet is spaghettified over weeks."

"Spaghettified? Does that mean what I think it means?" Sikorsky butted in, pulling his hands from his face and furrowing his brow.

"Cut into ribbons," I said, mustering the simplest explanation I could come up with. It didn't help. Sikorsky buried his face back into his hands. "I think also you'd have some radiation effects that would subtly alter human consciousness, causing memories and identities to fragment, and possibly other effects."

Isaac shifted beside me. "Yessir, you'd have the expected hysteria and pandemonium. Mass suicides. Stock market crashing. People selling off possessions. Looting. Civil unrest. Violence. Revolts against government and shelters. Anarchy, unless we can all collectively get a grip."

The SecDef rolled his eyes.

"As Norma — that's what Tidbinbilla labeled it — drifts closer, we might see other planets or moons pass us in orbit, being pulled toward it and sucked in. The sun would also be shifting toward it. Everything is going to become scorching hot. Norma's pull would start to steal our sun's energy. The sun might actually fragment but, that superheated core would be exposed and send out solar flares."

The SecDef studied me. "And we'd have no choice but to follow our programmed orbital course and then we're doomed. Just like a zebra migrating across a river. The croc is coming."

"Uh, yessir, sure. Something like that," I said, thrown by the crude analogy, although it somewhat made sense. Norma the croc would latch onto us, pull us down and drown us in the void of outer space.

The SecDef sighed. "Well, you've given me a powerful lot to think about. I've got a meeting with the president in an hour. I'll brief him in full from what you've told me. I'd like both of you to remain on standby for any further questions or updates. Who discovered it, by the way?"

Isaac reluctantly raised his hand behind me.

"Well, son," Donze said, "I guess we owe you a debt of gratitude for pointing it out, no matter its position. Relax, Ronald," he said to Sikorsky, "I realize now that it wasn't on anybody's radar until recently, given its trajectory and speed. There was nothing anyone could have done."

He turned back to Isaac, Dina and I.

"Norma will be the end of us, plain and simple. But we can busy ourselves with how we map out the end of our days well enough. I'll be in touch."

I nodded and sighed. "Thank you, Mr. Secretary."

He nodded and switched off. Sikorsky did as well.

I turned back to my team and just stared at them in uncomfortable silence. Dina broke it. She collapsed in a heap over herself, burying her face in her hands and slumping in her chair.

And there, in the dark of that room, I thought briefly to everyone I could. My own eyes watered. Do I tell them about *Courier 3.1* now? Would it even lift their spirits one iota?

I shook my head. It probably wouldn't matter. Not one iota. Soon, *nothing* would matter. Even *matter* wouldn't matter anymore, soon.

Norma would end us.

There was no disputing that now.

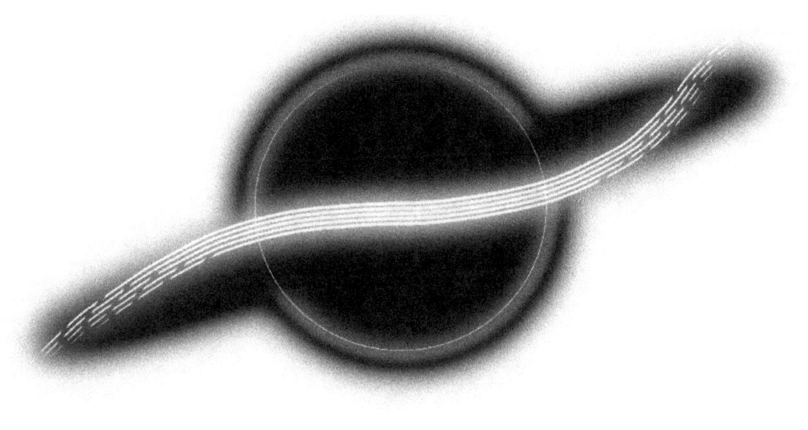

4 | News
November 7th, 2025

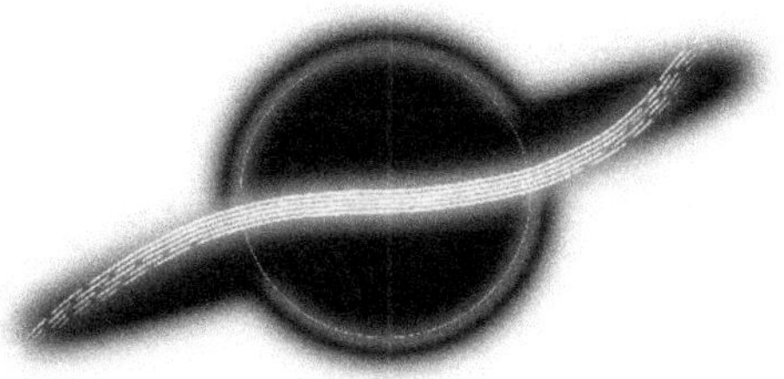

President Trump appeared before all of us.

"Here it is, here it is, quiet!" Isaac yelled.

We were all gathered together in droves before a giant screen. It was early. By now word had spread overnight, mainly by Dina, who simply couldn't contain her own grief and 'needed to talk to someone.' Several of our contemporaries, grads and undergrads, and various UW professors were now assembled down the hall from our lab, in UW Kane Hall. A tech had piped in the broadcast feed and we were now seated before it, waiting. There were dozens of us now in the know.

Many of them grasped just how bad it truly was, and how bad it truly was going to get.

I viciously chewed my nails, fighting back thoughts of *Courier 3.1* in the midst of all of this, and wondering how it would, or could, help us… or maybe just help me. The burps were coming, and my stomach was roiling.

The President.

There he was in the Oval Office, sitting at the Resolute Desk, flags flanking him representing nations and ideals that would soon be burnt to a crisp. I couldn't help but see the futility and eventual destruction of everything in… *everything.* Trump appeared drawn, sustained only by truckloads of information and caffeine.

"My fellow Americans," he began somberly, "good morning. I come to you today with some news."

News. An understatement of epic proportions.

"This morning, early, I was briefed on a development within our galaxy that has bearings on us all."

My mind was racing. This was not going to go down easily. People were going to freak out. Pandemonium would erupt in the streets. Civil unrest would consume us all, in every nation, unbridled and uncontrollable. Silence settled upon all of us, hanging on his every word. I glanced around the auditorium to try to gauge their tolerance levels.

"A few weeks ago, scientists at the University of Washington were alerted to a phenomenon drawing near to the Milky Way galaxy that was large: much too large to be some itinerant meteor, stray asteroid or cloud of wayward cosmic dust. They continued to monitor it, and have now confirmed that this object approaching our galaxy is, in fact," -here he paused, presumably perched on the fence of whether or not to deliver the news so decisively- "a black hole.

"Now, we've had black holes traversing the universe since the dawn of time, and some have come close to the Milky Way, continuing on their mysterious voyage. In fact, Sagittarius A, the closest one to us, lies at the galactic center of the Milky Way. It is what is known as a 'supermassive black hole,' near the border of the constellations Sagittarius and Scorpius, about 5.6 degrees south of the ecliptic, close to the Butterfly Cluster and Lambda Scorpii." He never spoke like this; he was clearly reading from a combination of notes and a teleprompter. His speed slowed and his diction was deliberately increased. "It was discovered in 1974 and has largely held a stationary position relative to our own orbit. It spans 26,000 light-years with a diameter of 32.2 million miles across. I give you those figures for comparison. Again, Sagittarius A is stationary."

Here it comes. I accidentally bit my fingertip instead of my nail, and hissed at the pain. Dina glanced at me.

"However, the one that was recently catalogued is mobile, and moving at over one-tenth the speed of light, averaging 21,300 miles per second. Its mass," he paused again, "is thirty-seven times the mass of Sagittarius A. Our scientists have run what are known as 'redundancy tests' to confirm mass, speed and heading, and agencies like DISCOVR, DSN and AARO have confirmed it."

He paused, taking a deep breath. "America, you're a smart collective of citizens. I assume you can already guess where I'm going with this, so let me be absolutely clear. It has now been confirmed that the trajectory of the black hole, which has been dubbed 'Norma' by the scientists who discovered it" -here I scoffed, as that wasn't technically true- "is unfortunately on a course that is set to intersect with Earth's orbit… in mid-to-late February of next year."

A collective gasp rose up all around us in the room. Someone screamed. My eyes flashed over, and a student was covering their face and bawling. They already guessed. The President wasn't being cryptic.

"Now, any one of a number of factors could potentially alter Norma's orbit, but at this point, it doesn't look likely, folks. Those factors include" -here he held a sheet of paper up below the screen and read off of bullet points- "galactic bodies and gravity, spatial turbulence, comets, meteors, asteroids with sufficient mass to pull it away from us. However, I've been assured that's highly unlikely. There is unfortunately nothing we can do to alter our own trajectory and push our planet beyond the collision path. Norma has a mass that will affect every single planet in our solar system, including our own sun, and those effects will be felt and observed even before late February of next year."

"Now," he said, releasing the papers he had been holding, and clasping his hands in front of him, "I realize this is not good news. Not good at all."

Again, understatement of the year, Mr. President.

"In simplest terms, what I am telling you today, is that, after all our pioneering research into Norma, where it's at, how big it is, how fast it is currently traveling, our scientists predict that we have a .005% chance of escaping this thing. It's very big." Trump shook his head. "Not good odds. Very, very bad. What that means for us is, most likely, sadly, the end of civilization as we know it. There is no escaping Norma. She will tear through our galaxy, sucking our planets – and our sun – into herself with destructive and irresistible magnetism that will effectively destroy our world. Life, as we know it on our beautiful planet Earth, will, sadly, end. This black hole is what is known as an 'ELE.' Extinction Level Event.

"None of us wants to see this happen, but after all research had been conducted and all ideas had been exhausted or proven futile, we must accept the inevitable if we are to bravely face our own demise. Our planet has survived comet and meteor strikes in its roughly six thousand years of existence, and we have outlasted them.

"But, sadly, Norma appears to be set to outlast us, and there is not much we can do about that. We must face this according to the power and maturity that is in each of us, and humbly accept that this is, unfortunately, the end. In three months, our beautiful planet will be no more, its citizens no more, this galaxy no more.

"What that means for all of you, all of us, myself included, from this point forward, is that I am implementing martial law. There will be no looting, no violence, no theft or advantage taken of our fellow citizens." He was reading again. "We will meet this thing together, bravely and with dignity, or we will not meet it at all. Those who cause discomfort or terror for our fellow man in the days leading up to Norma's intersection will be dealt with swiftly and severely. We are militarizing and mobilizing as we speak. Planet Earth will meet its doom," he said. His head drooped momentarily, and his eyes remained fixed on his desk. When he lifted his head once more, his eyes were shining. "Forgive me. I feel this too."

For a brief flicker of a moment, it felt choreographed; staged. Judgment passed through me – judgment over all of his business ventures that he was losing, his money, his fame, his power, and narcissistic bent, his self-proclaimed stature and opinion of himself. But whatever opinions I had formed of him, I had to put aside for the moment and trust that there was feeling behind those glistening eyes. We all stood to lose a lot here, not just money and power. All around me, people wept.

I choked up, and my chest spasmed. Dina leaned into me. Groans went up throughout the auditorium as the full weight of all of it – including seeing our President tear up – tore away our sense of hope.

"In partnership with the medical community, we are considering the best methods of psychological and medical help we can provide for all those who will, for obvious reasons, have difficulty facing such an inevitable scenario. In short order we will be providing updates from the United States Secretary of Health and Human Services, the CDC, the American Psychological Association, the National Institute of Mental Health, the National Register of Health Service Psychologists and anyone else who can provide hope, counseling, and measures of preparing for, and coping with, what is to come. Other countries will do the same as they see fit. We have a hard road ahead of us. All of us. However, as your President, I am confident that we are very,

very smart, and very, very capable. I believe in all those people that we have for so long entrusted our mental and emotional well-being to, that they will be able to help us see this event through."

Event? You mean the annihilation of our civilization? That event, Mr. President? I ruminated as my thoughts returned to pessimism and criticality.

Trump paused, and took a deep breath.

"The sad truth is that soon, our beloved planet will be no more, and for that reason I appeal to every one of you to *choose* to go out bravely. Admirably. With hope for the next life, and charity for your fellow man. Not with selfishness or acquisition, but with generosity and compassion, with malice toward none, and charity toward all," he finished, quoting Lincoln. He paused once more, sniffing. "That is all for now. Any updates we have will be provided as quickly as we can do so. God bless you all. God bless America. God bless Planet Earth. Thank you," he said with a clenched lip, and swiftly got up from his desk before the camera cut.

I felt a strange resolution surge through me. There truly was no way out.

The broadcast faded to a green background with the Presidential Seal.

The President was gone.

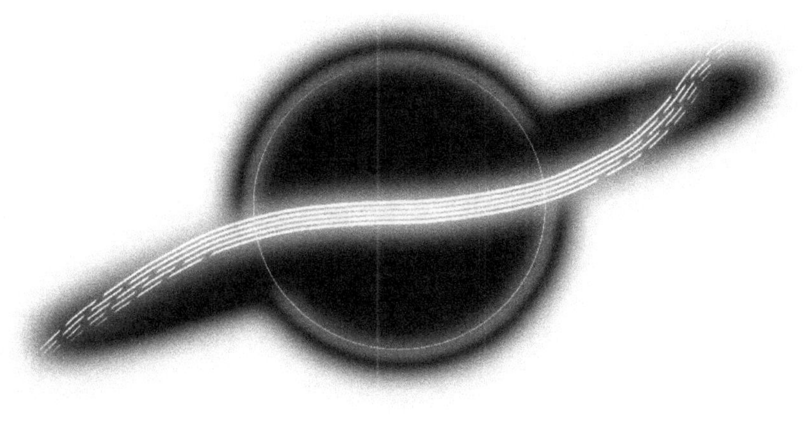

5 | Screw It
November 7th, 2025

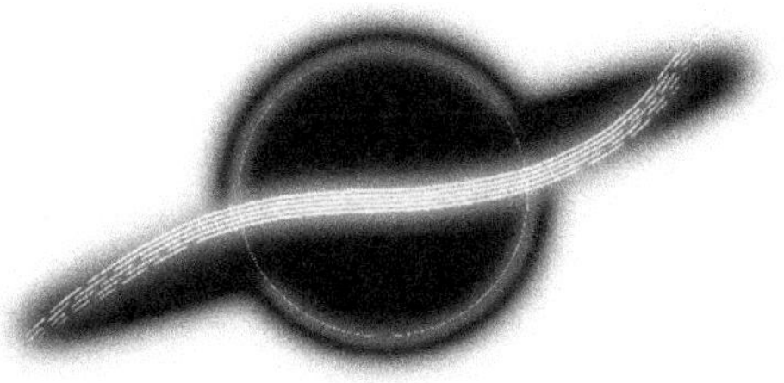

It was no use. We were doomed.

I couldn't resist it anymore. This *had* to be done. I returned to my apartment and slammed the door. Now, Macy and Jack Daniels were my company.

My dog looked fine; improved even. I stroked her ear with my left hand while I clutched my Jack Daniels bottle with my right. She watched me curiously, and I could swear she wanted a sip.

"Dogs have courage, right? You were brave enough to go through, right, Macy-girl?" I asked, staring her deep in the eyes. She blinked. "So, what's stopping me?"

Megan had been texting me incessantly since she heard the news. I told her I was stuck in meetings and would get back to her ASAP. She didn't sound convinced, and threatened to come over. But she didn't sound convincing either. My phone was blowing up. All kinds of people I'd never heard of or hadn't heard from in the longest time were now texting me with variations of *Is this for real? And PLEASE tell me they misread something and that we have a chance.* My mom was texting and calling every five minutes. She said dad was worried about me, and so was she. She pled with me to call her.

Yet, there I sat, naked as a jaybird on my sofa, drinking heartily. I wondered briefly, if I was drunk on this side, would I be drunk on the other? Would Nova tell Ava the exact content and volume of the alcohol coursing through my bloodstream? Surely it would read my BAC and interpret that correctly, re-inebriating me on the other side. I was shaking. This truly was the end, and, as they say, 'there's no time like the present.' So, what did I have to lose? A precious few more months? What futility and nonsense.

Screw it, I said to myself. I took one last ruffle of Macy's ear and gave her a kiss on the head, throwing the Jack Daniels bottle against the far wall. It shattered unceremoniously in the kitchen. Macy lifted her ears and then started, standing up with her tail between her legs, quickly ping-ponging her eyes from the kitchen and back to me.

"It's okay, baby girl," I assured her, scratching her scruff and hugging her tight. I could feel myself trembling.

Suddenly, I felt life within me, coursing through me as I stood up. A nervous stretch made itself known as my arms reached for the sky and my quads tensed. My hamstrings trembled, and I felt a frenetic shiver.

"Here goes nothing," I said to her, kissing her gently on the slight indentation at the bridge of her muzzle.

Nova was before me. I had already initiated the sequence just before I stripped. Now I tapped 'enter' and sent her into warmup mode. She wouldn't proceed until something was physically inside her and the door was locked. I had programmed her just so.

Suddenly, as I stood there, I was acutely aware of everything around me, almost in a trancelike séance, in touch with the universe. I held my hands out while Nova warmed up.

A police car wailed by outside. And another.

My phone buzzed again.

Someone down the street was hollering at someone else for God knows what minutiae that didn't even matter anymore.

The TV in my bedroom continued to drone on and on at low volume with CNN reports of this and that measure of hysteria that had erupted or unfolded somewhere.

A brief gust wafted the curtains to my left.

Macy laid down and rested her muzzle on her outstretched paws in front of her, still watching me.

Nova drew me in. The amber glow inside was beckoning, and the sterile walls were inviting. I felt eerily like I was re-enacting that scene from *The Fly*, but I learned well enough to ensure that the programming forbade multiple concurrent DNA strands; that was categorically disallowed so as to prevent any gene-splicing. I wanted my birds, my dog… *me*… to emerge on the other side still ourselves. That was crucial. There was no room for mistakes.

This was it. I hovered before the door, holding onto the titanium seal, and was suddenly aware of how greasy the tips of my fingers felt from sweat. I recoiled them to myself, clenched my fists, and wiped my hands on my hips, taking an overlong breath of the last oxygen Me 1.0 would take. On the other side, in Ava, Me 2.0 would take his first newborn breath.

I took one last pensive glance back at Macy. She didn't lift her muzzle, but she wagged her tail at me. A meager smile was all I could muster.

Nova practically called to me with her silent siren-song. The soft hum of the laptop could be heard behind me. All sounds faded as I stepped inside, slowly, and closed the door behind me.

It was so different. This was not how I wanted it. I knew what was about to happen, but I never intended to be in here myself. At least, not this early, and not under pressure by virtue of a destructive force coming to rip our galaxy, our very planet, apart. That was not my aim; nothing I ever envisioned for myself. But as St. Francis of Assisi once said, *Start by doing what's necessary, then do what's possible; and suddenly you are doing the impossible.*

Macy was still wagging her tail at me through the glass. I put my hand up to it and pressed, reaching out for her. She stayed put. *Good girl,* I thought. My hand returned to my side, but the foggy condensation of my fingers remained imprinted on the glass.

Beyond, perched on my dinner table, I could see that the countdown had begun. Nova determined I was the only one in here. Me and my fear. I wondered what the DNA of fear would look like if it was catalogued. Probably multi-stranded with long, strangling tentacles.

15… 14…

I didn't want to pray… to think… to compute… to fear… to be strong… to hope. I just wanted to get it over with.

Macy watched me.

11…

10…

The floor pad was getting hotter as I stood there, standing fully erect and ready to face oblivion.

Or rebirth?

7…

6…

I shut my eyes. It helped to have them closed and not watch the timer… watching it would only serve to increase my anxiety. The transfer would take a minute for me, presumably, as it had for Macy. The floor grew hotter.

I opened my eyes for just a flicker, gazing outside to the world that was. Macy had gotten up and was standing right outside Nova, staring at me, wagging her tail, panting with whatever she was feeling.

I smiled at her, lovingly.

A strange sensation enveloped me. A placid peace. Warmth, pinprick stabs of light, and a faint buzzing sound that filled my ears and my soul. Then, a powerful, percussive force flashed around me, and for a split-second it felt like my skeletal structure collapsed. And then, finally…

Silence.

I can't explain it, but everything felt so tranquil. Calm, quiet, as if all the air had been sucked out of the universe and sound waves were disallowed. I could hear my own breathing increase in volume, almost deafening; and then, nothing. All sounds were stilled. It was almost as if I blinked, and then I felt weightless as if drifting in a void, bereft of any time constraints. All seemed to slow.

Something smelled like it was burning.

A texture registered under my feet suddenly, and there were wisps of foglike smoke circling around me. I could suddenly detect the floor beneath my feet as the smoke entrails were vacuumed out of the chamber.

But which chamber?

My vision became clearer, and the swirling fog around me abated. I didn't presume I could move yet. The vacuum continued to suck out the smoke.

And there, beyond the pane, was Macy. Just as she had been, staring at the chamber.

The chamber that I *had* been in. Over there. She wiggled her tail as I watched her, silently, quietly, caught between astonishment and fear, hardly daring to breathe. She was staring into Nova, waiting excitedly for me to return in the very chamber I had stepped in.

But the door to Ava opened, and the remaining wisps of condensation and haze floated out. Macy's head whipped over to me excitedly, and then she got up and pranced over to the entrance to the other chamber, ducking her head and sniffing curiously.

I stepped out. She sniffed my legs.

I bent down. She watched me, with those beautiful, improved eyes. I knew it was her.

And she knew it was me.

She spared no expense, rushing into my embrace and licking my chin, my lips, my hands. Whatever electrostatic residue resided on them, she was interested in, and it tickled her fancy as she indulged in it.

"Hey, girl, remember me?" I asked, looking at her and straining my neck at my apartment.

The gust still blew.

CNN still played.

The sirens still wailed.

The man still bellowed.

My phone buzzed.

I was changed, yet they remained the same. Everything was as it was.

I pressed my hands against myself, feeling all over, giving myself a cursory once-over as I examined each part of my body with fervor, inspecting and pressing, feeling and registering, wondering and confirming. Everything was where it had been before.

I was still me. At least, Macy thought so.

"What do you think, baby girl? Am I still me? You know me?" Macy sat and stared up at me, panting and wagging. I leaned down toward her and said the magic word.

"Shake!"

She lifted up her paw, knowing what to do, and her old yet restored limb met my young yet restored limb. We embraced, and I shook her gingerly and kissed her head once more.

And, as if to dispel all doubt, leaning over toward her, I felt suddenly dizzy. In fact, a little nauseous.

But this was different…

It wasn't nausea from just having been teleported, disassembled particle by particle and then reassembled ten feet away.

No.

This wasn't brought on by motion.

It was from Jack Daniels. The Nova chamber read me, disassembled me, and then Ava put me back together from the information she was given, including my exact state of inebriation. That information included half a bottle of Jack Daniels in my stomach and my blood stream.

A smile crept across my face as I faced the second inevitability of the day.

It works. It works! *IT WORKS!!*

A gargantuan and irrepressible laugh escaped my lungs, and I howled toward the ceiling, stretching out my arms, and whirling back around to stare lovingly upon Nova and Ava. *I was there,* I observed silently, staring at Nova, *and then I was there*, I celebrated, my eyes darting over to Ava. I turned back and kissed the Ava chamber.

It had worked.

It was inevitable that it should work. Now I just had to figure out what to do with it.

Before I could summon my thoughts, I whirled back around as my door burst open and there came Megan Trapper, beholding me in all the glory of my birthday suit – quite literally, as I had just been given birth to in a completely and wholly new way.

She started to say something, but stopped, gawking, gazing around in disbelief and shock.

"Stuck in meetings, huh? *Liar,*" she said accusingly, nearly out of breath, her eyes scanning my new body, helplessly gazing downward. Her eyes fixed on my torso.

I did the same, and then brought my eyes back up to meet her, still laughing. "Trust me, it's the same one," I managed through a chortle, unable to contain my joy.

Courier 3.1 had just worked. I had been teleported.

It had worked. We were onto something here.

PAGE 74

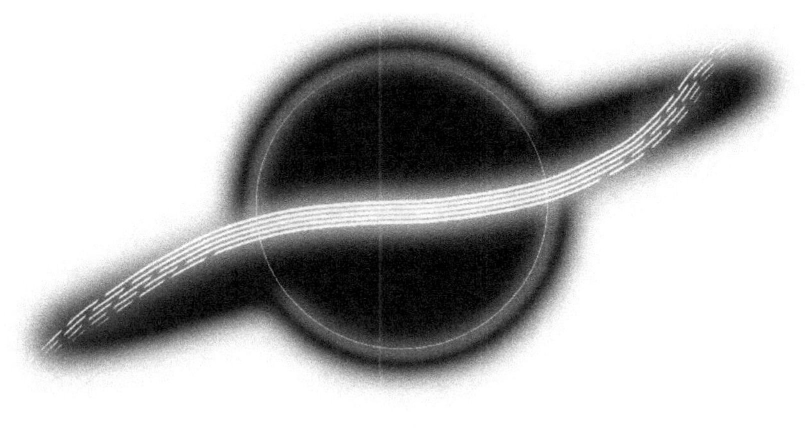

6 | *Potentials*
November 7th, 2025

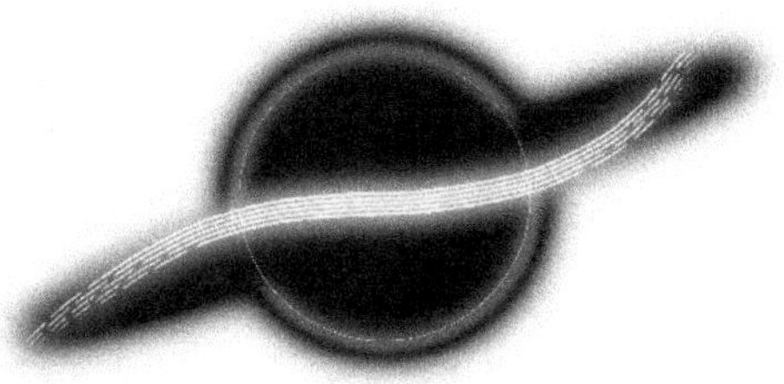

She just gawked at me, incredulous.

Megan asked me what I had been doing. However, it didn't take her long to put two and two together, so I came clean. Her jaw fell to the floor.

"I'm not kidding, Megs. Look at the logs," I said, pointing her over to my laptop. "Just, don't go into the kitchen; there's a broken bottle in there," I cautioned. "Don't worry, I have more. It's time to celebrate! It worked! Come here, Macy-girl!" Macy enthusiastically bounded up on the sofa next to me and gratefully allowed me to stroke her fur.

I had run to the bedroom and clothed myself, and now I was sitting on the sofa while she tapped away on my keyboard. I just stared at Nova and Ava, but I couldn't stop feeling uber-connected to my own skin, sensing everything: on the lookout for any signs of abnormality or change. I couldn't find anything. Even my stomach had stopped grumbling. It was a bizarre, almost cybernetic sort of computer diagnostic, a self-assessment that saw my mind whizzing through different sensors scanning my anatomy. Granted, joy and exhilaration were flooding through my core, so the readings were probably more optimistic than they would normally be; in the midst of such tragic news about Norma, I was riding high on the crest of this moment.

It appeared, in all likelihood, that Nova replicated the contents of my stomach, but it had idealized my organs and reintegrated them in a perfected state. Just like Macy. *So interesting,* I thought, while Megan tapped. I took another swig of my second bottle of JD.

"You *idiot*," she finally said to me. "Do you have any idea how foolhardy that was? We have three months left to live, Dane, and you wanna off yourself on the first day?"

"What do you mean?" I asked, incredulous. "Megan, it *worked!* Look at me!" I insisted. She didn't. "*Look at me,* Megs. I went through! Do I sound different, look different, act different?"

She reluctantly pulled her sour eyes away from my laptop and gave me a once-over up and down. "I've seen enough of Dane Currier today, if you know what I mean."

I shrugged and tilted my head.

"And…," she paused, "you're still pudgy." A faint trace of a vengeful smile stretched her lips.

I laughed, bolting up. "Megs, it's not an Ozempic machine, for crying out loud. It's a teleporter. It's me! I'm still me. Of *course* I'm going to still be pudgy, or," -here I threw my hands up helplessly- "*whatever* you think I am. Don't be such a negative Nellie, man!"

I just stood there in front of Ava, pondering the sheer implausibility of it all. But why not? I had programmed it to do exactly as it had just done. The system learned, and I'd gone through all those stages of testing that had led inexorably to this moment. I was riding high; pudgy or no, Negative Nellie or no.

Megan just shook her head. *Whatever, Toothpick,* I thought. Yet, as I took a swig of the Jack Daniels, I realized helplessly that that was what probably caused what little pudge she said I had. *Oh well, down the hatch*, I thought resignedly, unconcerned with her petty evaluations.

"This is actually pretty impressive, Dane," she relented. "I mean, all of these computations have you going way out there – somewhere – being put back together, and then you're back. When did you go?"

"Literally like twelve minutes ago!"

"And it was instantaneous?" she persisted.

"Nearly. I didn't notice any kind of time gap, but I forgot to check the time. It felt both instantaneous *and* interminable. I can't explain it."

She looked at me squarely. "How do you feel, really? I mean, anything different?"

I frowned. "Not that I- I mean, I don't really know of anything. Nothing's registered, not even the burps."

"They're gone?"

"Well, I mean, I haven't had any in the last twelve minutes, but it comes and goes. I need to give that more time. But nothing else feels out of the ordinary." My smile persisted.

She returned to my laptop. A siren went wailing by outside, briefly drawing her gaze. I mindlessly scratched the scruff of Macy's neck.

"Dane. Come here. Look."

I meandered over to her, taking another swig, feeling mighty proud of myself through all this.

"Look at this readout."

"What am I looking for?"

"The electrons. They're off the chart."

"So?"

"So? I mean *look at them!* They're still orbiting the atomic nuclei – at least that's what this is saying – but look!" She pointed at a figure in the column of metrics assessing my teleportation.

"The negative charge?"

She nodded. "Yep. Your protons look normal, but your electrons should be balanced from them so that you retain a neutral charge. Remember when we were assembling it? Programming *Courier* I mean." I nodded. "So, electrons are bound to the nucleus to different degrees. But look at these valence electrons, the outermost ones. There are maybe five, six times as many as there should be."

"So? What does that mean, Megs? In English please."

She sighed. "You're a dork. Listen to me! They're the least tightly bound. They form the chemical bonds with your atoms to create molecules and crystals. They facilitate chemical reactions through transfer or sharing between atoms. The inner ones make up the core. So what do the outer ones make up? The valence shell. By these valence readings, your shell's been reinforced to a quintuple degree. Even a sextuple one!"

"So I'm Iron Man now?"

"Not quite, pudgy. Move." She shoved past me and went over to investigate Ava, waving her hand around inside it and rubbing her fingers together. "Come here. You feel this?"

I followed her over to Ava and thrust my hand inside, waving it around as she was.

"Residual electrons. Reactive, but not bonding. Stranded. You can literally feel their presence."

"So Nova transferred me to Ava but gave me an extra dose of electron shells?"

"Maybe? I think so, yeah," she appealed to me. "That could have all kinds of bearings on what a lifeform can endure. That would explain the strengthening of Macy's eyes, her hair color, et cetera. Has she shown increased energy levels at all?"

"Yeah, I think so?"

"You should have been paying attention to this. You're really cavalier about it." She put her hands on her hips and glared.

"I'm not cavalier! I just needed to try whatever I could. But Megs, are you thinking what I think you're thinking?"

"I dunno. What am I thinking? Besides hungry."

"That if there's a surplus of electrons, it could mean increased travel fortitude, uh, resistance to gravitational forces, or speeds. Maybe even finding the ability to travel long distance, even…" I trailed off, hoping she would catch my drift.

She did, and her eyes widened. "…even away from earth. To another solar system."

"Hell, why not?" I squealed. "I mean, Ava doesn't *have* to receive the signal. She can act as a relay. She can bounce it. We programmed her with that capability. We've got signals floating out there residually from Internet transmissions sent via Wi-Fi that are just now reaching planets and solar systems light years from us, that were sent in the early 2000's, most likely. At the advent of the Internet."

"Yeah, but that's still a far cry from sending a human. Those are 1's and 0's, man. This doesn't just 'beam' you to wherever you want to go. You'd still need a receiver. You'd need *some* kind of receiver there."

I stopped, scratching my head. "I dunno, I feel like we're on to something here. Even if we were to find a way to transport some of us – perhaps a fraction of a colony of us – to some, some, I dunno, 'transition planet,' at least for a while, so that we could get a receiver somewhere habitable. It would be like leapfrogging through the galaxy, and it would take an incredible amount of time. They just discovered TOI-715b this year," I said, referencing the 'super-Earth' discovered this year that orbited a red star 137 light years away. It comprised a mass about 1.5 times as wide as Earth. It was in a conservative habitable zone. But there's no way we would get there in time, of course. Norma would destroy us in 3 months. "There have got to be other candidates out there too. What if," I thought, scrambling, "what if Neptune didn't get pulverized by Norma?"

"Neptune is *not* a habitable planet, Dane… not in the slightest. Extreme cold, windy, no oxygen, no solid surface mass."

"Okay, but, you know what I mean. If there was a planet in the Milky Way galaxy that was on the far orbit *away* from Norma, like, if Mars could sustain us – at least temporarily – we could use it as a jumping point. Uh, a staging ground or something like that."

She paused, considering, but ultimately shook her head. "I don't know. Nova and Ava are solar powered," she said, trailing off, lost in thought.

I nodded.

"Well, that's one thing that works for them. I'm actually thinking about one of our nearest star neighbors. Proxima Centauri b, in the Alpha Centauri system. Still, for the signal to travel through space, it would take about four light years for a signal to travel to PCb. That's a long time for a signal to be in suspended animation, shooting through the cosmos, one after the other. What if one got waylaid? What if we found a planet and somehow got a receiver there but people didn't clear out or, or, I don't know, *reintegrate* fast enough or something? You could risk gene splicing or inadvertent merging. It's a freakin' mess, man. I'm hungry."

She sat down in a huff. "The signals could get there, but they would have to wait until we could actually get a *receiver* there. They'd be waiting for light years. I don't know if we'd have enough valence electrons to sustain us that long."

"I admit, it's a longshot. All of it is. But you just hit on something," I said.

"What?" she asked, confused.

"Proxima Centauri."

"What about it?"

"Well, if Proxima Centauri is the nearest star and only 4 light years away, wouldn't it be somewhat habitable?"

She furrowed her brows. "Maybe. PCb is an exoplanet with an M-type star. It's bigger than Earth, I know that. 1.3 times the size. 4.24 light years away I think the prof said last time he talked about it." Megan was enrolled in Bioscience and they did discuss planets and other systems beyond our own. That was an invaluable asset right about now. "PCb would be a lot closer than that other one you mentioned, TOI-715b, for sure."

"That could be a logical contender then!"

She thought to herself. "Maybe. If Norma doesn't rip right through it as well someday. With the way our luck is going, I wouldn't count on it."

"There's not much left to count on. I'm open to suggestions. The point being that we need to do some heavy thinking and less drinking," I said, putting down my Jack Daniels. Optimism was coursing through my veins, jockeying for position with the JD now. "There are all kinds of potential things we could do to make something happen.

Anything happen," I urged. I sat back down on the couch, chewing my fingernails once more. They tasted strangely bitter.

"Yeah, but Dane," she countered, "that doesn't mean it would take us 4.24 years to get there. That's *light* years. That's if we could even travel at the speed of light. At our present speeds, our conventional poky spacecraft wouldn't get there for seventy *thousand* years, man." She paused, as if trying to recollect something deep in her memory.

"What is it?" I asked.

She held up a finger. "Hold on. There were flirtations documented by the American Nuclear Society with nuclear pulse propulsion in projects like Orion and Daedalus started in the 50's and 60's, but I don't know where they're at. I think Orion was abandoned due to the Nuclear Test Ban Treaty. I could look it up and see where it's at now? If someone were working on nuclear pulse propulsion? *Whoa.* That would *greatly* speed things up. We're talking under a century of travel to get there."

"Really?"

She nodded. "Mm-hmm. But that's *if* they're working on it. You'd have to find out. Dane, that could be the real thing that would work. Then the only questions are A, is PCb habitable, and B, could we sustain ourselves as data in transit? But we actually have a pretty freaking big saving grace here. Based on what we've seen of Norma, she's coming one way, and PCb is on the other side of us. That much I know. That means PCb isn't in line with Norma's projected path. That's *huge*, Dane. If the opposite were true, we wouldn't even be talking right now. We'd fly right into it. Thankfully, it's in the complete opposite direction."

I didn't reply; I was lost in thought, myself. Math was never my strong suit, and there was a lot to compute here.

Megs thought to herself again for a moment. "I mean, if you're fortified just going through Nova, then that might mean that you can withstand long-distance transit while in a disembodied state, I don't know. That's a long time in stasis. But it's a near scientific certainty that we'd survive stasis longer than we would in straight travel to PCb. We'd die on the way; we'd never make it in our current fragile flesh. But as data? We just might. It will take a lot of poring over all this data, Dane. A *lot* of poring over it. It might be doable, but none of us would ever be able to confirm it. A lot can happen in seventy thousand years… or even in a century. And we only have three months."

Silence consumed us. Outside, the world marched on in futility. More sirens. More people yelling.

Presently, Megan looked at me and stared hard.

"Hey. Ava is basically a receptacle," she said. "It didn't take us long to build her. We could build another one to hold *multiple* signals, couldn't we? I mean, as long as the power stayed on and it was protected, we could send *multiple* data streams to it and have it hold them indefinitely."

My eyes widened as I listened to her, considering. "Yeah? Yeah!" I snapped my thumbs. "We could load it up with drives and redundant arrays to store the signals until whatever craft carrying them reaches a habitation zone."

"We could program it to dispense the signal and reintegrate the teleportation subjects at preordained coordinates," she said, and a trace of a smile spread across her lips. "You could upgrade *Courier* to do that."

I smiled back.

"Ya think?" she asked me.

"I think! I really do. I mean, what other option do we have?"

She shook her head. "Beam me up, Scotty."

"Exactly. That's basically what they are. Who's to say that we didn't come up with the girls precisely for this scenario, Megs?"

"The girls?"

"Nova and Ava. Sorry, I refer to them that way collectively."

She nodded, and then frowned. "Dane?"

My eyebrows raised.

"I'm hungry." She stroked her stomach and frowned.

I shook my head and laughed. "Of course you are. I am too. Quieres Taco Bell?"

"Yo quiero."

"Well then let's go see what happened to my stomach, and see if I can take it. No grumbles yet."

"Sounds good," she said. "And Dane? You're not so pudgy. Maybe Ava improved you."

"We'll see, Megs. We'll see. You got your mace?"

"Yeah?" She looked at me confused. Megan could handle herself in a fight, but fights were undoubtedly brewing out there, no matter the caution that the President advised. She would need to be equipped.

"Good. I'll get my gun. There are crazies out there. And it's gonna get worse."

She smiled at me. "Then let's go get a bite to eat, get the stuff we need from the U, and start to make it better," she said with a grin.

I grinned back. "You said it. The universe has a way of balancing things out, Megs. Maybe this is our way out. Maybe this is the universe's way of keeping us in balance, by having you and me build these things, having them ready right when we needed them most? I'd like to believe it's more than just coincidence. More like destiny."

Macy, understanding nothing of this, just watched us and wagged endlessly, carefree and naïve.

But Trapper stared at me, hopeful.

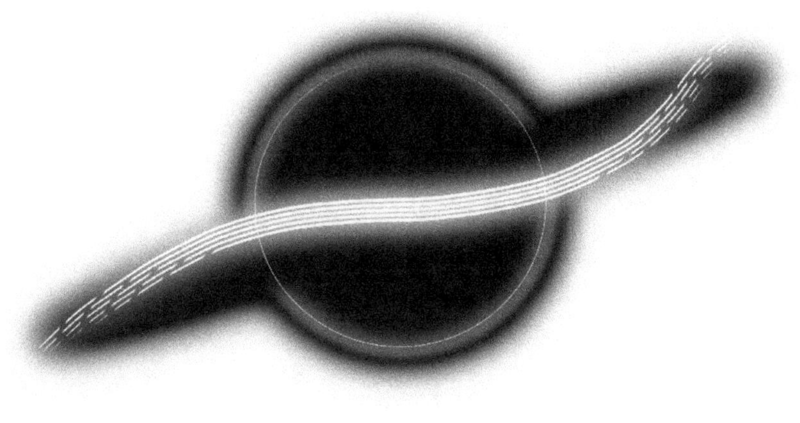

7 | *Travel Plans*
November 7th, 2025

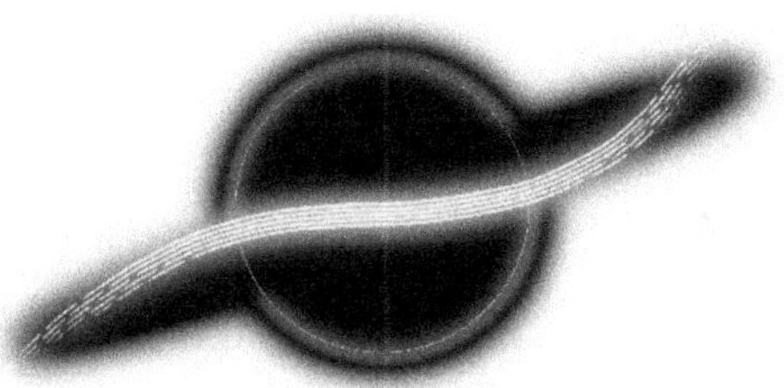

It was surreal out there.

People were calm, for the most part, and life was going on nearly as it always had been. A commentator known for psychiatry was on CNN speaking with the anchor about the emotional grappling with such an impending cataclysm, and what we as a species could handle.

We had pulled up and ordered. Megan bought my food, whispering me a quiet *my treat to congratulate you on Courier 3.1* my way. I thanked her, and then returned a quick call to my mom and dad to tell them that I was fine and catch up with them briefly. They were doing as good as could be expected, given the news. I texted Dina and Isaac as well. No news; no change in trajectory. They had also not heard from St. James, which they were a bit surprised about.

People ambled around us, some in a bit of a daze, most not talking, eyebrows folded downward in a bold and determined consternation as they sought to accept the news that blanketed our world with a stranglehold.

And now, Megan and I listened intently as we quietly munched on our Taco Bell. I grinned to myself as I noticed the distinct absence of any grumbles in my abdomen, and the burps were nowhere to be found, except on the coattails of a giant swig of Dr. Pepper.

"Coping with the inevitable," Dr. Brent Reinzell, MD, began, "is a fairly personal process, and there isn't really, empirically, a unique or singular ideal way to handle it. Some strategies can assist us with navigating challenges such as this, those challenges being either emotional or practical, such as group therapy, reading and assimilating information on black holes, because, as they say, *information is power*." He shrugged his shoulders. The anchor did the same. "And, when we have information, it better prepares us to understand the imminent threat, and to, thus, reconcile with it. It's crucial at this stage, for all of us, to truthfully acknowledge our feelings, seek out support from like-minded and affirming friends, family and the like, but, ultimately, the real trick is in focusing on what matters most, that being to acknowledge the gravity of the situation. To deny reality is pretty crippling in terms of advancing our personal health," Reinzell finished. "We have to seek an aurora out of our bleakness; a new beginning, if you will, even if that new beginning has an impending terminus."

Aurora. Didn't that mean beginning? *Nice try, Doc.* We're coming up on a most certain end.

My eyebrows flicked up as I looked away from the screen and back at Megan, who had nearly already finished her three soft tacos and two bean burritos with no onions. "Deny reality. Hmmph. No denying it now, eh?"

Trapper didn't answer me.

I looked around. "Look at everyone. Either they haven't heard, or they have and they don't care, or they realize caring is futile. You would think there would be something buzzing through the air other than apathy, wouldn't you?"

Megan looked around. "You totally missed the fourth conclusion," she said accusingly. "They *have* heard, and they've accepted it. I think that's why the shrink said that was the most important thing. I mean," -here she started to chuckle to herself- "where are we gonna go, huh? How you gonna outrun a supermassive black hole? Where are you even gonna go?"

The CNN broadcast, which included a panel of various other unnamed participants, concluded with a black screen and text encouraging those considering suicide to call the 988 Suicide and Crisis Lifeline, and then CNN cut to commercials.

I nodded in agreement. "But there's one thing that *they've* missed, right?"

Megan's eyes darted up to me briefly as she squeezed her last mild sauce packet into a waiting taco.

"They've missed *Courier 3.1,* Megs. I wonder what kind of shot of adrenaline it would send surging through them if they knew what we were potentially sitting on." I stared at her, beaming, awaiting her vote of confidence.

"Yeah," she said, nonchalantly, as a piece of taco fell from her lips. She wiped them. "But, Dane, first we have to get the materials right away and start building Number 3 – you have to figure out a name for it, by the way – and then we need to talk with someone about the logistics of making it all happen. Getting it to PCb. I mean, there's no easy way to make this happen. You can't line up a thousand naked people outside your door and ask them to patiently wait their turn to be zapped into data and then hurtled off into space."

Megan had a way of phrasing things with no BS. She was right. This would take some logistical planning, and it would be limited. A thousand? I wasn't even sure that that would be feasible. And she was also right – I needed to think of a name.

I just stared at her pensively, sipping my Dr. Pepper. "You're right. First things first, we get the requisition orders turned in, and obtain the equipment. We can start building tomorrow. Once we're confirmed that we have three working chambers, then I can maybe even talk with Donze. He would be a good-"

"Who? Donze who?"

"Sorry. Secretary of Defense Erick Donze. He's who Dina, Isaac and I linked up with when we confirmed Norma was a supermassive. We were initially talking with Doctor Ron Sikorsky with the AARO, but he's kind of a lame duck.

No power. Nothing to really get things moving, and no mental fortitude to do it with. We'd have to go higher than that. I can talk with Donze and brief him on our thoughts. If Proxima Centauri b is-"

"Just call it PCb please, we only have three months, Dane. I age a little each time you try to say its name."

I chuckled. "Fine. But if PCb is in fact a contender, then we better start planning on that. I'm excited just thinking about it! What else do you know about it?"

She shook her head and clenched her lip briefly, gathering a steely breath. "Takes 11-ish days to complete an orbit around PC. Discovered three years ago, I think. PCc too; that was reported even earlier, but it's not confirmed to even be there anymore. Might be a dust belt. But as for PCb, might have a large core, supposedly water-rich. Last I heard they were still running sims on its physical properties, but it should be Earth-like with similar orbit but a faster development. I think the prof said that it is tidally locked though, so only one side would face the star. That means cold, cold, *cold,* forever on the dark side, baby. If it does lack an atmosphere, it could be as low as negative forty Celsius. But if it does – and scientists *think* it does – the temperature could range from negative twenties to high eighties. There might be cold traps due to atmospheric circulation though. It would be like living in either Antarctica or Mexico, depending on which side you're on.

"*But* – the downside is that Proxima Centauri is a red dwarf, and that means potential radiation and solar flares on the hot side. Red dwarf stars aren't exactly ideal, Dane.

Those stellar flares can be a significant hazard for planets in their habitable zones. If it's tidally locked, we would just stay on the dark side, close to the terminator should we need to venture out into the heat for a while. Ya know, the twilight zone. We would need proper winter suits. All of us. But those flares can also affect their atmosphere.

"None of this is confirmed though," she ended. "Not much about it is confirmed at all. As of now it's just guesswork. PC is a much smaller star. Just a red dwarf with less than twenty percent of our Sun's energy."

"But it's way closer and more ideal than anything else catalogued, right?" I asked. "Right now, it sure sounds like our best shot. *Certainty* would be ideal, yes, as in, it could 'certainly' sustain life. But the only thing certain right now is that we're all going to die here."

"Yeah," she said, nonchalantly, with a thousand yard stare. "But you know what they're gonna do, right?"

Dina called me. I wasn't ready to pick up yet, so I silenced it. I stared at her blankly, confused. "No. What are *who* gonna do?"

"They're gonna handpick all the people they want to send. I mean, if *Courier 3.1* proves viable in that it can teleport somebody to a habitable system, they're gonna cherry pick the President, Donze will pick himself, probably you and your team since you guys discovered it, but it'll be government officials, top science dogs, agriculturists, agronomists, botanists, celebrities, artsy-fartsy snobs, all the top brass who could make a difference on a new planet."

"Well, maybe, but-"

"But nothing! They certainly wouldn't pick me. I'm a nobody who eats too much. I don't give a flip. No thanks. There wouldn't be any Taco Bell there anyway."

"You don't mean that. Come on," I chuckled as Dina called again. Still not ready. *Decline.* "Megs, if Norma doesn't kill us, Taco Bell eventually will. You can't survive on that stuff."

She shrugged her shoulders as my phone buzzed one more time. I rolled my eyes and looked down.

Dane. Pick up your phone! St. James is dead. Killed himself an hour ago.

I swallowed hard. I didn't know the man well, and the briefing that we just had with this Tidbinbilla contact of ours did little more than to confirm what we had already dreaded. Nonetheless, it felt like the sliding of tiny pebbles that eventually morphs into an avalanche. He had no doubt felt he had nothing left to live for, and that Norma would take the rest. So? He caved, and decided to take it back. I couldn't blame him, but my heart went out to him.

Trapper noticed my reaction. "What is it?"

"Megs, I gotta go. It's late anyway. I gotta get to the lab. I'll put in the requisition order tonight. Wanna meet me back at my pad tomorrow and we'll start building her?"

She nodded. "Only if you tell me who *her* is," she said, and sipped her drink, eyes glued to me.

I thought for a second. Didn't take long. The answer was right there.

"How about Aurora?"

Trapper squinted. "Nova, Ava, and Aurora. Yeah. Works for me."

I nodded. "OK. See you at the dock in a few hours and we'll start loading up the equipment. If you want to head out there ASAP and get started, I'll meet you. Just need to check in at the lab first and talk with the mucky mucks."

She gave me a thumbs up, and I was off, texting Dina as I scurried to the lab. It seemed like we were in a race against time itself.

Things were getting real here.

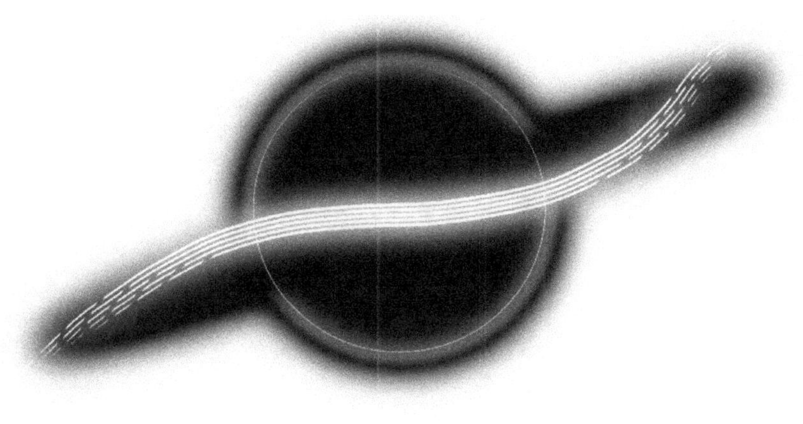

8 | *Pandemonium*
November 7th, 2025

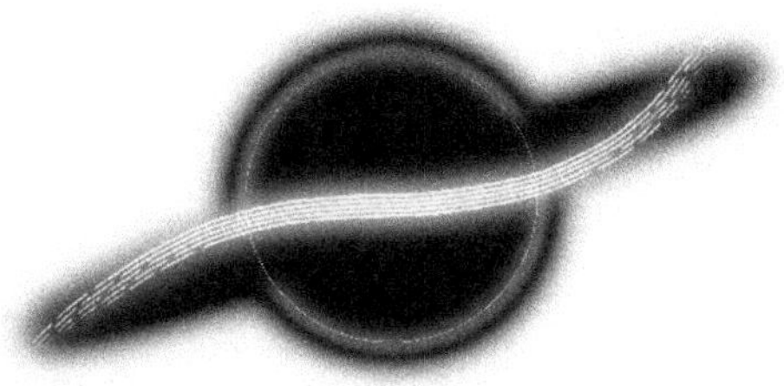

The mob was alive and well.

I heard the commotion before I even got there.

The scene was truly one of havoc and unbridled chaos. Students and professors were rioting against other faculty and security, and someone had evidently spearheaded an attempt to steal parts and supplies for makeshift bomb shelters. Apparently this was happening on a widespread basis at factories, universities, and various retail establishments that provided any kind of fabricated goods. As if constructing a makeshift bomb shelter would provide even a modicum of safety.

I tried to keep to the periphery, but even as I did so, placards were flying, Molotov cocktails were hurled in every direction, cars were overturned, and fires had broken out. Riot police were already on the scene, and someone with a loudspeaker was trying to pacify the crowds and reason with them. The whole scene was the furthest thing from what the president urged, and now my conversation with Trapper seemed so alien. *Some* people were resigned to their fate, yes, but not all. *Not all.* There were always going to be dissenters, and those that would go down in a blaze of glory, even if going down meant straight to their own deaths *and* taking others with them. As if impending death wasn't enough; they had to pull the whole house down on their head as well as others.'

A part of me felt supercharged as I whizzed through them, as if I was running on better batteries after having emerged safely from Ava. Just bordering on invulnerability, it was as if I felt somehow untouchable. Indeed, I hadn't had any sulfur burps since my teleportation, and that was a sign. I still *felt* like me, I still *thought* like me, I still *walked* like me, and all of that conveyed a sense of superior survivability.

Nonetheless, chaos erupted around me. *That didn't take long,* I thought morbidly to myself. *Bring on the anarchy.*

I carefully threaded my way, and narrowly missed some debris tossed in my direction as I hurried past the line of riot police, flashing my graduate school badge. I needed to get what these rioters were after… *before they did.*

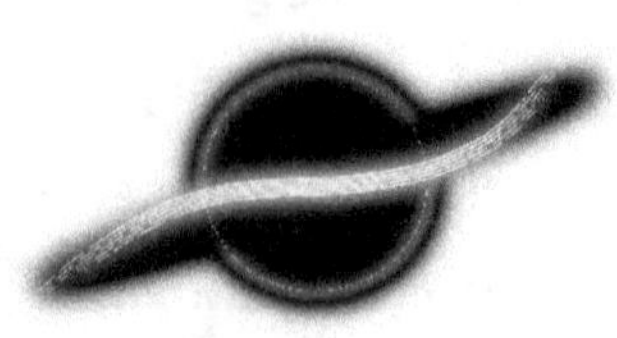

Dina melted into my arms the moment I saw her. She and Isaac were perched at their computers, still monitoring.

"How you two holding up?" I asked.

Dina shrugged, pulling away from me, as I rubbed her back. Isaac didn't even answer me, engrossed in metrics and data pouring from the monitors.

"That good, huh?"

"Predictive matrix doesn't suggest any deviation at all, Dane. This thing's gonna eat us. Maybe St. James had the right idea," he muttered, glumly.

"Hey, none of that, Isaac. We're at an ellipsis, not a period. Not yet. Chin up, okay?"

Isaac Farragut had always been one of those hard-to-read people who simply went about his business with the unflagging dedication of a servomotor. He just did what he knew he needed to do, and there was never any protest. But I'll be darned if there wasn't the slightest bit of complaint peeking through now. He was abysmal just like the rest of us. A few more punctuations of dreariness, and he might be out there hurling Molotov's like the rest of them.

Dina was another matter. She wore her heart on her sleeve, and here she was again, beside herself with sadness.

"Have you guys talked to your parents? Loved ones?" I posed. "Anyone you can reach out to locally and spend time with?"

"Doing what?" Isaac muttered again.

"I don't know... keeping you from un-aliving yourself like St. James," I said, playfully slugging him in the shoulder. Neither responded any further. I guessed now was the time.

"Why are you so peppy? Too many Cheerios in your bowl of sugar?" Isaac poked, eyeing me curiously.

"Listen," I started, pulling up a chair and sitting, facing them. "Can you guys take a quick break? I need to fill you in on something."

Isaac audibly rolled his eyes and rotated in his chair, abandoning his post. Dina had already plopped down sadly in her chair, resting her head in one palm on the desk. She stared at me mournfully. Isaac joined her with a bleak regard.

"Guys, listen. We're not done just yet. Not yet. We still have some time. I'm not going to tell you what to do with yours, but I want to finally clue you in to what I've been doing with mine. I haven't had the license to share it with anyone except a partner until now, but we've been doing some thinking, experimenting, and planning. And... building."

"Who's 'we'?" Dina asked.

"Me and Megan Trapper. Undergrad. Astronomy major, with bioscience and tech understudies," I replied.

"Oh, right. I've seen you with her at functions. Never met her though," she answered.

"She's pretty smart. She's been helping me with something... *novel.*"

"Is this what you've been so secretive about for the past few months?" Isaac asked.

"What do you mean?" I asked, curious.

"Dude. You're constantly stealing out of here, you can't wait to leave, and you never hang out with us anymore. You've been living under a rock since May. We already knew you were working on something, ahem, *novel,*" he said, sporting air quotes and donning a face of mockery.

Dina grinned at his retort.

"Yeah. Okay, you got me. Yes, this is it. I'm not sure you're going to believe me when I tell you, but, yes, I've been – *we've* been, Megan and I – working on something that just might," -here I paused, wanting to be careful not to convey false hope or overly raise their expectations- "might present an alternate scenario."

"How do you mean?" Isaac asked, leaning in. "Don't tease me."

I stared at him and took a deep breath. My eyes ventured over to Dina briefly as well, and there was a twinkle of curiosity in hers.

"It's hard to explain – and it's not. I've been working on a… *teleportation* system." I paused to let it sink in. "It's something novel, yes, but I didn't know just how novel until now."

"A teleportation system? You're kidding me. Have we all crossed over into fiction, now, Dane?" Dina mumbled.

"It's not fiction, Dina. It's not." Someone further back in the lab knocked over a beaker, or something, and I quickly jerked my head to assess whether someone was eaves-dropping. I leaned closer in to them, scooting my chair right next to Dina's.

"Guys, it works. *It works,*" I emphasized.

"How do you know?" Isaac quickly barked.

"Because it does, Isaac. I've sent things through. It wasn't perfect, but it does what it needs to. It's been perfected. And it… *perfects* the subjects that have gone through. I've sent three subjects through. The first were my birds. They didn't make it. But then I sent Macy through."

"Your dog?" Dina asked incredulously. "You put your poor dog through there?"

"Oh, she's not poor anymore. It actually *improved* her, Dina. She's younger, she's more agile, her eyes aren't cloudy anymore, she's got the vigor of a two-year-old pup."

"You said three subjects," Isaac persisted. "What was the third?"

I stared at him intently. "Not what. *Who.*"

It took him a second, but he understood. "No way. You? You went through?"

I nodded.

"What?" Dina exclaimed. "*You* went through? Do you have any idea how foolhardy that was?" She looked me up and down as if to assess whether I was still myself.

"I agree. It was. But I had enough proof. Enough proof and no time left to prove anything else," I defended. "I *had* to. You guys remember the burps?"

"Yeah. Disgusting." Isaac mock-gagged.

"They're gone?" Dina asked.

I nodded back to her. "So far. And I feel younger, I feel more energetic. It's like, somehow, Nova and Ava — those are what I named the teleporters…"

"Nice," Isaac interrupted, nonchalantly.

"…somehow, when I went through, Nova sent the data to Ava, and Ava disregarded anything in a less-than-ideal state, categorically 'upgrading' it. She did the same thing with me that she did with Macy. I had a big dinner and my stomach isn't even grumbling. And no burps."

They both looked me up and down.

"Guys, it's *me*," I said. "I swear to you."

"Even if I believed you, I'd have to go see it for myself," Dina said. "Anyway, what does all this have to do with your 'alternate scenario'?"

I took a deep breath. "It's hard to explain, but Megan and I have been spit-balling over some ideas. And now I need to talk with Defense Secretary Donze again, because we just might have a way through this."

"No friggin' way," Isaac muttered, his eyes squinting. He straightened up. I had been addressing Dina and hadn't noticed him. His jaw was dropped. "Teleportation *off* Planet Earth? That's what you're doing, isn't it?!"

I nodded. "Shhh, keep your voice down. We're not sure yet, and we haven't quite locked in how we would do it."

"To where? When? How?" Isaac asked, suddenly empowered with hope and raising his voice despite my pleas for him to keep it quiet. "When?!" he asked again, nearly yelling it.

"Isaac! Please. We don't have enough cookies for everybody," I said, laughing. "I don't know yet. We're discussing Proxima Centauri b. Sorry, I have to say 'PCb,' or Megan will hit me. It's in the next closest system."

"What?" he cried with a sneer. "That's over 4 light years away! We need something in our *own* system!"

I shook my head. "No way. Norma will swallow everything up here. Which is why we're focusing on PCb in the interim," I paused, "*or* figure out a way to get a receiving chamber there *before* Norma hits us. It's the closest."

"How can you do that?" Dina asked.

"That's exactly what I need to ask the SecDef about. And I want you on that call. Then, you can come over and see for yourself."

They eyed me curiously. The muffled sounds of the rioters persisted outside.

I smiled at them. "I call it *Courier 3.1*."

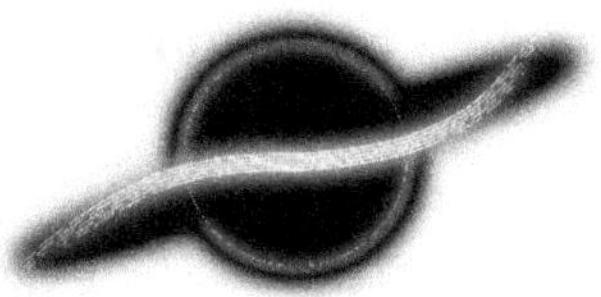

"Let me see if I understand this cockamamie plan in entirety," Donze said, his forehead propped by a tense hand. "You want us to jettison one of your receiving chambers toward this, this, 'Proxima Centauri b' planet – which I note, by the way, that you have provided *zero* guarantees of its ability to sustain life – and hope to God that it receives multiple human signals preserved inside one of your thingies back here on earth, wait patiently for seventy thousand years, while praying to whatever patron saint is in charge of hairbrained celestial travel plans that we actually *survive* this comedy of errors. Then, we get there, just in time for you to zap fry us back into a state of animation, and we all get to walk around like lethargic, nude sleep zombies in some new Garden of Eden. Do I understand your crackhead batshit crazy strategy correctly, Mr. Currier?"

"Mister Secretary, I realize it sounds far-fetched-"

"*Sounds* far-fetched!" he bellowed.

"Sir," I persisted, "believe me, if we had a better way, I would be presenting that. This is the best we can come up with, and I believe that what I've developed may have just come for such a time as this," I defended. "If you have a better option, sir, with all due respect, I'd genuinely love to hear it."

He just squinted at me stoically over Zoom. The time drug on interminably while we waited for his verdict.

I could feel the heat of Dina and Isaac repeatedly glancing back at me while Donze and I faced off.

The Secretary of Defense finally lurched his forehead away from his hand and pulled back from the screen. "What the hell. We *don't* have any better ideas. Our days are numbered and we're all dead men anyway. The President's son has fallen apart, which affects the President, and the rest of us now have to figure out what we're going to do."

This was news to us. Something must have happened; some emotional distress must have befallen the White House on the coattails of Norma.

"I'm sorry to hear it, sir."

"Well, you would be too if your future daughter-in-law killed herself."

I tilted my head, and then glanced at Dina and Isaac. "I'm sorry, sir?"

Donze paused. "Oh, of course. You wouldn't have heard yet. She put a gun through her mouth two hours ago. Couldn't take the Norma news. She was set to be married to Barron early next year." His brow furrowed, and he wiped his hands through the air as if to clear the slate. "Let's not talk about this right now, folks. We have, I think, more pressing things to attend to."

That makes two. St. James and the President's daughter-in-law. How tragic, I thought to myself.

"Yessir," I replied. "I'm sorry, sir."

"Hey, it's not *my* daughter-in-law," he said, dismissively and rather heartlessly, studying his notes on the desk in front of him. "Now, please explain to me in the simplest terms how this would work."

I cleared my throat. "Well, Mr. Secretary, my *Courier 3.1* chambers are called Nova and Ava. They're already operational. I've already gone through myself, sir. What you see before you is Dane Currier 2.0, if I can say that. I can have myself checked out by medical but I don't have any anomalies, any sickness, any extra limbs, lapsed memory, cognitive issues... nothing. We need to build a third, however. One of the teleportation chambers, Ava, can act as a relay extender, in order to jump the signals through time and space. We would send the subjects – as many as we can – through Nova. They get housed only temporarily in Ava, who then springboards the signals to another waiting chamber either here or even already on PCb. We just have to get this third one – we're calling her Aurora – there somehow. My colleague is in the process of securing the parts for the third chamber now."

"What do you need from us?" he asked briskly.

I gathered my breath. "Well, sir, what do you know about nuclear pulse propulsion?"

The SecDef just stared right through me. "Why do you ask that?" he finally asked, with a clear note of suspicion, which both encouraged me and confirmed that he knew about it.

"Well, sir, that seventy thousand years gets reduced to under a hundred years if we can mobilize it. Sir," I replied, "if the government has access to any tech or engineers who have any knowledge of the subject, it would greatly expedite our passage."

He continued to numbly regard me, a blank slate concealing dubious lines of thought scrolling behind his eyes. "Greatly – expedite – our – passage," he enunciated. "You mean to this other star."

"Yessir," I answered, and then I read him clearly. "Someone is still working on it, aren't they? Is that why you're looking at me that way? Has someone been working on it all along? Sir, I'm telling you that would *exponentially* increase our chances of survival."

"Hold your horses, Mr. Currier. I'm going to ask. There is someone, but this has been top-secret highest-priority government-clearance-only work, and there are considerations that need to be taken into account before I can divulge that or connect the two of you."

"Such as?"

"Is the fact that it's top-secret not enough, Currier?" he growled. "The short answer is *yes*, I can put you in touch with a team led by someone who can help you. The long answer is that the work they've been doing is classified; it was never supposed to be public knowledge."

"Understood," I replied. "Well, Mr. Secretary, time is running out. If we're going to start working on this and get our other chamber out there, we need to start talking *yesterday*."

The same cold disregard, the same icy standoffish bureaucratic red-tape-face. I couldn't imagine what lines he thought he might be crossing when our world was about to be stripped to ribbons and here we were talking about a potential way off this rock.

"What's your direct phone number, Mr. Currier?" he asked me. "I'll need to make some calls and get back to you."

I gave it to him, and he switched off, thanking us for our time. That was nice, at least.

I turned to Dina and Isaac. "Well?" I asked them.

"Seems impractical and a long shot," Isaac muttered. "But if you've already got these things working and you're still you," -here he stuck a finger and poked it into my chest to ensure I wasn't an apparition; I smiled as he sighed in relief- "then we're with you."

I put a hand on his shoulder. "I appreciate it. I'm sorry I couldn't tell you both. I didn't want it getting out. But you can see how timely it is." I watched them, and then got an idea. "Hey, you guys wanna try it?"

Isaac slowly brought his eyes over to Dina, eyebrows up. She smiled back at him.

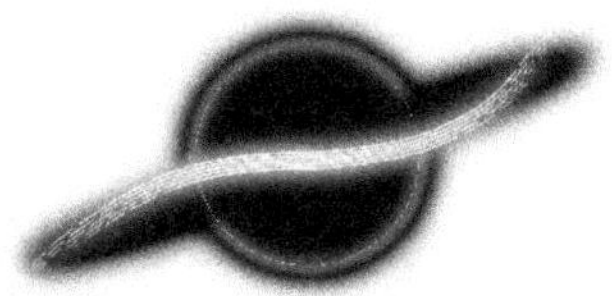

"That's Nova, and that's Ava," I said, pointing at them. "Pretty sexy, eh?"

Isaac had been sitting on the couch as soon as he had come in, loving all over Macy, adoring her and cooing to her, affirming to me that she was beautiful. I didn't know he was such a dog person. Now, he bounded up, removed his coat and strode toward them, examining Ava's exterior. Macy followed him and sniffed him curiously. "Wicked. What are they made of?" he asked, not taking his eyes off of them.

"Oh, DuroLast, 3M, insulated aluminum conduit, polyurethane, plastic, resin, and a partridge in a pear tree," I said. "I promise it's not atoms just holding hands."

"Insane," he said.

Dina was already inside Nova, feeling around and slowly revolving as her eyes took in the belly of the chamber around her. She closed the door, and her voice was muffled. "Tight seal! Vacuum?"

I nodded.

"No particle leakage. That's probably important," she observed.

"Well, I wouldn't want anyone appearing on the other side and missing something trivial, like, say, their brain."

She stifled a slight giggle. "Sure."

I looked back over at Isaac. "What do you think, Farragut? Pretty impressive, eh?"

"You went through this?" he asked me.

"Of course. Somebody had to try it. I wasn't going to let one of you go in case it decided to send you through with your right forearm poking out of your left nostril and your left knee where your right ear should be."

"You put your left knee in, and you shake it all about," he offered in a sing-song.

"Hokey pokey, sure enough," I said, grinning.

"And how do you facilitate the transfer?"

"Right here, buddy. *Courier 3.1.* Right on my laptop. Coded it myself."

"*You* did?" Dina asked, emerging from Nova.

"Well, I got some app and coding help from Kabat in computer science," I shrugged. "Man, did I have to give him the runaround in terms of why I was asking him the questions I was asking him for specific lines of code."

Dina was leaning over all my equipment. "And how did you tell it to recognize and understand you?"

"This," I said, pointing to the scanner. It was a small microwave-sized device off to the side of my laptop, with a simple USB-C interface. "I literally had to get a skin sample from Macy, same with me, and allow it to scan us and understand, on a cellular level, what we were made of."

"That's amazing," she said. "I could have told Nova what you were made of, easily enough."

"Yeah, but 'piss and vinegar' wouldn't have really sent the right message. She would have sent me into Ava's chamber as a toilet and a plastic jug," I smirked. "She needed to know precise details."

They studied both chambers, silently, reverently, with an earnest amount of hope swirling around them.

"You feel the same as before?" Farragut asked me.

I nodded. They remained quiet for a while after that.

"This is it, gang," I offered. "This is what I've been working on with Megan Trapper. If this works, we just might have a way out."

Isaac didn't waste any time. He quickly threw his backpack onto the couch, slipped off his shoes, and then strode over to Nova. "I wanna try it."

"Not so fast, buddy. Wait!" I exclaimed.

"What?" he asked, turning back around.

"You gotta go nude, remember?"

He rolled his eyes. "Fine. Look away, perverts," he growled, fidgeting for his belt.

"Hold up!" I said. "Nova needs to 'know you,' first, Isaac. Come here. Watch out, Macy girl." Macy had been sniffing Isaac's feet, but she now jumped out of the way.

He came to my little table with the laptop and the scanner. I fired everything up, and then reached into a small container where Trapper and I had deposited a few small medical lancets. "Give me your finger." He did so, and I poked it and took his blood sample, inserting it onto a slide from another container next to the lancets.

The scanner whirred. I quickly created a new profile in *Courier 3.1* for him. "What's your middle name, Isaac?"

"Cray."

"Cray? Like the big old computers? Wow. OK." I typed in *Farragut, Isaac Cray.* Gave it his general parameters and let the scanner do the rest. We waited for it to beep and Isaac's profile to be populated with data.

Isaac gasped as the screen lit up with his DNA profile. "So now you have a biological profile on me?"

"Yep. Okay, buddy, take it off."

"Look away!"

We did so. Isaac stepped into Nova, after having removed his clothes and placed them just outside the door to Ava. The lock on Nova clicked. I didn't wait for him to tell me when, whirling back around and moving to my laptop. He was inside cupping himself with a sheepish grin.

"Knock it off, Dina!" he exclaimed, muffled.

I glanced over at her. She was giggling and covering her face.

"Okay, you ready, buddy?" I looked back at him. He nodded.

"Here we go. Ten seconds." I programmed the countdown, and then let *Courier 3.1* do its thing.

The countdown seemed shorter than it actually was. In ten short seconds, Nova lit up blindingly just as it had when I had watched Macy and the birds and everything else go through. Shortly thereafter, Ava answered with a flash, and the inside swirled with foggy trails of wisp. A hand presently reached down to the door handle and unlocked it.

Isaac stepped out, fully nude, and fully himself. His face was plastered with a gigantic grin signifying absolute approval with zero shame. Macy went up to him and sniffed him, wagging her tail. He immediately bent down and stroked her. "Hey, Macy! It's me! Remember me?" She wagged and rubbed against his legs as he bent over and scratched her sides affectionately.

"Don't forget you're naked, buddy," I said to him.

He laughed and checked himself over. "Whoa! Are you serious? I don't even care! How do I look? It's me! Can you tell it's me?" He whirled around us.

"Uh, yep, still you, and still naked," Dina said. I chortled.

"Right!" he exclaimed, and then whipped down to the ground to fetch his clothes and get dressed, speaking frenetically as he did so. "That was insane! I mean, hot, and not hot – it felt like I was spinning down into this, this vortex, but it was like an arc, or like, no! Not an arc, but like of, like a parabola, ya know? In a weird, staticky way… but like, no pain! It felt like an hour or something. How long was I gone? That was *so* weird! Like a rush of pinpricks and crazy spots swimming in front of my eyes, and more colors than I could count. *How long?!*" He spoke with a spastic energy, unable to contain his amazement.

"You broke Isaac, Dane. He talks now. Send him back through," Dina joked, turning to me.

"No, no," Isaac protested, finishing up dressing. "Isaac.exe is very much functional and operating within parameters. Whoo! That was crazy! Can I see what it says?"

"Sure, take a look," I said, pointing him to the screen.

All he could mutter repeatedly was *Wow…* as he examined metrics of his position, polarity, electrons, protons, neutrons, space-time position, axis, mass, relative position in Ava to Nova, and all sorts of dizzying details that would be Greek to the layman. "It was nearly instantaneous, wasn't it? I swear I was in there close on an hour."

I looked at Dina. "Well, that's two down. Your turn, Dina!"

She shook her head. "No. No. Not just yet. I mean, I know I'm gonna have to if this is our way out, but… not yet, okay?" She nervously backed away from us. Out there, where pandemonium was breaking out in pockets, she was trying to reconcile with the pandemonium inside her own heart. I understood. Was this really a chance? Could it actually save us? She needed to be sure.

"Dina, serious, you gotta do it! I feel great! I'm still me! Right?" Isaac asked, turning to face me.

I nodded. "You're still you, buddy. But just… give her time. No rush."

Isaac snickered to himself, looking back and forth between the two of us, and then shook his head crazily and laughed heartily. "Unbelievable. That was wild. Put me on the next flight to Proxima Centauri *b!*" he exclaimed.

Dina turned to him. "Well, that's just it, right? It's not exactly a guaranteed flight, is it? Who's to say we'll even be included on the manifest?" she asked doubtfully.

I shrugged. "No, there's no way we'd be left out. Isaac, you discovered the damned thing. Dina, you're on that team. And I developed *Courier 3.1*. We're *going,* guys. All three of us. No way around it. I'll pull the plugs and format the laptop first."

Dina sneered. "Well, I'm not holding my breath. You know how the government works. Just listen to Donze! We're dead in less than 3 months – let's be honest, it won't take the full three – and even still, the United States Government is playing hard-to-get with their top-secret bullshit. Everything should be on the table now. *Everything.* If I sound mad, it's because I am. I believe *Courier 3.1* works, Dane. I do. I just saw Isaac teleport. It just never ceases to amaze me, the audacity of the holdouts." She crossed her arms as she spoke, increasing in speed and volume as she went. Something obviously nagged at her from the past, or some other issue. She was more heated than I had ever seen her. "Somebody said it in an old movie somewhere, I can't remember where exactly, but they said, 'scientists have always been pawns of the military.' It's so aggravatingly true!"

"Dina, what is it?" I asked.

"Nothing, I, *nothing*," she said, waving me away. "It's just stupid. This whole thing is stupid and so... final," she finished, with some heat. "I just... mark my words, Dane, they know now. They *know.* I wouldn't leave this place if I were you."

I tilted my head. "What do you mean?"

"Your apartment! I wouldn't leave it." Isaac straightened up, watching her quizzically. "You know what they'll do," she said. "You'll come home, and these won't be here. I guarantee it."

We both just watched her. I cast a quick glance to Isaac, and his eyes mirrored the sobering potentiality of what she was suggesting. Dina always struck me as a bit of a naysayer, a checks-and-balances sort of woman, opinionated to the point of devil's advocate, whereas Isaac was just a pessimistic mumbler – until the past five minutes, that is. What was coming from her now was deep-rooted suspicion that had its origins that certainly preceded our own friendship.

"You think they'll come in here and appropriate all of this now that it's on Donze's radar?" Isaac asked, but it was delivered more like a statement of certainty rather than a query.

She nodded. "'Appropriate'? That's not the word, Isaac. 'Steal' is the word!"

"There are many more self-important people in this world than the three of us. Norma is on her way. If there's now a chance that those people can be saved by the hair of their chinny-chin-chin while the rest of us burn up, and they can start their own new colony somewhere else without all the crazy rest of the planet? They'll take it. You heard Donze, Dane. *Cockamamie plan. Crackhead batshit crazy strategy.* Those aren't just words. Now he knows it works, watch him pivot and see the potential escape plan that he's privy to now. He'll endorse it like there's no tomorrow, and he'll take all of it and say it was the government's idea. Watch."

I suddenly thought of my gun, and the need to be armed. Was I just being reactive? Was Dina? Would Macy bark enough to wake us up and alert us, if we were sleeping?

"So, what do I do?" I asked her, throwing my arms up in helplessness. I wasn't ready to be deflated yet; to be deprived of my optimism, but she was, I felt, raising a valid concern.

"Yeah, what does he do, Dina?" Isaac supported.

Her eyes were wells of suspicion and fear. "I'm saying you'd be a fool to leave this place. Couple'a black Suburbans come rollin' up one day, park right outside your apartment, right? A bunch of them bust in with overwhelming numbers, hit you and Megan Trapper with chloroform, and make off with Nova, Ava, Aurora, your laptop, your scanner, all of it. You wake up and have *nothing*. I've seen it before, Dane."

"When?"

Dina sighed, and she crossed her arms. "My dad," she said, glumly. "He had a cold fusion plan that might have actually worked. He taught at Syracuse. Everything was fine, he was making progress on it, and somebody – he never found out who – spilled the beans to some government ne'er-do-wells. He was actually really close to getting funded! He was so optimistic. So full of joy. No. One day he comes home. Everything ransacked. Papers littered everywhere. All his research, *all* of it. Gone! He and his lab were on the trail of being the first to replicate it since the Pons-Fleischmann experiment in 1989. All of them signed an NDA. It didn't hold. Someone blabbed! And then," she trailed off with another labored sigh, "it was all over. That could have put us all through college and taken care of us for life."

Dina sat down hard on the couch.

"I didn't know that, Dina. I'm sorry."

"Me neither. I'm sorry, too," Isaac mumbled, reverting to his quiet self once more.

She shrugged. "History repeats itself. It always does. My dad used to always quote Ecclesiastes. *What has been will be again, what has been done will be done again; there is nothing new under the sun.* It's true."

"Well, there's one new thing at least. Norma. Never destroyed Earth before. That's new," I offered in a weak attempt at humor. It didn't work. She just stared at the floor.

"Hey," I said, correcting my approach, "I'm sorry about your dad. I truly am. I didn't know that. It makes sense that you're scared. We'll be careful, okay? I'll tell Megan the same thing. We won't leave."

I looked at Isaac, and a grin crept over my face. "I don't think we'll really want to, anyway, given what we have to do, and what we're on the verge of. Hell, I can survive on pizza and Mountain Dew until the cows come home. So can

Megan. She's getting some of the equipment as we speak. Requisitions."

Dina raised her eyes to meet mine. "Just be careful, Dane. That's all I'm saying. Be careful. This is important. It could be a way out. I don't want what happened to my dad to happen to you."

I didn't say anything in response. I just stared at Macy for a moment, lying on her pillow in the corner of the living room, eyeing us curiously. She registered me scanning her and began to wag.

All I could do was nod and appreciate Dina's warning. But the cold reality was that I was now more than a little skittish in my heart. Would the CIA and a bunch of hired guns burst in here and take what I've worked so hard for? Would they, in good conscience, steal what was mine, my breakthrough development, everything I've strived to achieve with *Courier 3.1*?

My heart told me she wasn't barking up the wrong tree. My heart told me her cynicism was well-founded.

"I'll be careful. I promise."

Dina's eyes finally dropped, and then moved over to Isaac. "Alright. I'll go through later. But I gotta get something to eat first. Isaac, wanna come with me?"

Isaac nodded. "Yeah. This new body needs some fresh air after *this* talk." He grinned at me. "Sorry, Macy, gotta go! Be good!" He pointed sternly at her, mockingly.

"You're staying here, right, Dane?" Dina asked.

"After *that* conversation? Definitely," I said, shaking my head. "Not hungry. I'm gonna go over some schematics in re-configuring Ava as a relay for when we get Aurora setup. Norma won't wait. You guys wanna get what you get and bring it back here, that works. Megan should be here in a while."

"Okay," Dina said, and they were off, out into the pandemonium and the fray.

"Be careful out there," I cautioned. "I mean it."

I locked the door behind them, and surveyed the room. There was a lot here, and a lot riding on it.

Like hell I was going to let some government cronies waltz in and make off with my girls. *Over my dead body… or yours,* I thought, coldly.

I went for my gun, checked it to make sure it was loaded, and put it in my back pocket. Now I was armed. No one would get *Courier 3.1* or my chambers without a fight.

After all, the government was still alive and well.

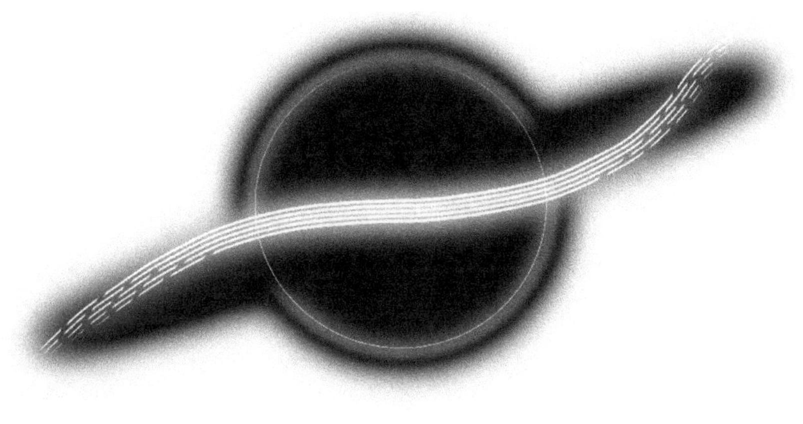

9 | *Construction*
November 8th, 2025

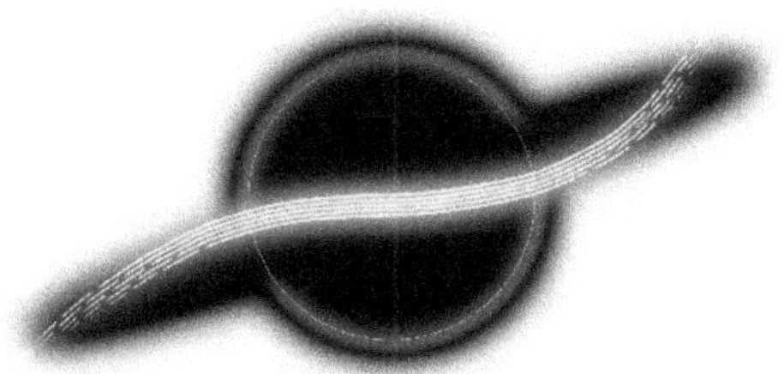

It was early, and we needed a break.

Trapper had returned; she finally got to meet Dina and Isaac, and vice versa.

Quickly, Megan devoured the rest of her food while she regaled everyone with stories of pandemonium and chaos, insanity and dread slowly creeping through the streets and waylaying as many poor souls as it could devour. The end was coming, and charlatans already stood out on the sidewalks with sandwich boards preaching of hellfire and damnation, crypto and comfort animals. People were starting to dot the streets everywhere, hawking various wares which attested to their own measures of belief in dubious forms of security.

The four of us bantered briefly about the end of the world, but that was that. We had work to do.

We all set to work, feverishly commiserating by the light of a dozen dazzlingly bright floor lamps. That was critical, because the schematics demanded that each part fit precisely, and we had to manually cut some pieces out on my 3D printer in order to make them all fit together. There couldn't be any breach in the chamber, though the inside would be filled and coated to create an impenetrable seal against leakage, and would then be thoroughly scanned and analyzed by *Courier 3.1* to ensure stability.

Through all of our work, Macy made her rounds and ensured that she received plenty of scruffs of her fur. Isaac was always the most affectionate with her. He really adored my dog, and she ate it all up.

At one point there was some kind of explosion a few blocks from us, and answering sirens. Macy yelped and stood erect, facing the door. I could only imagine what civil unrest might be unfolding. CNN was quietly droning on in the background, and we were trying not to give it any added focus. We knew the stakes.

The truth was that we had *Aurora* to build, and Norma wouldn't wait. *Funny,* I thought – all these girls getting ready to fight, three against one. We'd see how my girls would fare in the upcoming fracas against the certain supermassive heading our way.

Everyone had eaten, but, strangely, I wasn't really all that hungry. I also hadn't had a single sulfur burp since going through Nova, and I told them as much. Isaac was fascinated by that, and I could tell by the look in his eyes that he was running his own self-assessment, determining what previous flaws had been upgraded in himself to near perfected status: even *purged* from his new form.

We had a job to do, and we couldn't waste any time putting Aurora together. Patterned nearly identically as a baseline to Ava, she would be the relay receiver, and she is who would make the long journey out to Proxima Centauri b. But Aurora would be different.

For the first time, we were all sitting there brimming with hope. All of us. We knocked heads together, we slaved over the schematics and what the final blueprints would look like, and we knew what else we needed. Megan was bossy; no one cared. I think Isaac really appreciated her assertive personality because it bordered on snide aggression, though I caught occasional smile-heavy glances he gave toward Dina, and wondered if there was something there.

Megan, however, was putting everyone in their place. After all, she was the geek who knew how to take my vision and manifest it into plastic and resin through my 3D printer. I was the visionary; she was the wizard. We followed her lead and slaved away on ensuring that it would work.

The modifications that we were making to her would see expansion banks on her inner hull, between the inside chamber and the outer frame, in which we would insert SATA drives and redundant RAID arrays protected by ferromagnetic metals such as iron, copper and nickel in the outer plating. This would shield her from electromagnetic interference, radio frequency noise, magnetic radiation and the like. We also had conductive fabric layers to reinforce the shielding, and we were painting the outsides with conductive paints over the metal plating to create electromagnetic barriers. We also had to account for solar arrays to power her batteries for the long flight should she have to be jettisoned from whatever nuclear propulsion spacecraft we might get our hands on. That would be the contingency plan. As the spacecraft drew near to PCb, it would need to invert and drop her to the ground safely somehow, or all that human-data could be compromised.

In the middle of our commiseration and planning, my phone buzzed. I stopped everyone and showed them my phone. SecDef Donze texted me – it read, simply: *We have a green light. I'll be in touch. Let me know what you need, and tell no one. I mean it. –Erick Donze.*

That was it. That's what we needed to hear.

Two comforts emerged from that text. One, that nuclear propulsion *was* in fact still being tested and that we'd have access to the technology to transport Aurora to PCb. Thus, my suspicion was confirmed. It stood to reason – why abandon something so revolutionary when you can work on it in secret and emerge as the industry leader when the technology is actually called for? This seems to have been the *modus operandi* for the US Government for far too long. Maybe now it would be just in time to actually be useful for something other than bravado and self-aggrandizement.

And two, that we might just be left alone while doing so. No hired thugs to pull the wool out from under us. At least, that's what I was crossing my fingers for.

Time would tell.

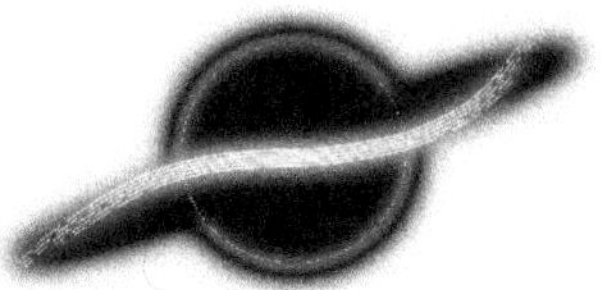

We were all napping in the middle of the day when another explosion sounded.

Macy jumped up and barked repeatedly at the window, then retreated, growling.

The building rocked suddenly, and there was a whooshing sound out on the street. I leapt to my feet. The others jumped up in a panic as well: Dina and Megan in my bedroom, Isaac and I out in the living room. Dina's hair was sticking straight up like a cat.

There's nothing worse than being jerked out of REM sleep. I remember that from my practicums… some of our biology studies required deep studies on REM and being 'dug in like a tick.' It's the most unpleasant thing to be yanked out of. My eyes were wide with alarm as I went to the window.

I had just missed a group of jeeps and cars barreling down Pacific Street, smashing other cars out of their way in their race to evade their pursuers. My eyes flashed back up the street they had just come. There, rolling noisily toward them, was a tank. A United States military tank, of all things! Right here in the middle of Seattle, pushing its way through. And there was another one! And another! A caravan of the iron maidens was rolling its way down the street.

Macy began growling vigorously, bristling.

"Holy sh-" a voice muttered beside me. It was Isaac, peering through the blinds to my left. I stared at him wide-eyed for a moment in alarm, and then returned my gaze.

"Dina, turn on the news!" I cried. "Macy, quiet!"

My dog put her tail between her legs and crept off, licking her lips nervously.

I glanced back up the street. Whatever unrest those fleeing in the jeeps had caused, it was enough to warrant a blast from a *tank.* The Fishery Science Building was in flames. That was nearly right across Pacific from us, slightly to the west.

I wondered what was going on in there… who the jeeps belonged to… or what they had done. Had they stolen something? Killed someone? Too many questions for a bleary, tired mind. Was this the beginning of unbridled anarchy? Would we be facing this every day?

The tanks rolled on down Pacific and were lost to view. I don't even remember what was said between Isaac and I, or the ladies, or any of us. All I remember is pouring myself back into my bed in an exhausted stupor, my heart racing at first, and then quietly slowing to a dull sludge.

Macy jumped up onto the couch with me and folded herself into a tight ball.

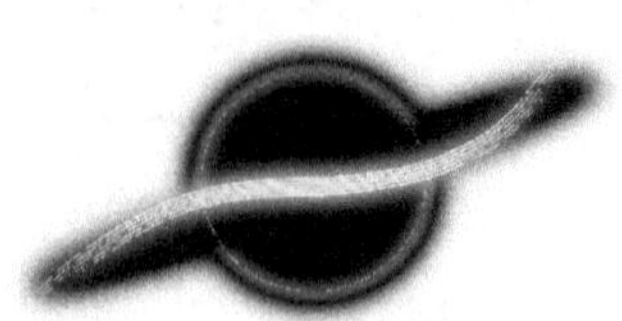

Trapper awoke first, gently nudging me on the shoulder. "Dane. Wake up, Dane. Dane!" Well, it *seemed* gentle at first.

"What? *What?*" I asked, blinking stupidly and trying to stow my irritation at the sudden urgency on her part.

"Time to get up, pudgy. Aurora's calling."

Macy jumped off of me as I stuck a knuckle into my eye and peeled out some gunk. A wicked yawn escaped me as I glanced around. The others were still passed out. I could see Dina at the end of the hall on my bed, and Isaac was face down on the couch, dirty socks protruding from a blanket loosely covering him that Dina must have covered him with before passing out again herself.

I glanced at the clock. 3:53 pm. *We certainly won't save the world working these hours,* I thought.

"Anything new with those tanks and jeeps?"

She shook her head and plopped down at the table, staring into my laptop. She picked up a piece of cold pizza next to her and began gnawing on it. "I'm just looking at these in your system. Where does your OS display the redundancies to mirror teleportation integrity?"

I stifled a giggle. "I love it when you talk *data* to me."

She sneered.

I couldn't get up yet, still stretching. "Are you on the main screen?"

"Yep."

"Hit Command F5. That's the main pulldown menu. Go under 'Arrays' and then down to 'Analyze.' You'll see the teleportation subject history. Isaac will be the last one, yesterday afternoon, somewhere around there." I yawned again, trembling slightly. A hunger welled up inside me – I was famished.

"Amazing," she said. "Everything is a one-to-one ratio. I wonder what would happen if something was not quite mirroring up. Would Ava send the subject back to Nova?"

"Yes. But it would happen before anything got sent. It enters a holding state where the handshake is made, and if it's not identical, the signal gets sent back to Nova."

She frowned, and looked at me. "Ava rejects it?"

I nodded to her, yawning again through my fist.

"That could be a huge problem on the receiving end."

My turn to frown, confused.

"Well, what happens if for some reason the transfers are rejected entirely? Would they compile and fuse back in Nova?" she asked.

"Ew. That doesn't sound healthy. I wouldn't want to reappear with Isaac's stinky feet coming out of my face," I joked, standing up and walking toward the kitchen to brew some coffee. I grabbed a jerky treat from the puppy cookie jar and tossed it to Macy. "But no, I modified that last night during our assembly, given what we're planning on doing. *Courier 3.1* has been updated. They don't reform, they're sent back to a holding pattern, essentially."

"So, the code for each DNA profile gets resuspended until called for once more?"

"Yep."

I craned my neck, working out a kink.

"Hmm. Well that sounds necessary," she ended, and then fell silent.

"Yeah, that's what happened with nearly every original attempt. It happened with Macy as well before I figured out what was happening. I had to program in some lines of code for recall."

Macy heard her name and started wagging.

"Got it," Trapper replied.

I inserted a Gloria Jean's butter toffee coffee K-Cup in the machine and hit 'brew.'

"Uh, *Daaane*?" Megan droned, slowly.

Her curious tone of voice and drawn-out beckoning of me caused me to turn and face her.

"What's this?" she asked, almost accusingly.

"What's what?"

"You said the last one was Isaac yesterday afternoon."

"Yeah, I did. He went through."

"Come here."

My brow furrowed as I strode over to her. Prescience ate at me; I almost knew what she was going to say before she said it.

"Then what's this transfer profile at 4:03 am?"

I leaned over her and studied the monitor. My jaw dropped.

It wasn't Isaac.

The mass suggested a smaller subject. Human biological DNA, certainly, but slighter build and far less dense, muscularly.

And female.

"It wasn't me," Trapper defended. She and I gawked at each other in amazement and then scurried to the bedroom, gazing down upon the figure lying there.

"Dina?" She stirred slightly but didn't acknowledge me. "Dina, wake up." My undergrad mumbled some incoherent response, and then slowly shifted her head to look at us staring down upon her. "You went through!"

She blinked in confusion for a moment, and then smiled and slowly nodded through a yawn.

"Yeah, I did."

"Did you really?" Trapper asked her. "How do you feel?" Megan and I both looked her up and down. I knelt down beside her bed, well, *my* bed.

"Fine. Headache, but only because of lack of sleep," she breathed through another yawn, slowly sitting up and staring at the floor. Dina ran her hands through her hair and tousled them into place. "Because someone woke me up too early." She mock-glared at us.

"It's four in the afternoon. Nice try. Time to get up, my friend," I said, sitting down next to her. "Seriously, why'd you do it? They should be supervised. You waited until we were all asleep?"

She nodded, blinking at the light coming through the blinds in the bedroom. "I did."

"Why?"

Dina looked sheepishly back and forth between us. "Don't be coy. You have to go nude. You think I wanted to put on a *show*?" Dina recoiled into a shy grin.

I smiled back at her. "Well, you're clearly still you," I said, smiling approvingly up at Trapper. "You feel okay? The same?"

She thought to herself for a moment. "Yeah, I mean, I don't feel any different, if that means 'the same.' It was a weird feeling. I felt exhilarated, like Isaac was when he came out. It was a crazy experience, Dane. You really did it. I couldn't sleep for another few hours afterward."

"So did you," Megan said. "You really did it while we were all asleep. Glad you're okay."

"The run sequence was simple enough," Dina replied. "I figured, if we're all gonna go through this thing eventually anyway, I might as well get in a practice run before we're all standing around nude assessing each other up and down. I don't want to be rated a 1 or a 0 before I'm reduced to 1's and 0's."

I chuckled. "Maybe Trapper here can develop some bio-undies that Nova wouldn't stitch into our DNA in Ava or Aurora. That way we can preserve a modicum of decency and not have to put on a mass strip tease."

Dina giggled now. "Sure."

Trapper spoke up. "Girlfriend, don't worry about ratings. I'd kill for your butt. It's an 8 on my scale."

"Yeah, well, your boobs are a 9.5 on mine, so there," Dina shot back. They fist-bumped and giggled as I watched and smiled approvingly. Dina got up and hugged Megan.

"I'll go rouse Dirty Socks Boy," I said, rising and heading back toward the living room. "We gotta get started again. Who wants coffee?"

Me they both chimed simultaneously. "But I need to get a shower in, first," Dina said. "With *no one* watching," she clarified.

I smiled back at her. "Where's the fun in that?"

We would need to get a good breakfast in us even though it was four in the afternoon. If we didn't have calories, we weren't going anywhere.

It was late, and we needed a break.

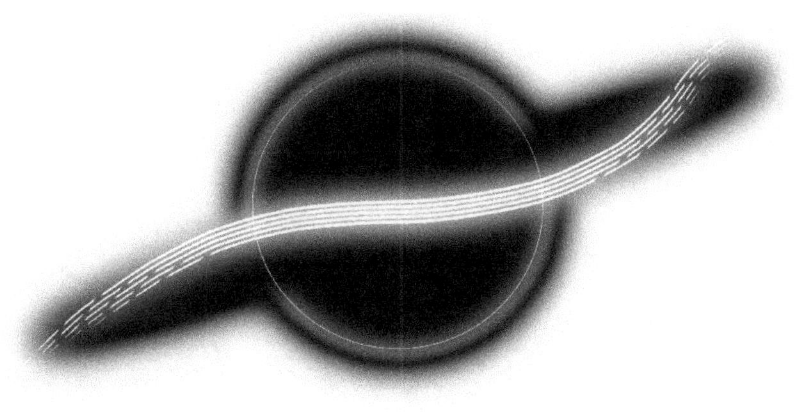

10 | Setback
November 9th, 2025

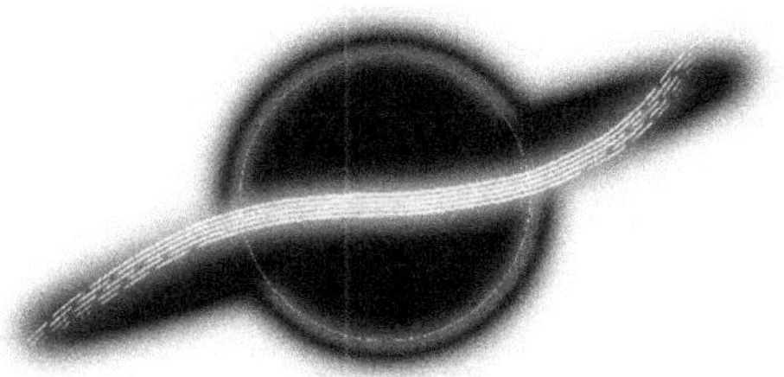

Once more into the late night hours we went.

I glanced at the clock. It was now 1:37 am on November 9th.

We'd all showered, fed ourselves, and I put on more coffee. Thankfully, our little jaunt out to Subway for fresh air and sandwiches took only forty-five minutes.

Trapper stayed behind and guarded the place with my gun. I showed it to her. She'd been target shooting before, so it wasn't a dry run for her at least. This way, our place, our research, and the last best hope for humanity's survival could stay protected.

We returned to find her – or, at least, someone who *looked* like her – in one piece. I thought she might test out the teleporters while we were away, but she insisted she hadn't. She asserted that she wasn't scared, just didn't see the need yet; besides, she said, "I trust you, Dane." That little vote of confidence went straight to my heart. And then she added a quippy addendum, "Besides, none of you are deformed mutants yet, so, there's that." She definitely had a way with words.

We had labored far into the night and were about to wind down, but we had to make plans to test something the following day. The obvious choice was Macy, but I had some hesitation, for reasons clearly beside the fact that I loved her, and she was my pup.

The cold reality, however, was that I'd never tested Nova to Ava to Aurora, and was tremendously reluctant to send Macy through. We would be in undiscovered country on this new venture.

Donze had warned us not to tell anyone about what we were doing, and none of us wanted to be the first to try the relay yet, no matter the fact that three of us had now gone through Nova to Ava.

A relay was something else entirely, because we would be entering a state of suspended animation on a timed duration, held as data on a RAID array of solid state drives, awaiting reintegration back through Aurora. That whole concept was entirely new, and brimming with loads of uncertainty.

In short, we would be tempting fate if either the relay *or* the reintegration failed. I suggested we sleep on it and get to bed earlier than yesterday.

We finally gave up and collectively crashed just under 2 am.

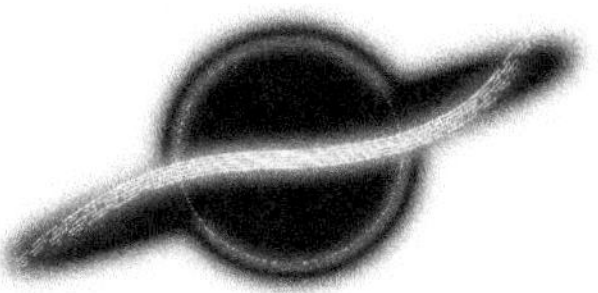

November 10th, 2025

I awoke to my alarm at 7 am. Sunlight streamed through the blinds in the bedroom, and left simmering stripes of heat across my chest.

Aurora was half-complete. She would be fully assembled, the four of us working feverishly on her, by this evening. And then, we would perform the test.

I texted Donze for an update on the nuclear propulsion while everyone else slept: *Please advise on nuclear propulsion status. We are approaching completion of third chamber, ETA this evening sometime, hopefully. Will perform subject transfer test ASAP following. Fingers crossed.*

I tossed my phone aside and combed my hair with my hands. Macy hopped up on the sofa and just stared at me. She had that look in her eyes that said, *It's been literally three days since you've walked me, so I'm about to bite your face off. I hope that's okay?*

I grabbed her and pulled her near, silently ruffling her fur. She was right. She *had* been exceedingly patient.

We had let her out in the backyard of the apartment complex; it was fenced in and grassy, but beyond that she hadn't been walked in a while. "I'm sorry, baby girl, I've neglected you, huh? Yeah. She's a good girl. We should get you moving, huh?"

Her ears perked up.

We should get you moving. Perhaps those words held more significance, more trust, than I cared to assign them or realize. I took a deep breath, and Macy watched me as she began to pant.

"Yeah, you're right, girl. It's a bit stuffy in here. Let's go. You wanna go? Go for walk?" I said, eagerly, and her eyes widened and head tilted as her ears went up. Macy bounded from the couch and ran to the door, staring up at the doorknob and wagging endlessly.

As soundlessly as possible, I threw on a shirt, shorts, my coat and shoes, then grabbed her harness and leash, but not before I left a quick note that we would be back in a few. Stuffing my cellphone in my pocket, we slipped out.

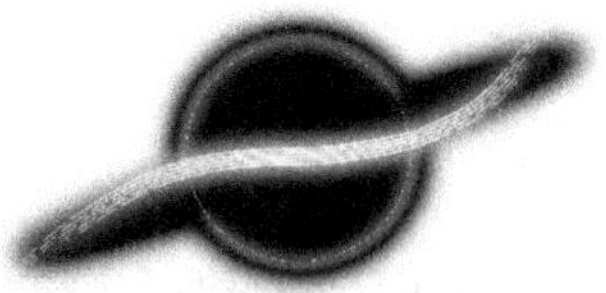

It felt like it should be even colder than it was. I wondered if that was Norma calling: radiation extending outward toward us even now. The temperature said that it was 61 degrees. But this was November.

The world was quiet, but the Fishery Science Building bore testament to loud, violent scars from those tanks. I wondered what had become of those jeeps and what the authorities did to them once they found them. The news had said nothing. I would catch a better view of it when we wrapped around Boat Street on our way back from the walk.

Macy and I traipsed up Pacific. Cars dotted the roadways, people going to and fro and fulfilling whatever mission they felt they had left.

A tangible calm had descended on Seattle at least, following the past few days of anarchic outbursts. However, it belied the storm that was coming. Calm for now, yes, but the air was so thick you could chew it. I think Macy sensed it as well.

We walked our usual route, east on Pacific, down to 15th, hanging a right at UW Children's Center at Portage Bay, and then all the way down to the water off Boat Street. We hung another right and went up to Fritz Hedges Waterway Park, and I let her off her leash to run around a bit. She was always friendly, wagging and never chased other dogs; her nose was always to the ground.

Macy took care of business and then we were back up toward home. Trapper texted me. *Hey, pudgy. Got your note. The others are still nuked. See you back here soon.*

There was a boatload of other texts I had missed. Mom, Dad, fellow graduate students, friends from another life, relatives, old contacts who had heard I was involved in Norma's discovery.

I stopped in my tracks. There it was:

Hey, bloke. Sorry I haven't texted before now. Wanted to thank you for all you've done. Keep doing it, eh? This thing will destroy our planet, for sure, but you're young, and it doesn't have to destroy you. For me? I've lived long enough, and have outlived both usefulness and desire to be useful. Nothing left to live for. Don't want to be destroyed by TWO Norma's in one lifetime. Sorry we couldn't be friends longer. I wish you well, and I'll put in a good word for your deliverance from this thing. Take risks, even with what you love. Live. Cheers, mate. -Henry

It was dated November 7th at 12:07 pm.

Henry St. James. My heart leapt into my throat as I read his final missive. A man I had hardly known but had talked to on occasion, who had helped us confirm the supermassive black hole that was on its way to us, sent literally moments before he had killed himself.

My breath held interminably; I was afraid to let it out. The world spun. What a final act of goodwill and blessing before he exited the stage of life. His comment about 'two Norma's killing him' hit me hard. His ex-wife, and now this world killer. Both had killed his world. Poor guy.

All I could do was sigh. It took me a while before my feet registered that it was time to move again, but they did, reluctantly. Slowly, heavily, we trudged up the road. Macy was tugging on her leash, leading me.

We passed up Boat Street, her leading the way as usual, angling back up north toward Pacific, as I simmered in my thoughts.

Through the parking lot, in a clearing through the trees, there was the west front of the Fisheries Building. A gigantic, blackened scar fanned outward from the point of impact, and the building had caved in at the corner. Concrete and plaster rubble littered the parking lot. Two of the trees surrounding the perimeter of the curving parking lot were scorched near to the building. Rebar poked out of the structure's wound.

My thoughts went back once more to that tank and those jeeps, wondering what had become of it all. Silently, I prayed for more God-fearing people that would keep the peace as we hurtled toward our own destruction. Or, well, as Norma's destructive forces hurtled toward us. I shook my head.

God. Where was he in all of this? Did he even hear my prayer just now? Was he seeing what was coming our way? Did he even care? I was never really a believer, other than Sunday School as a kid and having it drilled into me by my God-fearing parents. It didn't tend to play nice with science, and so I had to choose one over the other. But now, it seems, maybe there would be a reckoning. An ELE tends to force humanity's eyes and hearts upward to connect with the almighty. I just wondered if it wasn't too late.

We rounded the corner, and Building C loomed up at the corner of Pacific and Brooklyn.

The Fishery Science Building, the park, the quiet lull of the morning, St. James' text, all of it, slid into the past as I glumly trudged up the steps.

Macy followed me, reluctant for the walk to be over.

I reached the apartment door and unlocked it, heading inside. There was Trapper, sitting at her laptop next to mine, glancing up at me with a slight smile. Isaac was unmoving on the couch, but he saw me and grinned.

"Morning," he said.

I waved to him, freeing Macy from her harness and throwing my phone and keys to the side as I plopped down into my beanbag chair next to the couch, staring at the half-shell that was Aurora. Soon, we'd have triplets in here, and soon I would have to send Macy through them. That was the only way. It was what I had to do.

"You okay?" Isaac asked. Megan looked at me.

"Yeah. Just thinking," I replied softly.

This thing will destroy our planet, for sure, but you're young, and it doesn't have to destroy you.

His words came back to me, ringing true. Norma didn't have to destroy us. But, even more than that, Nova and Ava didn't have to destroy Macy. It doesn't have to destroy us. *Take risks,* he said, *even with what you love. Live,* he had said. Was this some cryptic unintentional hint that I should be willing to risk Macy, even Macy? After all, I had done it once before. I needed to do what needed to be done. And the truth was that she had not outlived either 'usefulness or desire to be useful.'

I brought my eyes to my beloved dog. She stood by the kitchen counter, expectantly, watching me and wagging, waiting for a treat. She always got a treat after a walk. She would get one now.

"Come here, girl," I said to her softly, and I think both Megan and Isaac registered that my tone was subdued; concerned; downcast.

"Dane? What is it?" Trapper now asked.

I sighed, retrieving my phone and scrolling to the text from St. James. At that point, Dina had entered the hallway, wrapped in a blanket like a walking burrito. She eyed me curiously.

"Hey, bloke," I started. "Sorry I haven't texted before now. Wanted to thank you for all you've done. Keep doing it, eh? This thing will destroy our planet, for sure, but you're young, and it doesn't have to destroy you. For me? I've lived long enough, and have outlived both usefulness and desire to be useful. Nothing left to live for. Don't want to be destroyed by TWO Norma's in one lifetime. Sorry we couldn't be friends longer. I wish you well, and I'll put in a good word for your deliverance from this thing. Take risks, even with what you love. Live. Cheers, mate. Henry," I ended, and I confess my eyes were watering. "He sent that to me right before he killed himself. I just now saw it."

I swallowed hard. The gravitational weight of the room made its presence known, descending upon us as if Norma were already here.

"It's a blessing, Dane," Dina said, walking over and sitting down next to me. "A blessing from a stranger. How fortunate are you to have gotten that? His text is right where we are in this very moment."

She was right, and I knew it. We all knew it. I glanced over at Macy. *Take risks, even with what you love.*

There was only one thing to do, after getting her a treat, of course.

Send her through.

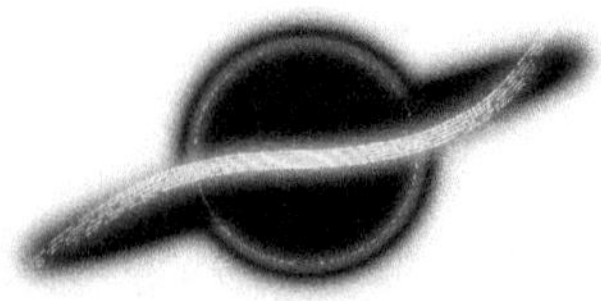

Evening approached, and we still weren't quite done. The light was fading outside, and reddish-orange beams once more lasered through the blinds in my bedroom, shafting down upon my bed, bathing Macy in amber arcs.

We were close, but we just needed the drives.

The DNA makeup of humans, descrambled and interpolated by *Courier 3.1*, amounted to roughly two terabytes of data per lifeform. That was a *lot* of data. That data contained height, weight, mass, skin color, hair color, eye color, pigmentation, imperfections such as moles and rogue hairs, skin elasticity, organ placement, blood type, anatomy, brain composition, memory modules, behavioral traits, socio-emotional makeup, intellectual quotient, artistic traits, synapse patterns, cognition, and *so* much more. Nothing could be left out! And we would need RAID arrays, so that would be doubled. There was no way in hell the UW would approve the kind of funding required to procure such large solid state drives. Some manufacturers produced SSDs up to 122 TB in size. That would be 30.5 humans, because with RAID, the space needed would have to be doubled in the redundant array of independent disks. As far as we knew, no one possessed the technology to produce petabyte drives of one thousand terabytes yet, so the best we could do until then was just daisy chain the terabyte drives together.

Doing the math, we figured if we got ahold of 100 of those drives, that would be three-thousand fifty lives. Would that be enough to jumpstart the human race on PCb? I didn't know, and I wondered, comically, who the 'half-human,' the 'point five' would be.

The humans would have to be a good representation of life here on earth, young and old, rich and poor, slave and free, famous and unknown, and they would have to represent a diverse palette of who we were… who we became… how we evolved… what humanity truly means.

Along with that, we would have to find a way to send along food, not knowing what kind of resources awaited us on Proxima Centauri b. We would need chickens, pigs, and animals small enough to fit within the confines of each chamber… or we would have to build bigger chambers for both Nova *and* Aurora, since Ava was simply acting as a bounce point. Those bigger chambers could then incorporate oxen, cows, larger livestock and cattle, as well as whatever other animals we would want to bring along.

On the spacecraft Aurora would be traveling in, we would need to also transport grain, nutrients, plants, grass seed, water filtration devices, vegetables, fiber, tools and supplies for building, weapons, a supply of basic medicines and how to replicate them, earth records, historical artifacts revealing where we came from, and so much more. It would be a renaissance… a complete reboot. But this time, we would have the advantage of bringing along what worked. The only unpredictable variable was the humans. It would always be the humans. New societal norms would have to be adopted; rules and laws would need to be strictly upheld.

The philosophical underpinnings of this were going to be enormous. We were just providing the *Courier* system as vehicles. They were physical. But it was the *intangible* things we would be bringing with us that would require a lot of work and coordination. The belief systems, the religions, the socio-political perspectives, civilization norms, laws, familial relations, practices, and all of that. Thankfully, we'd be able to leave that to someone else.

Call us, simply, 'chauffeurs.'

Isaac had gone back to the lab to check on any updates with Norma's telemetry, or see if we'd missed any landline messages. Calls were supposed to be forwarding to his phone, and autoreplies instructed people to call or text him, but they had stopped. His voice mail was probably full. Presumably, much higher agencies than a little podunk lab at the University of Washington were now on it, and didn't need us anymore, but nonetheless, he still wanted to stay on top of things and connect with any contacts or colleagues that might need our input… or we might need theirs.

He would be back tomorrow morning. Besides, if we didn't regularly show up at the UW lab and log some kind of hours or credentialed work, things would get suspect and our tenure might be revoked or suspended. Doubtful, given the fact that Isaac, especially, was the one who discovered Norma. That would be bad form to cut us out of the picture just like that. And tenure revocation is generally considered a hollow threat in light of impending complete annihilation.

It was hard to believe that life had changed so much in only nearly five days. We had catalogued Norma early on November 6th. Since then, the denizens of planet Earth appeared to have wrestled briefly with it and then resigned themselves to the fact that we were, quite inescapably, doomed. There was a certain peace in that resignation; a certain futility in attempting to bargain with it. Maybe we had all learned the five stages of grief by now and were coping with it by effectively saying, *Oh well, screw it.*

Donze sent me another message that night out of the blue. I snapped the others to attention and read it aloud to them.

President advises quicker progress and would like to meet. I would accompany him. We'll be flying out on Friday the 14th and would like to get acquainted with your team and see your technology up close, firsthand.

Thankfully, I was reading ahead in my brain, and noticed it before I read it aloud to the others. There were Donze's words, cold and clear: *Farragut-322 isn't slowing down. Neither should we.*

I knew in my heart that I couldn't relay Norma's official scientific name to them. Isaac would be crushed knowing that the supermassive was named after him since he was the one who had discovered it. Thankfully, he wasn't here right now, but I didn't want them relaying it to him.

"Dane? What is it?" Trapper asked.

I glanced up at her. "Nothing. Just… surreal," I said, meaning the naming, not the President's impending visit.

"Holy crap," Dina said. "The President, here?"

"*And* the SecDef," I replied, eyes wide.

"Are they sure that's safe? Wouldn't that attract unwanted attention to us?" she asked.

"Probably, unless they came in a cover car or something," Trapper replied.

"Only one way to find out," I replied, and then began hammering out a text.

Glad to show you what we're doing. Test subject going through the relay tonight. 87% complete with the third chamber. What time Friday?

Will advise, standby came the reply.

"He'll advise. I guess we're at their beck and call," I said, flicking my eyebrows up. "No worries, that gives us plenty of time to finish up Aurora."

"But seriously, the President of the United States, here, in your apartment. *Whoa*," Trapper said, exhaling hot hair in amazement. "Hail to the Chief," she said half-jokingly, with a mock salute.

"Tell me about it. We'll be fine, though. Let's just make sure everything works, gang," I said. "I'm not relishing the test we have coming up, and the sooner we get that win under our belts, the sooner we'll know where we stand with all of this."

Farragut-322. Ouch. Would Isaac be fine? Would any of us?

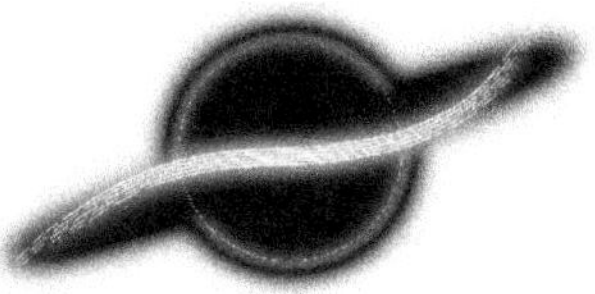

Isaac called me.

The Event Horizon Telescope, in conjunction with the Center for Astrophysics at Harvard & Smithsonian, was working overtime along with NASA and the European Space Agency to monitor Norma. EHT telemetry had her still on track to intersect with our orbital plane in late February, possibly even a bit sooner. Disappointing, of course, but the hope now conveyed to the four of us via *Courier 3.1* and our three, beautiful girls allowed us to see beyond the present calamity, whereas most people's vision stopped short.

NuSTAR and Chandra telescopes said her hot gas readings were off the chart. Other stellar orbits outside our immediate galactic neighborhood were having their orbits disrupted in its vicinity. The event horizon was strong; the singularity at the center was having its way with all things around it. Hawking radiation was no longer speculation; Norma was definitely putting out a faint stream of particles due to quantum effects near the event horizon. I could only imagine what the tidal forces were around it.

Isaac was answering a few messages and then he'd head home to pack some things and return. He would not be with us for the test tonight… if we were to even conduct it tonight. I informed him of the president's upcoming visit.

By our estimation, we were now about 95% ready. Teleporting Macy would require less than 2TB of data storage due to dogs' more simplistic makeup. We had a 2TB drive on hand, no problem. Dina had brought a few from the lab, so we slapped a Samsung 10TB drive into a spare bay in Aurora, wired it up to one of the switches that was connected to the motherboard, and it was partitioned and reading solidly. Once we knew that it worked, we'd firm up the bay assembly.

Ava had been retrofit with much more memory and a faster CPU and motherboard in order to handle the transfer speeds and preserve integrity across the board. If we didn't have that, we could risk all those lifeform signals racing through her becoming a jumbled, tangled mess... and the end result would be a dripping pile of oozing jelly that was once human life, deposited haphazardly onto PCb without a wish or a prayer, to slowly decompose in the heat of a red dwarf star far from home.

"You guys hungry? I'm hungry. And nervous," I added, and I discovered that I was, in fact, trembling a bit, the closer we got to Macy's test.

"Pizza sounds good," Megan said nonchalantly. Dina looked up at me and nodded.

"Pizza *again*?" I asked.

Trapper stared at me quizzically. "What?"

I held up my hands helplessly. "Okay. Fine. Pizza... *again.* We gotta save some for Isaac though. And that's one of the first things I'm sending through, way before Macy. I'm gonna run down to the bird store real quick as well."

"You can send pizza through?" Dina asked.

"Yeah, but it won't reintegrate perfectly on the other side. It's not biological. A steak would be reintegrated; an orange would be, celery would be. Pizza isn't a living organism," I said, chuckling. "It's made up of a bunch of *once*-living things. Anyway, I'll send a slice or two, and then a bird or two. If all goes well, Macy goes through. Not before."

Trapper chuckled. "I think you should try to send a bird through while sitting on a piece of pizza, Dane. If it comes through all jumbled on the other end, we can call it a *pecker pie*."

"I'm ignoring you," I insisted. "Except to say that I'm ignoring you."

I grabbed my keys and phone and headed out, locking the door behind me. Trapper chuckled again.

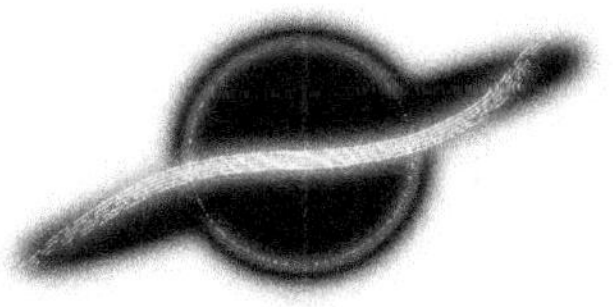

Forty-five minutes later, I was back, three pizzas under one arm, and a few small cardboard bird carriers clasped together under the other, loaded up with four society finches. My dog greeted me at the door, picked up the pizza scent right away and eagerly followed me inside.

"Got the food. And the pizzas," I joked. Dina made a revolted face. Megan quickly jumped up from her laptop and seized the pizzas from me, whisking them the rest of the way into my kitchen, and throwing one open.

Macy jumped out of her way, but then became interested in the small boxes of finches I was carrying.

"Thanks. Starving," was all Trapper mumbled through dough, sauce, cheese and pepperoni, ripping open a twenty-ounce Mountain Dew and chugging it like it was gasoline and she was a souped-up Ducati.

Dina rose. "We're pretty much done, Dane. Slapped the last few innards on a few minutes ago, it's fully insulated, and the seal's nice and tight. Vacuumed it out and Aurora is ready to rock. The other girls are prepped and ready."

"Right on," I said. "I'll ready the birds."

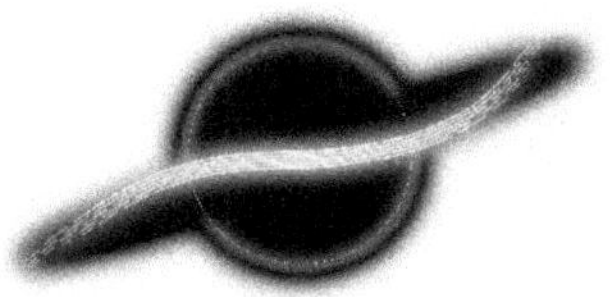

Dinner finished, I put Macy in the bedroom and shut the door so that she wouldn't get any ideas about the birds. She had licked her lips enough while sniffing their boxes. Next, I fetched one of the tiny, white society finches. The boxes were flimsy cardboard, allowing fairly easy extraction. The first bird pecked at me vigorously in self-defense.

I plucked one feather without so much as a squawk from the finch, inserted the feather into the scanner, and let *Courier 3.1* do its thing. The bird's DNA profile was created with an answering beep. Dina and Megan watched in fascination; only Dina had seen this done, briefly, with Isaac before he went through.

Next stop for the tiny fowl was setting it down gently on the floor of Nova and quickly closing the door before it could fly out. It flitted around, glancing off the walls a few times, its miniscule heart beating frantically, before it finally settled on the floor and awaited the teleportation sequence along with the rest of us.

I sat down facing the laptop, adjusting the traffic and relay settings to read from Nova, and then send to Ava and bounce to Aurora in a holding pattern.

Courier 3.1 did its thing. All three chambers fired up properly. The countdown tracked. White hot light filled Nova. Ava was silent except for her whirring and clicking motherboard, and the slight vibration emitted by the singular SSD drive installed therein.

Aurora didn't light up. For a second my stomach lurched, wondering what went wrong. And then it hit me. This was protocol and to be expected; there was nothing wrong. Aurora was simply awaiting the 'go' code to reintegrate the tiny finch. Exactly as we had programmed it to do. This was a failsafe line of code that I had intentionally programmed in to ensure that there would be a controlled sequence, reintegrating upon command. Once we could ensure that the holding pattern was secure, we could then program automation to deliver them, one after the other, allowing the subject sufficient time to exit the receiving unit.

I hit *Commence Relay* in *Courier 3.1* and whirled around to face Aurora.

It mirrored Nova's sending transmission light flash, and then…

…there was the bird.

Good as new – or as old – and flitting about in the same panic, it finally landed and looked around erratically, its chest reverberating with the same frenetic heartbeat.

I crept up to the window slowly so as not to frighten it and send it fluttering around again. I could feel Dina and Megan peering over my shoulder curiously, all of our eyes trained on the bird.

There it was! It had worked. Ava had successfully bounced it over to Aurora. Our newest girl had listened and heard, and replicated the little society finch with the same precision as Ava would have. And the beauty of it all? Aurora was wireless. Ava sent the signal over the air, and Aurora grabbed it and reproduced the finch with the same data integrity as Ava would have.

I slowly stood up and took a quick look at Megan and then Dina. Before we knew what hit us, we erupted into a joyful holler and enveloped each other with celebratory hugs, enraptured with joy at the prospect of sending humans through soon.

Without delay, I texted Isaac that it worked.

Momentarily, a smiley face appeared in the chat below my message, followed by Isaac's text. *Great work! See you soon.*

I don't know how I managed to get the bird out of Aurora and back into its box, but I did. It took some work, but that part was done. It felt a little overly warm, but that didn't register any sort of nuanced confusion on my part. After all, it was a frightened little thing. I put that box aside from the others to keep the transferred ones separate.

Next up, the pizza.

I wasn't sure what to expect by sending a slice of pizza through, but figured that might show us what kind of effect the chambers would have on non-biological organic material as well. Worth a shot. Inanimate objects wouldn't be teleported; things like grain and seed would be housed in vacuum-sealed carriers inside the spacecraft, and then deposited along with the rest of us. But it would be nice to see what it would do with this.

All three girls were running. Pepperoni and cheese in the scanner. Profile created. Sequence initiated.

We watched, curiously, as Nova sent it through, and I hit *Commence Relay* once more.

We opened the door. Aromatic steam rolled out. There, on the floor of the Aurora chamber, lay a smoking molten mess of goo: a steaming fusion of pepperoni and cheese, ingredients indistinguishable from one another. I glanced over at the ladies, and all they could do was offer a concerned expression. "See? Told ya. I guess we stick to live subjects?" I asked, and they nodded. "Anybody wanna try some of that?" They shook their heads. "Cowards.

"Alright," I conceded. "I'll clean it up and then we'll get Finch Number Two and then Number Three in there for the sequence. Then we can try Macy. Okay?"

It wasn't long before we were cleaned up and reset for the second finch. Nova's sequence was running. Ava and Aurora were fired up and ready to go. We sent the first one through and kept it in a holding pattern, with a timing separation of one minute between reintegration and reset so that we could extract it and ensure that Aurora was ready for the second finch.

The first one was through! I didn't hit *Commence Relay* this time. We were testing the holding sequence. I hit *Commence Suspend*. If all went well, little Finch Number Two was now loaded into a partition of our SSD inside of Aurora. Without delay – purely out of excitement – I got Finch Number Three out of its box…

… *and it escaped!*

It wiggled out of my grip and flew around the room in a panic, smashing into the sliding glass door and thudding to the ground before launching again. The girls tried to help as well, cornering it. The thing was fast, flitting about and jumping into the air with a frightened *beep* just as I went to cup it in my palms.

"Dina, grab it, there it is!" I cried. "Wait, don't – just, don't move too quickly. Here, Megan, head it off and, just, look out!" She nearly tripped over the power receptacle and thick insulated power cable for Aurora. "Careful!"

"Dane, you stay there. Here it comes, I've got it!" Dina cried.

"No, don't! It's coming to me. You wait there, and no! Dane, don't move, stay there! It's coming to me. Haha! It's behind the couch. Hang on," Trapper exclaimed.

Indeed, Finch Number Three had hit the wall and was flapping its way down behind the couch. Megan hurled herself over the back of it and clutched in vain. It hopped out and began a new, fatigued and desperate flight.

Dina waved her hands in the air in a vain attempt to ward it off from the kitchen as I moved into view.

It was growing exhausted and was losing altitude. It flew scattershot into the kitchen and plopped down into the sink. I moved in quickly and cupped my hands over it, trapping it.

"Got it!" I exclaimed with joy. "Come here, ya trouble maker," I said, bringing it over quickly to Nova. I gently opened the door and placed it inside. It hopped around slowly, unable to fly due to fatigue. Its beak was reverberating with quick frightened breaths as it sat, fazed.

"Poor thing," Dina voiced with sympathy.

"I hate birds," Megan chimed in, remorselessly.

I laughed. "Me too. They're irritating." I chuckled once more. "Okay, Round Two, Finch Number Three. Here we go. Commencing suspend!"

Nova lit up. Ava didn't. Aurora didn't. Finch Number Three was gone. My laptop beeped a chime of success, and a prompt filled my screen of a successful teleportation and storage.

We surveyed each other again with high hopes.

"Alright, this is what it all boils down to, folks," I said with a chest full of hopeful air. "You guys ready?"

They nodded.

"I wish Isaac was here to see this," I said.

I hit a third button this time labeled, *Commence Relay Series.* If all went well, Finch Number Two would reintegrate in Aurora in fifteen seconds, and Finch Number Three would then reintegrate in Aurora exactly one minute after that, allowing us to extract the first bird and reset.

Countdown. Fifteen seconds seemed interminable, a few minutes at least.

Aurora flashed white. A countdown displayed on my laptop, starting at one minute.

"Okay, move, move! Get in position to block it if it tries to fly out, you guys!" I opened the door, and steam poured out. I batted it away from me, clearing a path for my vision. It was hard to see. I knelt down and peered through the swirling mist.

I couldn't see the bird! It was nowhere to be found. I felt all along the bottom of the chamber, running my hand around, and wildly looking up and around to see if it leapt up and was clutching the side wall, or ceiling, or... something.

"Dane! What are you doing? Get it out of there, the clock's ticking!" Dina cried.

"I'm looking, I'm looking!" I cried. "I don't see it, do you see it?"

No! they both cried, peering in with me.

"Check the laptop, check it quick! Does the transfer say complete?" I hollered.

Megan dashed over to my laptop. She didn't answer.

"Trapper!"

"I'm *looking!* Where do I look?" she cried.

"Under, under-" I tried, but suddenly I couldn't remember. "Forget it! What about...?" I tried to think.

"Dane! Is there an abort button?"

I panicked, wondering why I hadn't put in an abort sequence button. Why the hell hadn't I put one in?

"Dane!" Megan cried again.

"You have fourteen seconds, get *out* of there, Dane!" Dina cried. She began pulling on my arm to pull me back.

I whirled back to Megan. "Look under Reports, and, uh, it should be…" I struggled. "I can't remember, I can't remember!"

"Dane! Nine seconds!" Dina tugged at me, her fingernails shredding my arm as she wrenched.

"Ow, Dina, stop! *Megan?!*" I cried.

"I can't find it! Dane, get out of there, close the door!"

I jerked myself up and out of there, slamming the door closed as gently as I could. I feared what would come next.

"Three seconds! Lock it!"

I pressed the outer lock button.

Aurora lit up white. We recoiled and covered our eyes, turning away. The inside of the chamber flashed twice, and we just stared at it. I swallowed hard.

On the credenza against the wall, Finches Number One and Four must have heard something, because they began beeping erratically. Almost frantically.

I slowly reached out and opened the door. It slid open with an airy mechanical whistle.

The smoke filtered out. The air swirled around it.

I swallowed once more.

The smoke cleared.

There, on the floor, lay the mangled carcass of two birds. At its neck, two appendages stemmed out, culminating in two distinct heads. Two overlapping sets of wings spanned out, intersecting bizarrely, painting a gruesome picture of fusion. One leg was bent backward behind it; the other three were crumpled up beneath it or off to the side. Its splayed form was a gelatinous mutation, oozing fluids and membranes; a splicing together of two distinct DNA patterns, joined together because that's precisely what the code told Aurora to do.

Or… was it because that was what *I* told it to do?

I was convinced I had missed something. *What had I missed?* I meticulously coded this process through all of last night and this morning!

Those poor birds. Joined together forever in some spastic metamorphosis, utterly lacking symmetry and bereft of life. Part of its delicate, misshapen skeleton protruded unnaturally through its back.

Two birds. Dead. Just like that.

"Sorry, Dane," Megan whispered emotionlessly. Dina stifled a cry and turned away.

"Yeah. Me too. I… must have forgotten something."

Dina moved away from us and sat down on the couch. I took a heavy sigh. Trapper went to the laptop.

I knelt down, staring at the disgusting new creation, wondering what I had done wrong. I would need to look through the code and heavily debug it.

And, slowly, the awful horror of what would have happened had I sent Macy through settled upon me. What if that had been a bird and… Macy? Or Macy and… Dina? What if I had accidentally spliced together two forms of life in an appalling and unnatural grotesque mutation?

I gazed down upon the creature in pity, wondering if it had died in pain, or if it was instantaneous.

I wouldn't have my answers soon. This was a setback. I was just glad it didn't cost Macy her life… or any of ours. But I suddenly cared about birds.

I should have learned my lesson from the pizza. Had I grown cavalier? At the edge of death, we had been cavalier, joking about pizza and irritating little birds. All life was precious now, even the tiniest. Even the lives of two tiny, seemingly insignificant finches.

I had killed enough birds, and now the other test subjects I had sent through recalled to my mind. Those poor, innocent finches… all of them. Hopefully, their deaths wouldn't be in vain. Hopefully, this would mean something and I would figure this all out.

I stared at Macy, full of fear and trepidation that I would someday, soon, inadvertently kill her as well.

And perhaps even kill the remainder of the human race, desperate to escape Norma. If I couldn't get this right, we were all doomed.

Once more, into sadness I went.

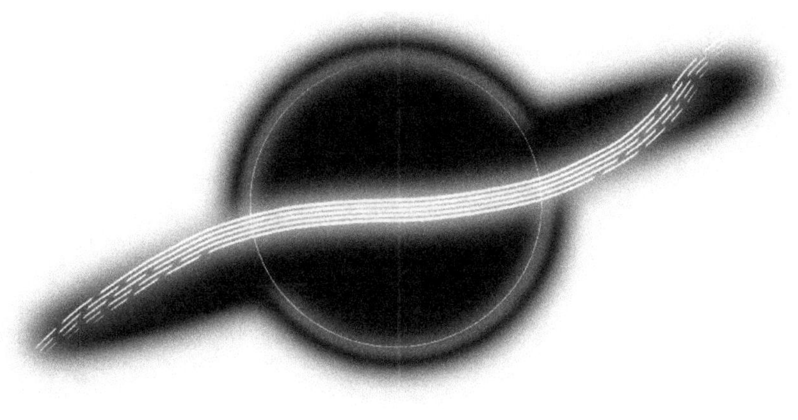

PART TWO:
THE END IS NIGH

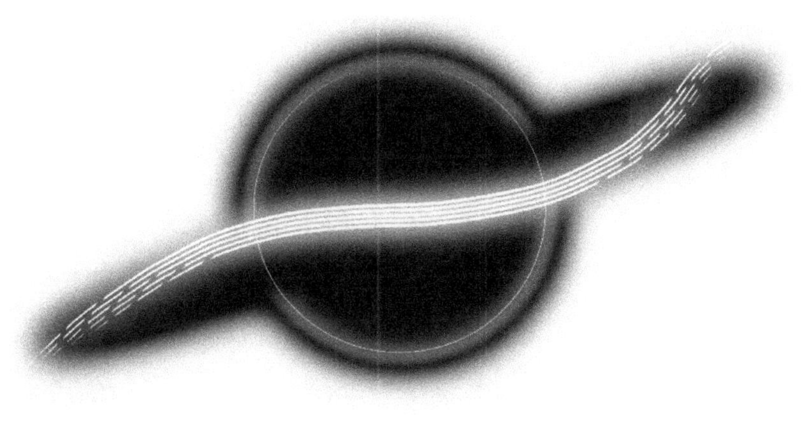

11 | *Mr. President*
November 14th, 2025

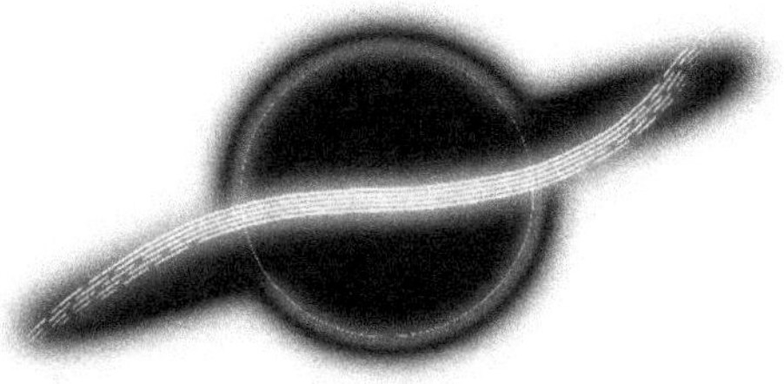

He was coming.

The text had just come through from Donze, and they were on their way here. The President of the United States was coming to see me, in my little apartment.

It had been four days since the birds. Norma was inching closer – the word 'inching' of course being a gross understatement here – and Macy had finally gone through after six more birds. I had purchased more, definitely: after all, there was no way in hell I was sending my dog through Nova and having her come out like that gruesome abomination we beheld on the floor pad of Aurora.

Macy's teleportation was a nailbiter, and I was trembling so hard my leg was bouncing off the floor; Dina had to restrain me in my chair. There was a strange delay in the reintegration that messed with my emotions *hard*. Time moved at a snail's pace, and I grew frantic. But then, finally, *mercifully*, Aurora lit up, and there she was. Same beautiful eyes, same nonstop tail, same beautiful dog, following all six birds in the sequence: all seven creatures held for ten minutes in Aurora. She hopped into my arms, and she even still reeked of the Beggin' Strips that I had given her just before she went through Nova.

The truth of the matter is that I had messed up badly. I had forgotten to program in some crucial and indispensable lines of code. The sequence was programmed correctly in that it held the teleportation subjects in stasis for one minute, but I had written incorrect syntax forcing what essentially resulted in a batch delivery, releasing all of them at the same time. An assimilation. *A mistake.*

In short, Aurora simply did what I told her to do. In short, she *combined* the subjects into a horrid fusion.

I recoded *Courier 3.1* on Wednesday, and then we sent two more birds through. It worked. Following that, we freed the ones we previously teleported, bought six more, and then reran the tests. The sequence was corrected to specify reintegration of the first signal, and then a double-verification to ensure that reintegration signal matched the original disintegration signal, two minutes to allow for extraction, and then reintegration of the next signal and double-verification of it as well.

Everything worked, finally. Cumbersome and laborious, to be sure, but it worked. I just hoped the President wouldn't ask me to test it in front of him, and that he wouldn't *himself* ask to go through. If it failed, I would be guilty of assassinating the President of the United States. I wondered if they would execute me before Norma would.

All of us were gathered now, in my little apartment, awaiting a single suburban to pull up. The President couldn't risk traveling in a caravan; he would attract too much attention to himself. However, a Secret Service advance detail had actually shown up earlier this morning, and now two of their men remained here with us, standing guard and awaiting his arrival with us.

Waiting was nerve-wracking. Waiting for Norma, waiting for Macy, waiting on the nuclear propulsion craft and news on it, waiting for the President.

Life had become all about nervous waiting anymore.

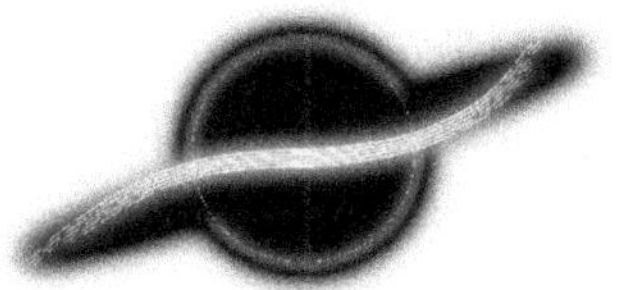

"Nice to meet you, Mr. President, Mr. Donze," I said, extending my hand after they had entered. They both greeted me enthusiastically.

"These are my colleagues, Isaac Farragut and Dina Jensen from the UW. And this," I said, motioning to Trapper, who had ambled over to me, "is Megan Trapper, also an undergrad from the U… she's been my right-hand woman in all of this. She helped me build everything you see."

Macy sat on the floor between Isaac's legs as he relentlessly stroked her and patted her.

The President was wearing a nondescript black cap and a black jacket over his white shirt and red tie. SecDef Donze was pretty much the same. I had never had a high opinion of Donald Trump, but here, standing before him, I was a citizen of the country that he was in charge of, and I was answerable to him. I just wanted to do my job and have what we needed to so we could save as many lives as possible. What my thoughts were on the people I had to interact with to get us to that goal was irrelevant. And, if I had to admit, it was actually an honor to have him here, knowing that we had achieved such a level of notoriety with something so incredibly novel and potentially life-saving.

"So these are the girls?" the President asked me in an inquisitive tone, removing his hat and smoothing back his wispy, Capellini-like yellow hair.

"Yessir, here they are," I said, motioning him toward them.

Donze approached me as Trump went to investigate the chambers close up. "Mr. Currier, nice work. Thanks for your patience as we've tried to get all of this underway. We appreciate all you've done so far."

He seemed nicer in person, actually. I was grateful for his comments, but, for some reason, the very statement put me a bit on edge, portending of some imminent shift in plans… or even a change of venue. I shook it off. "Thank you, Mr. Donze. The only question is where do we go from here?"

He smiled. "Well, it's of 'going' that I'd like to converse with you. The President as well. Can we sit?" He motioned me over to my couch, and then I realized that it wasn't a question.

I walked over to the couch and sat next to Isaac and Dina. Trapper had retreated to the table with her laptop next to mine, eyeballing Trump skeptically.

Donze remained standing, glancing back a single time at the President, and then back at me. Trump continued to inspect the chambers, inside and out.

"Let me be as succinct as possible," Donze began. Strangely, I felt suddenly like we were erring children sitting before a stern, remonstrative parent. "We're of course in an unprecedented situation, and we're going to need to take proper precautions," he said.

"Precautions against what?" I asked.

"Well, against the general population finding out what's going on here. What you're doing has bearings on the survival – correction, the *future*, to sound less bleak – of the American people. So I'll cut to the chase. We're going to need to relocate you and your team – and your equipment – to a secure location as soon as possible."

I looked at my team, and they looked nervously back at me. Trapper squinted her eyes.

"Okay," I said, "what does that mean for us, personally? You did say 'you and your team.'"

"Correct, we need-" he started, but then Trump walked over to him and stood beside him, hands at his side with those stiff pursed lips.

"Secretary Donze, allow me," Trump said, gazing down upon us. "We appreciate everything you've done.

We're not taking you off of this assignment or this project. This is your baby, okay? What you've done here is truly, truly magnificent, the most important thing ever, really. Nothing has ever come close to how important this is."

Ah, here comes the signature bloviating, I thought as he spoke, and I found myself wondering if we would be able to find a hard drive with enough space just for him.

"We just need you closer to home, which, for us, is Washington, DC. So we're going to relocate you – all of you, your whole team here, all your equipment, even your beautiful dog if you'd like – so you can work from a secure environment without any threat of being discovered or interfered with."

Sounded reasonable enough. We all figured this might happen, but at least we were being included. "Got it," I said. "What is your timeline, may I ask?"

"As soon as possible," he said, waving me down. "If you can be ready in the next few days, that would be ideal." He stared at me pointedly, squinting his eyes and awaiting my reply.

"I don't see any trouble with that." I looked around at my team, awaiting their reply. They shook their heads, in agreement that it wouldn't be an issue. "May I ask what the progress is with the other part of our plan?"

"What other part is that?" Trump asked.

"The issue of how we're supposed to get Aurora to Proxima Centauri b."

"Aurora?" Trump asked.

Apparently he didn't know their names, but it seemed now as if he was even oblivious to the plans Donze and I had discussed regarding nuclear propulsion. "Well, sir, Aurora is the name of the teleportation chamber on the far right there." I was talking to Trump, but my eyes were on Donze, fearing that I might be overstepping some line by sharing too much. Surely the President knew of our plans? "That is the one that we would be sending to receive our signals."

"Mr. President," Donze interjected, "if I may, sir, Mr. Currier is referring to the 'travel program' you and I had discussed" -here he enunciated *travel program* to clue in Trump- "which of course involves the special technology."

Trump nodded briskly, looking ever in-the-know. "Yes. We're making progress, and it's very, very good. If you have an update, why don't you share it with them, Erick?"

"Yessir," Donze replied, and he couldn't suppress a bit of a smirk. Apparently, he thought the same of Trump as I did. I glanced over at Megan, and her face was wrapped in contempt and judgment, shaking her head slightly. "*Yes*, Mr. Currier, we're making progress. We have a private hangar and laboratory at Chantilly Air Jet Center. That's where we'll be moving your systems."

"And us," I said. It wasn't a question.

"Yes. *And* your team, of course," he replied. "Our spacecraft is being constructed onsite, and it's being rigorously tested to ensure all systems are functioning correctly. We're calling it 'Genesis,' for obvious reasons.

We will be using a conventional launch vehicle – a rocket – to get Genesis up into a preliminary lower orbit around Earth. Our craft would be shielded during launch to protect against radiation exposure. Once initial orbit has been achieved, Genesis will employ rocket burns to maneuver it to a more remote, nuclear-safe orbit. Safety checks will be performed prior to reactor activation, then the propellant gets heated, and then we await the go-code. It will contain your third teleportation chamber, and then? Well, God help us on the journey."

"So," Trapper piped up, "I've previously confirmed that PCb does not lie in Norma's direct path. We'd have to hope for optimum timing of earth's rotation, and getting out of here before everything is destroyed. Otherwise we'd be sucked in along with everything else."

"Possibly," Donze said. "Timing would be critical, yes. However, that's thinking along the lines of conventional propulsion. Nuclear propulsion changes the game entirely. To that end, folks, and Mr. President, we're making great progress."

"So the programs that were working on nuclear pulse propulsion prior to Norma were never suspended?" Isaac asked.

Donze looked at him and smiled patronizingly. "I'm afraid I can't answer that question, you understand."

"Fine," Isaac relented. "But it's safe to say that we've got the technology – or *almost* got it – to the point of usability?"

"We're almost there," the SecDef replied heartily.

"What is your timeline, do you think, given the countdown that has been set upon us by Norma?" Isaac persisted.

"I should think that, with you there, and all key components in place, we'll have the capability within a month, ready to execute."

A month. That's pushing it, I thought, and my eyes went wider with a sigh. The truth is that would put us in mid-December, and things never happen on time when you factor in the US Government. The truer answer would be sometime after the first of the year. 2026. The year of Norma.

"Trust me, folks, we've got qualified teams working on it. We'll relocate you and station you nearby with full DOD-credentialed access to the premises. You'll receive a CAC and be considered DoD civilian employees and contractors."

"CAC?" I asked.

"Sorry. Common Access Card. We also have DBIDS cards, those are Defense Biometric Identification System cards, you'll probably be set up with those as well," Donze clarified. "We'll get you housing nearby, and arrange for all your equipment to be transported. We'll have a special contract team in touch with you soon to arrange for that. I assume you can break these down speedily and be ready in a few days' time?"

"Shouldn't be a problem," I said, although we had literally just put Aurora together a few days ago. Shame to have to break her down right away, and there was always more testing we could do, including an actual human volunteer. Who that would be yet, we had no idea.

"Wouldn't it be nice if we had one gigantic one you could fit all these little ones in and just whisk them over to the other side of the country, right? Sort of like a Russian Matryoshka doll, right?" He laughed immaturely.

"Uh, sure," I said, the joke lost on me as I remained somewhat fazed by all this. However, I resolved to trust that it would all work out.

"Ah well, you'll have to disassemble them, of course, that's the best way to get them out the door, but I trust you have schematics for quick reassembly?" I nodded. "You can then continue your testing on the new premises. We'll provide shipping containers, proper packing materials and labels to keep things organized and separated."

He glanced over at Trump for his approval. Trump nodded, trying to look both important and fully informed. The Secret Service guys started bustling around, holding their fingers to their ears.

"Alright, that's it, folks. Good work. We'll be in touch, okay? Keep at it," Trump said, and moved toward the door after shooting two thumbs up at us with that clenched-lip grin of his.

"Thank you, Mr. President," I said. Isaac echoed me.

"I'm sorry about your future daughter-in-law," Dina offered.

Trump clenched his lips once more, forcing a fake smile at her as he walked out with Donze. The agents nodded at us and followed the bigwigs out of our apartment.

We were now on our own to finish up testing and commence disassembly. I watched them load up into their Suburban and sundry Secret Service car entourage.

They were leaving.

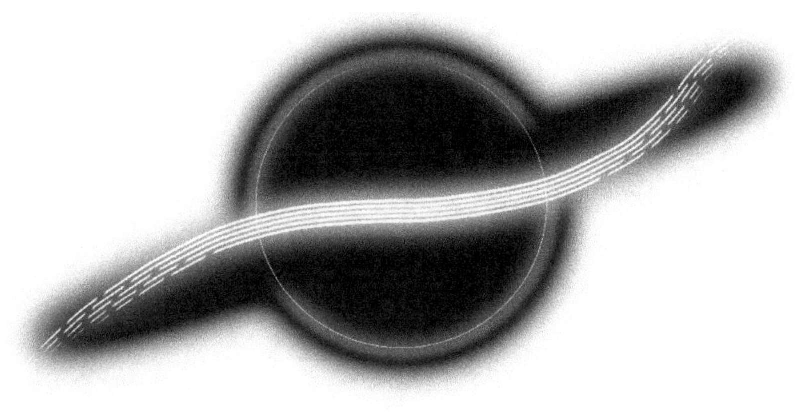

12 | *A Brave Soul*
November 16th, 2025

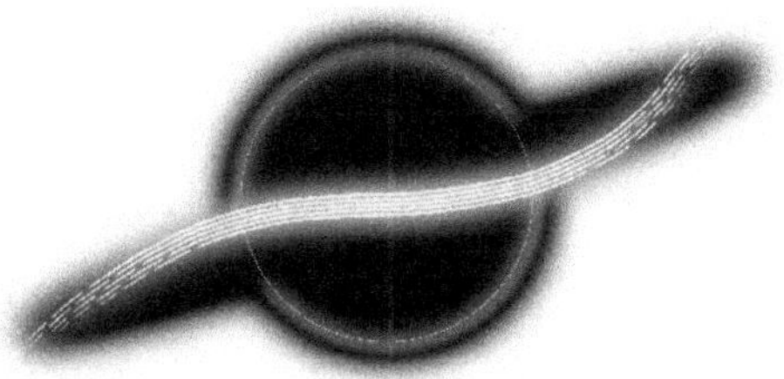

Everything was being torn down and prepared for reassembly.

The apartment was a mess. I hadn't packed all of my things. I didn't need to… why would I? Where we were going would be our final destination on planet Earth, and from there, we'd launch out across the galaxy, fleeing from a supermassive black hole that wanted to gobble us all up.

The only thing I really packed was a small box of collectibles to bring with us onboard Genesis. Thought it might serve as a time capsule of sorts.

Other than that, the rest was pointless.

The government contractors would be here tomorrow at 9 am to start moving us out, and then we would fly out the next day for Washington, DC.

We had performed a few more tests… not with any of us. Not yet. More birds, and more Macy trips. I was growing a bit anxious about Macy due to the sheer number of times she had gone through Nova. I had confidence in our chambers, but it was nonetheless unnerving to see her go through so many teleportations. As such, I watched her closely to ensure she remained healthy.

The signs were starting. Here we were now in mid-November, and it was already unusually hot for this time of year. Undoubtedly an effect of Norma drawing near, climatologists were regularly documenting increased temperatures that were atypical of November.

But that was just in the upper hemisphere. Up here in Seattle, we had always had a good mix of hot and cold, sun and rain. We had actual seasons here. Closer to the equator, it was growing even hotter, testing even the metrics and patience of diehard tree-huggers and global warming activists. And it was only going to get worse.

Additionally, on the outskirts of the solar system, DSN and DISCOVR both confirmed that Pluto was starting to exhibit strain. It had shifted its rotation – or, more accurately, it's orbit had *been* shifted – and it was now creeping nearer toward Norma's vortex, splitting off from its natural orbital plane into the vacuuming path of the hungry supermassive. It wouldn't be long, they said, before other planets followed suit, especially the little ones. At times, the sky appeared irregular in sparse patches, with bursts of color spilling through the heavens at odd hours, as if wisps of galactic strata were gently being tugged toward our invader.

Pluto was declared not a 'planet' in 2006. It was relegated to dwarf planet status, and, as the smallest – and, unfortunately, at this time one of the closest orbits to Norma – there was nothing it could do. It was gently shifting, being pulled off its axis at the aphelion, in an apogee at its orbit around the sun. It would be the first to go. DISCOVR was reporting that we'd soon be able to witness its demise.

But poor Pluto – as if there was any doubt that Norma was a solar system killer, Pluto's destruction would cement for our whole planet just how deadly this supermassive was going to prove.

Many more signs would come. This was only the beginning of the death pains.

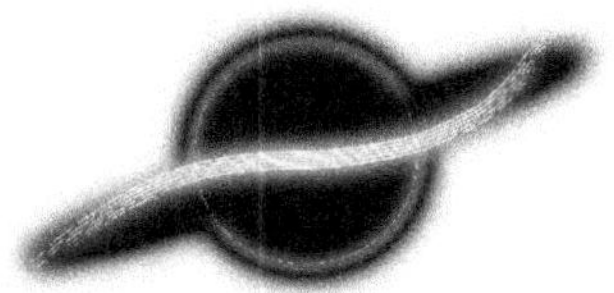

Isaac sat across from me. I couldn't believe his words. They fell from his lips decisively and assertively, and there was no mistaking them. I just wished I could actually 'mistake them.'

"You can't be serious," I protested.

"I am. More than I've ever been about anything."

"But Isaac," I said, "it's untested, man. You'd be the first human held in data storage, in stasis, and if we lose you, we've lost the very person who discovered Norma in the first place."

"That's exactly why I have to go first. You didn't have anyone contest your *own* volunteering when you went."

"That's totally different! I was going from there to there!" I practically shouted, pointing at the places where Nova and Ava had stood. The floors were marked with ghostly diameters where they had long stood: depressions in the carpet under their weight. Only the faintest depression showed from Aurora. She hadn't sat there long enough. "And I was hardwired, passing through an eight foot conduit via a LAN, Isaac. You'd be the first to be completely disintegrated, sent wirelessly, and transferred into a hard drive for stasis."

"There's no difference. You became data in your LAN, I'd be data on the SSD. No difference. The only difference here is that it involves three chambers instead of two. And as far as losing me?" He shrugged. "Sure. You might. The risk is always real. But isn't that why you went through? I know that's why I went through before, Dane. To make sure it works. We need to know."

I stared at him solemnly. "Yes, we do, Isaac, I agree. But once we get up and running, we can find volunteers. People with less to lose. We need you to help us continue to monitor Norma, to continue the prep of the chambers, to play devil's advocate and bounce ideas off of as we get nearer to the launch date. Why does it have to be you?"

He just stared right back, unmoved and stoic. "Dane. I discovered Norma. I hate myself for it. I need to discover *this.*"

And that was all he said. No begging, no pleading, no power plays. But in my heart, I knew this would be the reason. When St. James suggested Norma's name, I knew it then. Though we were all still collectively referring to her as Norma, I had seen Donze's text.

It was clear now that Isaac had also come across something, some report somewhere, in the scientific or monitoring community, that had updated her name with *Farragut-322.* He had seen it, and he was trying to reconcile with it. He didn't want it named after him.

I didn't envy him.

"Well, I don't know about you, bud," I said, "but I'm still gonna call her Norma."

He sighed slightly, realizing that I had perceived his thoughts. "I wish everyone would."

Briefly, I wondered about all the discoverers of horrors this planet had seen. Those who had identified toxic materials, scandals, comets, murders, atrocities, and other undesirable elements. They would forever be associated with them in one way or another, willing or no. I couldn't hold it against Isaac for wanting, in a sense, to 'clear his name.' Maybe he would be remembered for being the first human to test out the teleportation relay, to bravely volunteer where none other had.

In truth, he wanted to be remembered for that, not for being associated with the force that destroyed the earth.

"I hear you. You really want to do this?" I asked him pointedly. "I mean, really?"

There wasn't a wasted second. "I do," he replied, firmly. "I really do." He grinned slightly yet confidently. "I never told you this, but I'm in love with Dina."

I frowned at him, taken aback and blinking. "Wow… uh… really? Since when? I thought you were in love with Macy." I thought back to when I had noticed the smile-heavy glances he had sent Dina's way. It made sense in hindsight.

He chuckled. "Well, there's that, sure." He grinned and shrugged. "But with Dina, since, like, forever. I dunno… you work with people and you tell them that you love them, and if that's unrequited, that can make for a pretty awkward working environment, right? So I just stowed it."

"Well, maybe now's the time that you let her know how you feel?" I offered. "Before you go through."

He shook his head. "No," he said firmly. "*Afterward.* I'll carry that love through with me while I have it. If she rejects me, I probably wouldn't want to come back. This way, I'll have a reason to return."

I knew what he was saying. I didn't have anyone at the moment, but if I did, it would probably be Trapper. She always seemed a little too independent and quippy for me, but, hey, no time like the present. I supposed I should say something to her as well, so I wasn't really in a place to give counsel about relationships to Isaac.

I nodded to him. That sounded like a very good reason indeed. I clenched my jaw and gave him the best grin I could. "Well, looks like I can't talk you out of it."

He grimly shook his head, but his confident grin remained. I nodded.

"Well, let's get you through first thing once we get them all setup again. You wanna break the news to the ladies, or should I?"

"You can do it."

"Will do, my friend," I said, as I reached out to shake his hand. He took it slowly, regarding it, and then met my eyes once more.

"Thanks for hearing me," he said.

I nodded. "I hear you. I'm proud of you, Isaac."

I watched the brave soul before me, knowing full well what would happen to Isaac Farragut, and knowing that he knew it too and desired to face it anyway.

He would be torn down and reassembled before our very eyes.

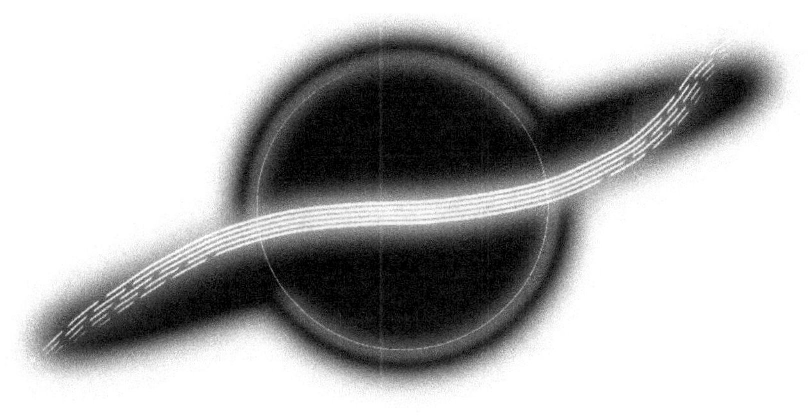

13 | *The First*
November 20th, 2025

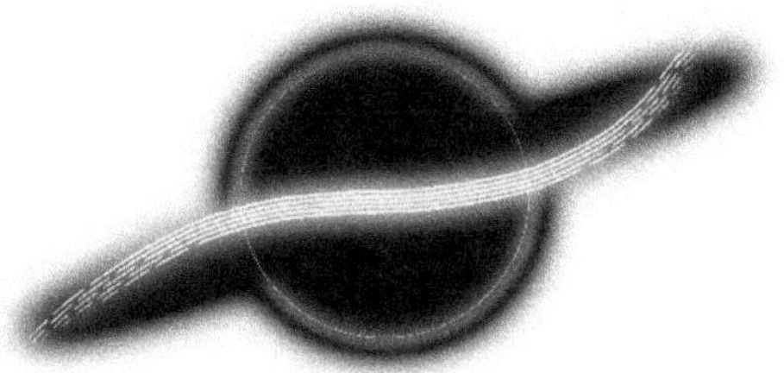

Time was ticking down.

We were drawing closer and closer to the new year… 2026… the year of Earth's doom.

But here, in our private lab at Chantilly Air Jet Center in Washington, DC, the four of us watched another countdown with bated breath and hopes filling our hearts. It was just our original team in the observation room, static and sterile, white and nondescript, allowing us to see everything with clarity, and work in optimum conditions. A far cry from the comforts of my old haunts, where in my apartment a delicious slice of pizza and a cold beer were only a few steps away. It was a certifiable step up, indeed, however: neat and clean, and reserved for us.

The naked man stood with his back to the remaining three of us, facing the newly-reassembled Nova chamber.

As with Aurora, Nova needed to be greatly enlarged to accommodate the animals we would be bringing with us. I had cartoonish imaginings of what it would be like when they brought them in. Maybe they would lead them in two by two and there would be some guy with a beard stewarding the whole process as they were loaded onto this 21st-century ark while the floodwaters rose.

To Nova's left stood the reformed Ava chamber. Ava looked identical to her former self. And, parallel to both of them, yet seventy-five feet down the lab and connected only via Wi-Fi stood the completion of the trifecta: our newest chamber, Aurora. She had been greatly enlarged to accommodate not just humans, but livestock and other larger animals that we would need to populate our new planet with. Whether or not they would survive remained to be seen. It would require quick work setting everything up for them to have what they needed in their new 'zoo.'

We had run preliminary tests once more. *Courier 4.0* – I had now made enough upgrades worthy of a substantial numeration change – had confirmed readiness of all three chambers, and all birds as well as Macy had gone through safely once more. The General even sent his wife's dog through. A tiny little Maltese named Coco. Pure white and affectionate, it came out just fine. He was a staunch and tough-built man; I think he was secretly hoping Coco would vanish into the ether so he could get a pit-bull. But she came out, and we were all rejoicing. Except the General.

Today, we would send our first human subject through. Isaac Farragut, discoverer of *Farragut-322*, strode confidently toward Nova, solemnly entering the chamber and closing the glass door behind him. It locked.

The countdown was on.

Sixty seconds.

Isaac smiled from within, pressing his hands up against the glass toward us. We all walked forward, extended our hands toward him and pressed them firmly through the door, mirroring his in symmetry. He smiled faintly and playfully glanced down, shifting his hips to further block himself from view. The ladies snickered.

We retreated and stood motionless, ten feet from the reassembled chambers, watching him, all of our hopes along for the ride in there with him. Macy sat on her haunches beside us.

Ten seconds. Nine…

Dina took a deep breath and walked down to Aurora to meet him upon reintegration.

Eight… Seven…

Isaac bowed his head and closed his eyes.

Macy stood and wagged her tail beside us, her ears up as she watched the man in the chamber.

Six… Five…

A beep sounded from Ava and Aurora, signifying readiness to receive.

Four… Three… Two…

Isaac looked back up at me. I nodded to him. He nodded…

One…

…and then he was gone. Nova lit up bright white, and then faded back to ambient light.

The chamber was empty.

Ava stood next to her, whirring and clicking. As expected, Aurora kicked into gear down the way, and did the same. There was no light flash, nothing spectacular about Aurora other than the slight audio emissions signifying her SSDs were being coded with data. She had been greatly souped up by the government, and retrofit with not one hundred, but *two* hundred 122-terabyte SSDs. This would enable us to transport roughly six thousand souls to PCb. But she was super heavy now. They would have to take great care loading her into the rocket, and launching and achieving orbit were another matter entirely.

The only thing we were lacking, which we would not be able to definitely prove, is successful life on PCb. If those stellar flares from Proxima Centauri were frequent enough, they could potentially strip away the atmosphere over time, increase radiation exposure, alter atmospheric chemistry, and more. It would be a potential negative impact, and we would be stranded there forever.

Time would tell.

But humans are known for adapting. Since the dawn of time, that's been true. And here before us, Isaac was, himself, adapting. The first human to volunteer for the teleportation relay sequence, reduced to a data stream, he had put his own soul forth at great risk to himself.

Isaac.

It was time to reintegrate him. I took a quick glance down to Dina, positioned in front of Aurora. He had been in there for thirty seconds. The plan was to go for one whole minute. We would test longer durations later. Hopefully, I or one of us would survive those tests as well. That was the clincher: we had a long journey ahead of us, and needed to survive it.

He was in there, somewhere. I whipped around and checked *Courier 4.0*. Isaac's DNA profile was right there in Partition 36 on SSD Number 135. We needed to test a random partition rather than go sequentially, and that's what *Courier 4.0* selected. He was there. All of him. Or, at least, that's what my OS reported.

"Go for reintegration, Dina," I yelled down to her, and she nodded, returning her gaze to Aurora. A knot formed in my stomach. *Please let him be okay,* I thought. I pulled my eyes away from my laptop and ran down to the final chamber. Trapper was already there with her, eagerly waiting outside the glass door for Isaac to show. Macy followed me.

Once more, the countdown.

Twelve… Eleven…

We all took a deep breath. Trapper put her arm around my shoulder. "Hey, relax. It's gonna be okay."

I nodded briskly. "Okay. Thanks, Megs."

Eight… Seven…

My mind raced, thinking back to all of the upgrades and codes I had run through *Courier 4.0* to upgrade it to the new version. Debugging and poring over all those lines of code. I hadn't missed anything… had I? I chewed my nails once more, running lines of code through my mind and scrutinizing them mercilessly.

Four… Three…

Of course I hadn't. The birds and Macy had gone through just fine, and the other dog, Coco as well.

Two… One…

Aurora illuminated from within. My heart skipped a beat. Flashes of light and arcs of energy flickered, and then a darker silhouette materialized amidst the swirling fog.

Isaac!

There he was. The door sounded and turned green, and Dina unlocked it, opening it out toward us.

The fog swirled out, and our undergrad stood there in front of us in all his glory. It had worked! He had been reintegrated! In my unbridled joy I shouted a massive *whoo-hoo!* and pumped my fist in the air, running toward him. Macy got frightened and bolted.

The fog was cold as I approached him. He had the minutest amount of sparkly coating covering his skin – crystalline fragments. His appearance was a bit ashen.

And his face drooped.

The knot in my stomach tightened.

"Isaac?" I asked him. "Buddy?" I snapped my fingers in front of his unblinking face.

There was no reaction.

Dina stifled a cry and brought her hands to her face, covering her mouth. Megan retreated to her laptop on a table behind us. Her system mirrored mine, with a cloud-based network access to *Courier 4.0.*

"Isaac?" I asked again.

Still, no response from him.

He fell forward into my arms, stiff and rigid: his body cold as ice.

"Dina... *Dina!* Trapper, help me! He's so cold!" Isaac was deceptively heavy, and he toppled over onto me as I desperately tried to lift him back up and not catch frostbite. He was *that* hypothermic. "Get a blanket!" I yelled to both of them. Dina reached for me and then did a double-take, torn between a desire to flee and a desire to comply.

Megan muttered, "Oh, no... oh, no... Dane, look," she stuttered, gazing into her laptop.

"What! I can't look, Trapper, help me! Dina! Where's that blanket?"

Isaac was frighteningly cold; icy to the touch. His face was devoid of emotion, inches from mine, and there was no sign of life within. Indeed, his pupils were dilated, and his blood vessels were distended under his skin.

"Isaac!" I cried, beginning to weep. Footsteps behind me as Dina came running back up from a medical cart against the far wall. She clutched a blanket and threw it over Isaac's shoulders. "Trapper, get the First Aid kit, get it now! *Trapper!*" She reluctantly ripped herself away from the laptop and fled to the cart Dina had just come from.

"Isaac, come on, are you okay? Talk to us!" Dina pled, rubbing his back and then recoiling from the touch. His hair was covered in glistening frozen specks, and it was solid to the touch, as if frozen concretely under the weight of ten containers of gel. "Isaac!" she pled again, and her voice cracked through her anguish.

"Megan! Where's that first aid kit?!" I cried, fiercely heaving Isaac off of me and then laying him down on the solid lab floor. No part of him relaxed to let gravity do its work and settle his weight evenly, distributing his fatty deposits around him to lay comfortably. He was statuesque, covered in a glistening cold, and morbidly unresponsive.

Macy walked up to him and sniffed him suspiciously. She growled and backed away, her tail between her legs.

Megan scurried up to us with the crash cart.

"Turn on the AED, turn it on, Megs, we're gonna lose him!" I yelled at her.

"If we haven't already," Dina muttered.

"Dina, stop that! Don't you say that!" I hovered over him and performed chest compressions, 100 to 120 per minute as we had been taught in that wretched CPR class at UW. I performed 30 compressions – his chest barely gave an inch – and then relocated and provided two rescue breaths.

"Hurry, Dane, hurry!" Dina yelled through her tears. Indeed, as I pulled away from him, my own tears fell on his face, freezing instantly into tiny circlets on his cheek.

"Dammit, Isaac, *no!*" I yelled at him. "Don't you die on me, you're supposed to live! You've got to live! Meg?"

"Here, go ahead. Wait!" she cried, turning back to the AED. "Put these on his chest." She handed me the AED pads to attach to his chest. It wasn't dry, but it was bare. He was already appearing to thaw.

I glanced back. The AED rhythm… there was none. No pulse. My face squinted in anguish, crunching into a desperate grimace. The AED beeped at me, advising a shock.

"Clear!" I cried to the others. Dina backed off. Megan just stood at the machine. "Clear!" I cried again, pressing the defibrillators to his chest and administering the shock. Crazily, my mind was thinking how futile this could be once we arrived on PCb; there would be no one conscious to administer the shock, no AED kit, just bodies all reintegrating one by one in Aurora until it burst. Cold bodies, frozen solid and in the throes of death, shattering into fragments inside my third chamber as the weight of more bodies compressed them, the glass cracked, and dead human upon dead human spilled out onto the alien terrain.

No! I had to focus. *Come on, Isaac,* I thought. *Come on!*

The AED beeped again. "Clear… clear! Dina, back off!" Dina had bowed her head and lain her hands on his knees… it looked like she was praying for him.

"Clear!" I yelled once more for good measure, and then shocked him.

The faintest beep came from the AED. A slight pulse. A sign of life flickered once and then vanished. Dina gasped, lurching up toward the machine, as if to will it to continue sounding. Trapper watched it, lightly undulating up and down, beckoning to it to continue reporting signs of life.

"Hit him again, Dane. Dane, do it!" Dina yelled, and her face was awash with warm tears.

I waited for the beep.

Once more the AED sounded.

Once more I zapped him.

Once more the machine erupted into a quick pulse of heart rhythm. Then, nothing.

I threw the paddles aside and cursed. "Dammit, Isaac, no! *No!*" I yelled at him, and then resumed with more compressions, leaning over him. As I straddled him, my own weight pushed his down, and I could hear what sounded like a faint crack from his body as it slightly shifted in the thaw, its frozen form giving way to flexibility.

30 compressions…

Two rescue breaths…

30 compressions…

Two rescue breaths…

Isaac could not die. I was not going to let him! "Come *on*, buddy, don't do this!" I yelled.

I was just going to go for the defibrillators again when his body flinched. His lifeless eyes stared upward into nothingness, but as we watched, his pupils contracted slowly, and the faintest wisp of breath emerged from his lips.

Dina choked back a cry. Megan ran over to us.

"Isaac?" pled Megan.

Dina echoed it. "Isaac, come on, buddy. You can do it, Isaac. Come on!"

I watched him, waiting. His chest slowly sunk with the speed of a turtle through thick sludge. And then it

increased in speed. His eyes contracted even more.
Another flinch.

The ECG started to pulse. Completely seized by arrhythmia at first, it slowly settled into a human tempo.

"That's it! That's it, Isaac. Come back to us. Come on buddy," I said, my hands on his chest, gently shaking him. Megan actually began to cry.

Isaac's chest rose and fell erratically, and a trace of a wheeze morphed into a cough as his body slowly came back to life. His pupils contracted somewhat. Dina grabbed the blanket under her hands and began to rub him all over with it, desperate to warm him up.

"Come on, my friend. You got this," I urged.

His pupils finally contracted fully, and his eyebrows furrowed as he blinked. His body spasmed several times in the clutches of a synapse misfire… or an epileptic seizure… or something. I wasn't sure. All I cared about was that there were signs of life now, and they were strong.

Isaac moaned, and a hot trail of air emerged from his lips until it was expended. And then, as if he were a newborn freshly delivered from his mother's womb, he took his first new breath of life on the other side of data, and his lungs expanded. Color slowly returned to his face. Tiny glistening crystals, by now thawed, dripped from his hardened body, the icy grip now relinquishing its grip to the onrush of warmth. Grey gradually gave way to healthy flesh tones. I looked him up and down. Dina continued to rub him.

The ECG started to quicken its pace.

"That's it! That's it! Welcome back, buddy!"

Isaac inhaled fully and then let out a horrendous cry as if stabbed by a thousand swords. His face contorted as the AED heart rhythm went absolutely berserk. Sounding as if he had the heart of a hummingbird, it pulsed wildly and then settled into a slow and steady rhythm once more.

"Isaac? Isaac? Talk to me, buddy. Trapper! Oxygen!" I barked. I hovered over our friend. "Buddy? Can you hear me?"

His eyes ever so slowly migrated from their thousand-yard stare through the ceiling to meet mine. His breathing slowed and then normalized.

Megan ran over with the oxygen and mask, and fitted it over his face. His hair was less crinkly now, with the slightest amount of give as she lifted him up and slipped it behind his head. She turned it on. The slow hiss sounded from the tank and we could hear it entering into his lungs.

Isaac looked at me. He nodded ever so slowly, blinking as his brow compressed into hardened wrinkles.

I hear you.

The words we spoke to each other when he volunteered. With that expression, he both acknowledged my question and showed that he was still himself, remembering our previous conversation.

I couldn't hold back the tears anymore, and nearly convulsed with joy. "You hear me," I said. "I hear you."

His eyes creased slightly, and there was the slightest trace of a twinkle in them as his cheeks rose into a grin.

I tousled his hair. "You're back. You made it. You *made* it, buddy."

He nodded again.

He had made it.

Dina let out a gigantic sigh of relief, and then burst into fresh tears. Trapper descended to her and put her arm around her. The ECG continued to sound out life.

Isaac was back.

His heart was ticking well.

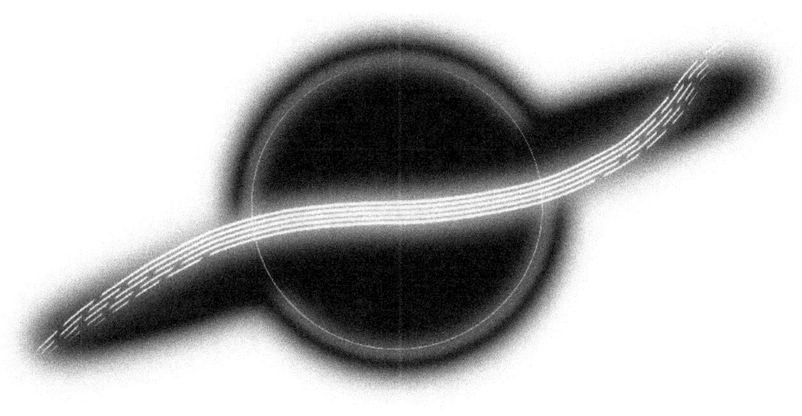

14 | Ups and Downs
November 21st, 2025

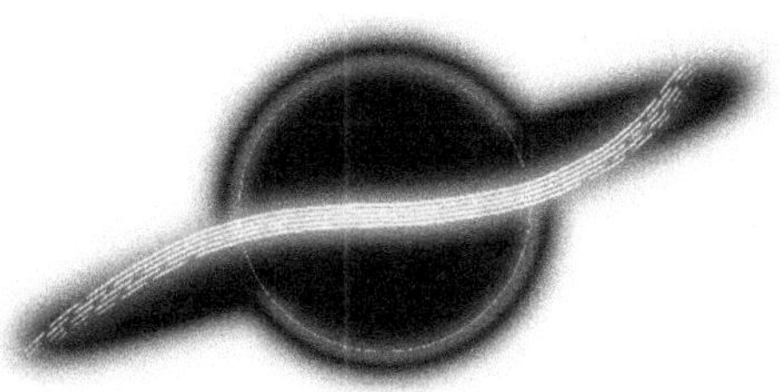

I just had so many questions.

Isaac was recovering, but we had nearly lost him. He was still in medical and was being attended to, but that event rattled and scarred us. It should have worked. All of it should have worked! Why hadn't it fully worked?

My faith was rocked, but that only served to force me into some uncomfortable introspection. What was faith, anyway? Did I have any? Surely I had *belief* in *Courier* and the chambers. Clearly, they had already worked. But was my belief in them only *because* they worked? Or, conversely, did they work because I *already* believed in them? I wasn't sure. Either way, this episode with Isaac rocked me, and that gnawed at my mind, my sense of self-assurance, *and* at this whole escape plan of ours.

If there was no one to rehabilitate a teleported soul, then everyone would perish. If we all issued out of Aurora as frozen bodies suspended in animation and in need of an AED, then there we would stay: icy corpses dumped on a faraway world, doomed to thaw and rot, fodder for whatever roaming animal life might happen upon us. Six thousand of us dead in the course of a few hours.

Furthermore, the whole prospect was tainted by an alien environment on PCb that would be potentially hostile to life... at least, eventually. That solar radiation could doom all of us someday, even if we stayed on the dark side as Megan and I had discussed.

Would we just be escaping the frying pan only to dive headlong right into the fire? Would we be living on borrowed time, marooned on a desolate planet that would provide just enough to support our small numbers, but eventually would be unsustainable for the long term?

Would Norma – or, rather, *Farragut-322* – circle around and destroy PCb as well?

Certainly, by teleporting a contingent of our population onto this planet in an entirely different system, we would cheat death for a while. But for how long?

Isaac had cheated death. He had reintegrated, but in a frightening way, requiring human intervention through resuscitation. That was a luxury we wouldn't have on PCb.

He was improving, and he was all there, cognitively and with his memory. He was still himself. Those were all good signs. However, none of us had any idea what this would all mean in practical application.

I went back to the drawing board once more while he recuperated. Something had gone wrong in *Courier 4.0* yet again. Why hadn't I learned with the birds? Why hadn't I buttoned it all up to perfection? Something had suspended Isaac in that he had not only been reduced to data streams, but placed in a stasis similar to cryo-freeze. His system had been deliberately slowed near catatonia in order to preserve him. The question swirled around in my head: *how to keep a human being at equilibrium as data?* How do I do that?

Trapper was occupied with more ethereal matters. What did Isaac see while in stasis? Where did his mind go? Was he awake? Alert? Did he dream? What sorts of dreams did he have? But - it wasn't time to debrief Isaac. Not yet. He slept a lot, which suggested another matter. Depending on where we were all deposited, we would need to allow for time to recover. That would not be possible on the dark side, freezing in subzero temperatures.

We would have our answers soon.

Meanwhile, Pluto had disappeared. It was nowhere to be found, and the charts showed full well what did it. And soon, our system would only have seven planets. Saturn, a colossal, ringed beauty unfortunately was in an orbit close to Norma's path. It would soon pass through her to the other side, where death reigned. The earth was warming up, and this day, late in November, was an unearthly 69 degrees.

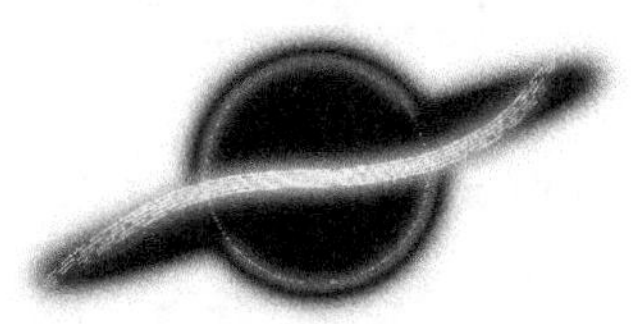

"It was surreal, guys. Just… surreal," Isaac said. We watched him as he shook his head, lost in thought. "I'd never experienced such peace before. Never. It was like the best sleep you've ever had," he said, and then he grinned a giant toothy, contented smile.

We mirrored it.

"Well, you were dug in like a frozen tick when you came back, that's for sure," Trapper said. "Had to shock you three times."

"I know, I remember! That hurt."

"You remember?" I asked him.

"Oh yeah. It was like when you're dreaming and you fall, you have a reflex spasm? Like that. Only it felt like alarm bells ringing inside my head. *Time to get up!* Like your mom is yelling at you on a school day to get moving and come downstairs for breakfast. It was jarring. Jolted me back. Dane, you've gotta find a way to expedite reintegration because I don't think I would have come back otherwise."

"Well, you had other reasons," I said cryptically to him, and his eyes darted over to Dina briefly, and then back to me. I winked at him, keeping his secret safe.

The ladies looked at me quizzically for a moment.

"Anyway, tell us more," I urged, "as long as you have the energy for it."

He grew momentarily silent, and stared off into the distance as we surrounded him there, lying peacefully upon his gurney. An IV sputtered momentarily amidst the faint, ambient beeps of his ECG. I glanced up. Heart rate, blood pressure, oxygen levels, body temp, all of them were nominal now, with only an occasional palpitation spike.

"Going through Nova was the same as before, right? It seemed like I was in there for an hour. I know it wasn't instantaneous; I know there was a bit of a delay before Ava grabbed me, but not an hour's worth." He blinked, trying to recall it. "This time though, it seemed like weeks, months, even years. I can't begin to parse out all my dreams, but there were many. Dreams I remember from my youth, mostly. Dreams of people, you guys," -here he looked at Dina and grinned, and I wondered how enjoyable that memory was- "I don't recall any nightmares or anything scary. I also don't think Norma even existed in my dreams. Like… it wasn't a factor. It was just a state of bliss and suspended animation, and just *really* good sleep."

"That's so interesting," Dina said, "that it seemed like years. I wonder when your REM state kicked in during all that. They say that most of your dreaming is done right before you wake up. I wonder if there's a way to monitor when that kicked in." I frowned, not understanding. "I mean, did his dreams happen during resuscitation or during stasis? Before or after reintegration, I mean."

I nodded. "Yeah, that would be good to know. I can try to code some enhanced brainwave monitoring into *Courier 4.0.* Might be time for another upgrade, methinks. By the time we're ready to launch I think I'll have to call it *Courier 392.7.*" Dina smiled.

"Yeah, I don't know," Isaac replied. "It was really luminescent, swirling, serene, ethereal, esoteric, intangible, every other word you can use to describe something so peaceful. Like one of those white noise machines you're powerless against as a baby, ya know? Riding in a car for a long trip and falling asleep to the steady hum. It was just…"

He trailed off so long that my eyebrows went up, watching and waiting.

"…*perfect*," he finished, grinning again, and he closed his eyes.

"Until the very end," I said.

His eyes opened slowly, as if out of a dream. Isaac nodded. "Yeah," he said, his nose crinkling, "it was just jarring. I don't know if that was from the reintegration or the AED though. You lose track of time and space."

I nodded, patting his chest. "It's okay, man. We're just glad you're back. *All* of us," I said, raising an eyebrow to him. I let him see my eyes darting over to Dina. He grinned again. "I've gotta check on the OS and see what went wrong this time, but before that I've got an update meeting with Donze. You rest. We'll catch up soon. Isaac," I said, pausing and staring intently at him, "I'm really sorry. We almost lost you. Everything worked for the birds, the dogs, I don't know what happened. We humans are just so much more complex, I just need to… I don't know… figure out what changed with you. We'll get there."

"You should also look into really speeding up the entries," Trapper said. "The critical part is getting people *in*. Once they're in and they're in stasis on the drives, Genesis has to launch, and it has to get out of here, even if it's fleeing from a dying planet right when it's being spaghettified. If we're now accommodating roughly 6,000 people, we need to have them hop on board the Genesis train with no delay." She cocked an eyebrow at me and tilted her head.

I nodded in agreement. "Right. Sounds good. Come with me, Trapper, yeah? You can help me with the coding after we see Genesis and talk with Donze. See ya, Isaac. Welcome back, buddy." I tapped him on the chest.

Dina started to follow us, but Isaac called her back and asked her to stay. I didn't turn around to gawk, but the smile spread across the length of my face.

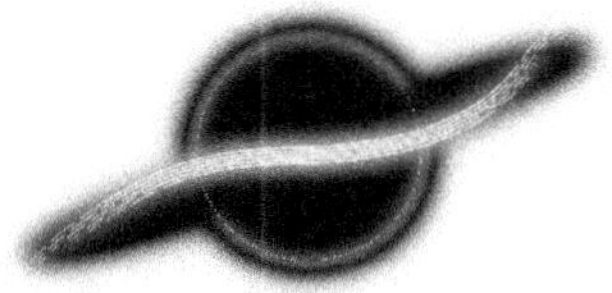

It was a thing of beauty, truly. Genesis was coming along really well. Gorgeous and sleek, it would be able to house Aurora and *much* more. There were building materials and tools for shelters, crop seed, animal pens and cages, agriculture supplies, weapons, fuel, enough bottled water to fill a stadium to the brim, tinder and flint, storage containers, medical provisions, and so much more, all compressed into the smallest real estate possible so as to be able to transport as much as possible to PCb.

The Genesis craft was similar in body type to any other NASA shuttle humanity had ever deployed, space-ready and designed for long stays. It was simply massively longer. The previous regulation shuttles were 122 feet long and flaunting a gorgeous wingspan of 78 feet. Genesis was alike them only in form factor. *This* getaway craft was 167 feet long with a wingspan of 92 feet. It was breathtakingly huge, and its cargo bay vast.

It was fully autonomous, requiring no pilot, and it was also differentiated from previous shuttle craft in that it had Harrier Jet-like propulsion, enabling vertical launches and landings. In this way, it would be able to follow a sequence for landing on PCb that required no human intervention, and could safely touch down with all aboard.

I didn't care to ask what the sticker price was on it.

Trapper and I paced around it and nodded approvingly. And, like a lightning bolt, it suddenly hit both of us at the same time.

This ship exists because of us.

The only reason they were building this was because we had developed a teleportation system for PCb that required a craft to get it there. This was that craft, and here we stood.

I wished Isaac could be with us right now.

Genesis would be mounted to the side of the conventional booster rocket for initial launch, and then the nuclear propulsion technology would take over from there once at a safe orbit around Earth. All of that was beyond my paygrade and over my head, but the technicians working on it were bustling about in white coats and skittering across the floor of the hangar as if Norma were coming *today*.

The bright lights of the hangar were piercing, leaving nothing to darkness. This thing needed to be airtight, that's for sure, and it needed to be foolproof. To that end they labored.

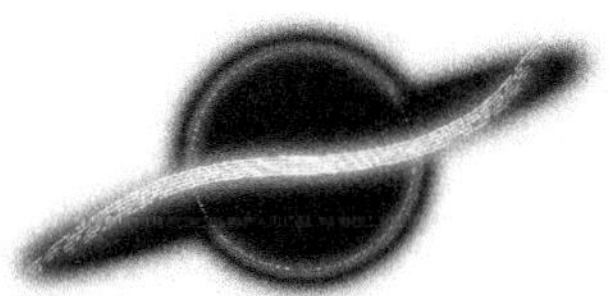

The SecDef was red-faced and bustling just as much as the techs were in the hangar. Something was up.

"Mr. Secretary?" I asked, after we were let in to the conference room he was sitting at. He held up a finger toward me, and pointed to a Bluetooth headset in his ear. I nodded and waited.

"Yes, Mr. Vice President, well, they're running me ragged as it is. Crews here are working as fast as they can." He paused. "And I told you that we'd be on schedule. You still have my promise on that." Another pause. "Well, unfortunately, the only thing that moves at that speed around here is that supermassive black hole. Besides, we still have more testing to do with the teleportation subj-"

He stopped, and rolled his eyes, balling his hand up into a fist and ready to thump it down hard on his desk.

"Fine. You do that," he said, curtly. "No, thank *you*, Mr. Vice President. A pleasure as always," he said, and then practically ripped out his headset and tossed it haphazardly onto the table. "Prick," he finalized.

Donze took a quick but deep breath, and then stood, greeting us. "Mr. Currier. Ms. Trapper. Good to see you," he said. "That was our illustrious and highly patient Vice President. Sorry you had to hear that."

I shrugged, ready to wave it away. "It's fine, Mr. Donze, I-"

"It's not, but whatever. I admit, hearing of your plans early on, I was not a believer, myself. Quite the pessimist, actually. I'm sure you remember our call. But now, it seems that certain unbelievers at the top of the pecking order are more comfortable wielding a hammer than joining in belief."

"Sir?" I asked, confused.

Donze now shrugged. "They'd rather wield a sword than a ploughshare. Anyway," he said tiredly, sitting back down in a huff. We sat as well.

Donze rubbed his face and then continued. "Looks like you've seen Genesis. They've got me stationed down here for a week overseeing it. It's a beaut,' ain't it?" Strangely, he donned a Texas drawl for that line. "The rocket itself is down at KSC in Florida at Launch Complex 39. It's coming along as well. The nuclear propulsion tech is nearby, but we can't disclose where that is, for security reasons. It'll be retrofit onto the rocket soon. Can you give me an update on your progress, please?"

I straightened up. "Certainly. Well, I texted you after the teleportation subject – our partner, Isaac Farragut – went through. He's healing nicely and he's making a great recovery. He shared about the journey in stasis and what it was like for him, how long it took, all of that. It was a peaceful passage, but not necessarily a tranquil return. My partner Megan, here, and I will need to further isolate how to refine that process, and we're working on that right after our meeting with you."

"What happened to him, exactly, Mr. Currier?"

I took a breath. "Well, it appears that for him the journey took longer. When he went through back in my apartment using only the initial two chambers, he reported that it felt like close on an hour. I would concur with that; my experience felt the same. But with the new system using all three chambers and teleporting over wireless streams, and then being kept in stasis on the drives, even though it was approximately one minute, to him it felt more like *years*, he said."

"Years?"

"Yes, sir, maybe more."

"Did he appear any older? Had he aged?"

"Not visibly, sir, no. He looks, acts, and talks the same. All of his bodily functions are normal, his metrics and DNA profile matched to his original with no degradation or degeneration, and he's clearly himself, just tired. My colleague Megan and I – as well as Dina Jensen – believe that he's recovering more from the revival post-transit. Having to resuscitate him was physically taxing. He expressed that himself."

"Oh, he did?"

"Yes. He reported it was jarring. He was really dug in there like a frozen tick, to quote Megan here."

"Is that right?" Donze said to Trapper.

Megan nodded. "Definitely. Flesh was frozen; hair was glistening with crystalline specks from the cold; pupils contracted, vessels distended, catatonic, sir. He came out like a human popsicle."

"Fascinating. I assume that throws a wrench into the process, of course."

"It does."

"I'm sorry to hear it. I'm sure you'll get back on track."

I nodded vigorously. "Oh, most definitely, sir. We will, and soon. The relays need to get everyone out of Aurora and reintegrated in an identical state to their previous makeup, or we'll have a logjam, and possibly...," I trailed off, unwilling to give voice to the word.

Donze squinted and leaned toward me. "Possibly...?"

"Possibly," I started again, "fusion. As in, multiple subjects becoming reintegrated together, over and over and over, all of them assimilated into one giant mass, which eventually would fill up the Aurora chamber to maximum capacity, causing it to burst. It would be an utter failure, of course, and we would leave this calamity for another one of our own making."

"Well, you better solve that problem right quick, Mr. Currier. Ms. Trapper," he growled. "That's an end result that the President and Vice President will not accept, most assuredly. Nor will I."

"Yessir," I said.

Donze's phone rang. "Donze," he greeted. "Could you say that again?" he asked in a stunted fashion, and then he turned to us and rose quickly. "Go. You need to go. Now. Back to your friend. He's coding."

My heart jumped into my throat, and my eyes morphed into wide circles. Trapper and I jumped up and flew out of Donze's office to find Isaac and Dina.

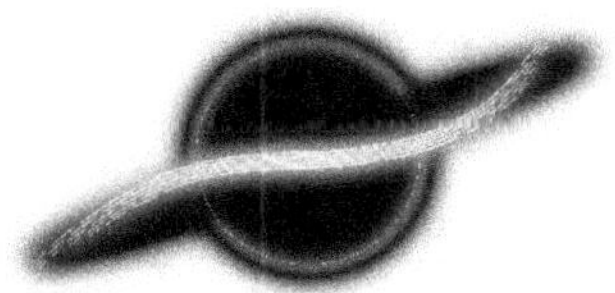

The medics had been alerted. They were working on him feverishly. Dina was off to one side, inconsolable. She covered her face and shook.

The AED was out. They shocked him.

Over and over again, they brought the paddles to his chest. But this time, there was no life. There was nothing.

Flatline.

Dina turned away and sunk into my arms as I wept. There Isaac lay, mouth agape, staring upward into the ceiling and beyond. His skin looked pallid and weak, his chest sunk. Yet, at the corners of his mouth, a faint trace of a smile teased.

Isaac, come on buddy. Don't do this to us. You were supposed to be well. I hear you, my friend. Come back. I hear you.

But Isaac heard nothing, and before we knew it, he was gone. The medics backed away and called it. Dina buried her head into my chest and sobbed, heartbroken. My own heart was ripped.

I let him go through. Me. This is my fault.

I didn't code everything properly.

And now, he was dead.

The connection was clear. Isaac was dead because of a problem with *Courier 4.0*. He had bravely volunteered to go through, and we had failed to bring back that brave soul. And now, he had suffered from a fatal heart attack on the coattails of what was to be his new identity, as the first person to travel through a teleportation system, be frozen in stasis, and emerge healthy in victory to show it could be done.

Through Dina's sobs, I distinctly heard one phrase, over and over again, and I lost it.

"He loved me, Dane. He told me… he loved me. He… told me he loved me! No! Isaac!"

I bit my lip, which was trembling, as all the air was sucked out of me. There, lying before us and turning a shade of purple, was the dead body of a brave soul who had grown even braver. He had told Dina. He told her how he felt about her.

For Dina, I was glad.

For Isaac, I was devastated. My faith had been rocked after his traumatic return. Now, I didn't even know if I had any at all. You could say my faith was annihilated, and I didn't know where to turn now. If I had any faith whatsoever, it was most definitely in a tailspin; and, potentially, in all likelihood, an unrecoverable one.

I needed to fix this damned system 'right quick,' as Donze had said, or no one would be able to tell *anyone* they loved them anymore.

Questions stacked perilously high in my brain as far as how to make this work successfully, and in time. I was not at a loss for questions.

I just had so few answers.

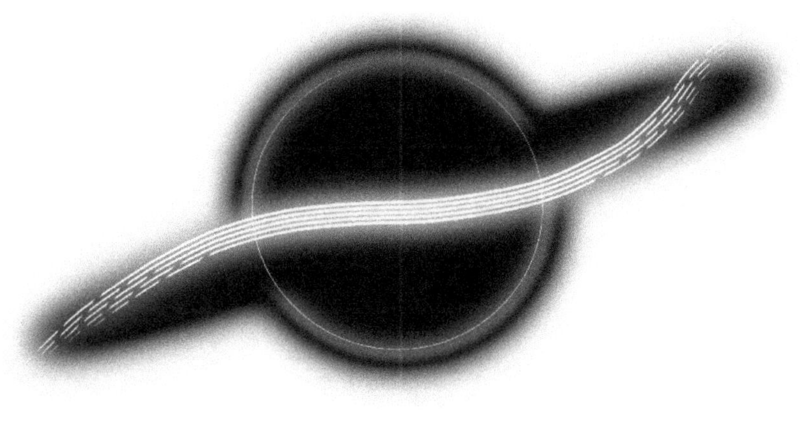

15 | Breakthrough
December 1st, 2025

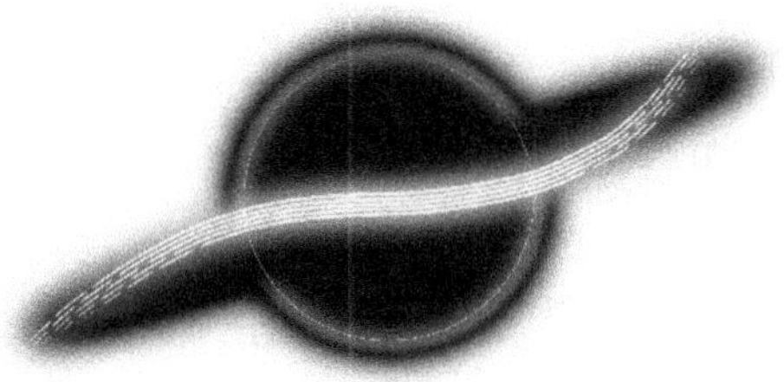

Hungry and driven, it was coming.

We all watched the feed, live, where Saturn was literally ripped apart. Its glorious rings of ice and rock disintegrated long before the planet itself did, skimming and ricocheting off Saturn's surface as they barreled across the stars into the black void that was Farragut-322. The planet went next, splintering and fracturing into large chunks, spinning and whirling crazily into the void. The molten core of the planet was exposed as portions of the crust broke off, and the temperature differential caused massive cave-ins and explosions as the quiet gas giant bellowed, gusted, and then was extinguished forever.

Our sun was also now gently being pulled toward the supermassive, helpless to resist. Its gravitational forces strove against the hungry beast drifting our way, and, at least for the present, was positioned relatively close to where it had always been. But the clock was ticking…

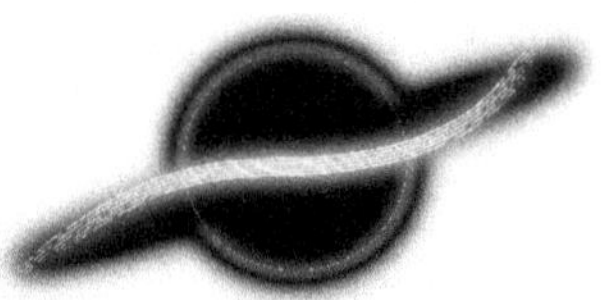

Dina was coming around again. She had to acknowledge that she loved Isaac, and it was hard for her to commit to a love she'd only just glanced off of. Her heart had been massaged by joy, only to be shattered by pain.

And as for Isaac's heart, what had caused the attack? The coroner reported that he hadn't had any congenital heart disease or defects. I sort of already figured that: in truth, going through Nova and Ava, he should have been perfected. But had the relay to Aurora degenerated something that was originally perfected in Ava? The coroner didn't think so. He had arteriosclerosis, as if he had had a high cholesterol diet or diabetes. That *had* to have happened 'coming out of the thaw,' as we called it. Something just hadn't reintegrated or settled correctly, and it was only a matter of time.

That killed me, frankly. Going through Nova had always *improved* the subject, or, at least that was initially true of Isaac when he first went through. I know it was true of Macy and me. Every time I thought about his demise I could only shake my head in frustration. What went wrong? And more importantly, *why?* I had such belief in my system, but, if pressed to be super honest, my faith in it had been perilously tested. If we were to make it, then I needed to have faith. It was that simple.

Trapper and I *did* go back and debug *CourierOS,* and we finally figured it out. It was now dubbed *Courier 5.1*, two evolutionary upgrades beyond the original success. It took us a while, but we finally discovered what caused Isaac's traumatic reintegration, and thus, would have prompted his subsequent heart attack. There were lines of subcode that could have caused my chambers – and thus, the SSD drives – to act as a cryo-freeze containment system, reducing the body's functions to the barest minimum. In all honesty, I had programmed in coding to strip the human element down to its core functions for stasis, but I had not reduced the pattern to all zeros. There were ones in there, not just zeros.

Something got lost in translation in the relay, and it took us a while to figure out where the breakdown occurred. Eventually, we determined, that in the handoff from Ava to Aurora and in the RAID array of the drives, the pattern was being split unevenly between the two drive partitions, and in the reintegration process, *Courier 4.0* had been simply trying to parse out both drives and stitch them back together. However, what it was ultimately doing was *pausing* the second partition's data and only reading the first. When the second partition was then assimilated, it overwrote the first partition, effectively resetting it to a cold state.

Thus, if we had used only single, and not *mirrored* partitions, Isaac would have emerged from Aurora as whole and alive as he had been when he was sent to Ava. I had to rethink the whole process and ensure that both partitions were read *and* assimilated simultaneously.

For now, however, neither one of us were willing to go through the teleportation relay that was Nova-Ava-Aurora. Not yet. After seeing what happened to Isaac, Dina certainly was out of the running, and we would never ask that of her. Nonetheless, a clock was ticking there as well: someone would eventually *have* to step up and volunteer, or we would never know if this whole 'cockamamie plan,' as Donze had once referred to it, would work.

In my heart, I knew who would have to volunteer. There was one person who screwed it up, and there was only one person who could redeem their mistake.

In my heart, I knew it was going to have to be me.

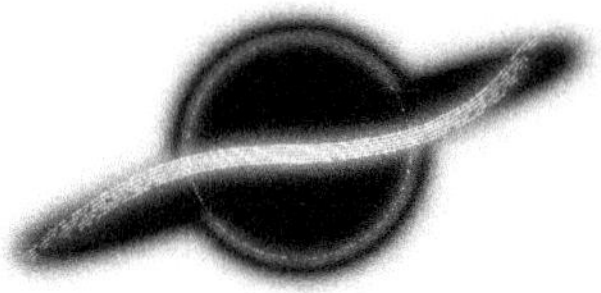

After the autopsy, we had Isaac buried outside the base on a beautiful, hot, late November day. The very phrase, 'hot, late November day' seemed so oxymoronic. And it was getting hotter, even with the sun drifting toward the black hole, because we were now *also* drifting toward it – and the sun – as well.

Farragut-322 was named as such in honor of its finder. This was something that Isaac had not wanted, and we all knew that he would be rolling over in his grave if he knew that the scientific community, and indeed the whole world, was now referring to it as such. It would have been the death of him all over again.

As for us, we resolved in our hearts never to call it that. We resolved to still call it Norma. After all, naming it after a horrible ex-wife seemed far better than naming it after a beloved colleague and friend whose research of it, and escape plan from it, had killed him.

The President held another national address, but was mumbling and incoherent. Something was happening to him – and, arbitrarily, to others around us, we had noticed – as if our very lives and consciousness were also being pulled toward Norma, in some kind of inadvertent and unwilling tug into a diminished consciousness that was not representative of their original selves.

Their mental acuity was being eroded, as if the oncoming gravity of Norma could work on the soul, and they slowly slipped into a dementia-like state. I had talked with my mom and dad at intervals, and I noticed it with them as well. A few of our techs stationed at the lab here exhibited some warning signs. It seemed to strike indiscriminately.

The medical community documented it and started referring to it, informally, as 'the slide.' Those who showed initial signs of the slide were monitored and prescribed things like Modafinil and Piracetam: nootropics and wakefulness-promoting agents, almost as if they suffered from narcolepsy.

Just as the galaxy was being affected, so were its citizens, pulled irresistibly toward a miserable end.

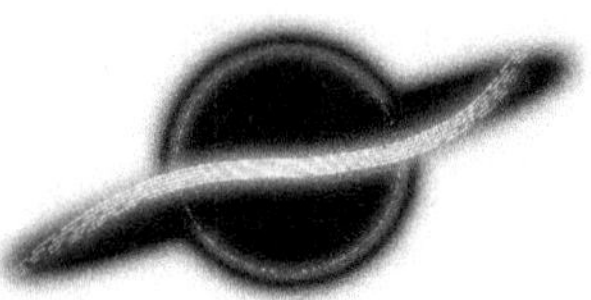

December 2nd, 2025

And now, early this morning, I sat in my Washington, DC apartment, brooding over, literally, everything.

Macy came up to me, and for some reason was extra affectionate. She would not leave my side.

"Hey, baby girl," I said to her, reaching out and enveloping her with a giant hug. She was doing fine here, which was something I feared. I'm sure she missed the familiar sights and scents of Seattle. We had been able to walk her in the narrow gaps between fierce research.

As I sat on the couch, I looked her deep in the eyes and rubbed her ears, remembering how much Isaac loved to do that. He really loved my dog, and I'm sure she missed him in some canine sentience.

I thought back to the UW lab, and all the days Dina, Isaac and I spent working together monitoring the stars and the systems out there. That dark room pinpricked with light from all of those monitors full of celestial maps and charts, wondering what we were looking at, or even looking for.

A memory of Isaac suddenly came rushing back at me from the recesses of my memory. It was from the early days of our tenure at the lab, just the two of us, talking freely.

"What do you plan to do once you graduate?"

"Me?" I asked. "I'm not sure yet. My family's down in Alameda, that's where I grew up. Just always loved the Pacific Northwest and wanted to go to the U. I think I'll try for something around here. I like it here. How about you?"

Isaac shook his head. "I don't think I'll stay. I want to get out and see the world. I'd love to chase extraterrestrial life, ya know? Ever seen *Contact* with Jodie Foster? Great movie."

"Oh yeah, that's a good one."

"Yeah," Isaac replied, "her dad said something to her at one point, like 'if we're the only ones out here, it seems like an awful waste of space.' I'd love to visit other worlds and prove or disprove their existence. Don't know until ya go, right?"

"Definitely. Don't know until ya go."

And just like that, the reverie faded, but Isaac's words remained in me, reverberating through my memory.

Don't know until ya go.

Was that why he wanted to be the first through the relay? I knew that he didn't appreciate the association with Norma, but had he also gone through because he wanted to be the first to get out of his own body and test this whole process of interplanetary space travel?

Regardless of the reason, I was moved, and once again found myself choking up. That old conversation motivated and inspired me. As before, when it was just Nova and Ava, a sudden resolve washed over me to see it through. We couldn't afford to wait, and I couldn't afford to carry the shame of what had happened to Isaac. We didn't need shame on PCb. We would need to start our new lives there whole and confident, ready to start anew.

I scratched Macy on the head and gave her some Isaac-worthy ear rubs, grabbed my things, and headed back to the lab, texting Trapper to meet me there as soon as she could.

No time like the present, right, Isaac? Norma wouldn't wait, and there was only one simple truth here:

Don't know until ya go.

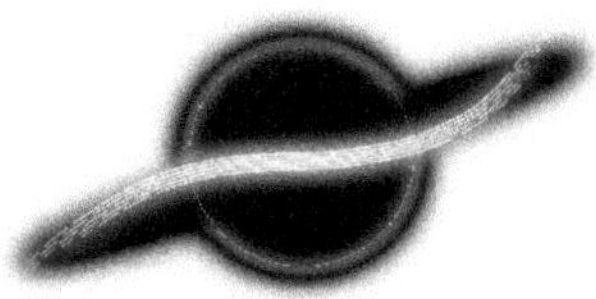

I stood before her, unashamed, and unafraid.

Correction: I was afraid. Yes. There was no denying that. What I was about to do was scary. But I was definitely unashamed. I *had* been ashamed over what had happened to Isaac, but frustrated rumination finally gave way to action and ownership. So, now I stood before Megan Trapper, with her at my laptop, ready to send me into the great unknown. Afraid, yes.

Ashamed, no.

Only she and I knew the game plan. I would be gone for a week. We needed to test this out at greater intervals. If we couldn't stand a week, then we wouldn't be able to stand a month. If not a month, then not a few years. And if not a few years, then we wouldn't be able to stand the approximately eighty-five years it would take to reach PCb.

Someone had to go, and that someone was me.

Don't know until ya go.

She didn't argue, she didn't protest, and she didn't try to talk me out of it. Megan Trapper knew what needed to be done, and she, like me, had the innate sense that I was the one who had to do it. This wasn't nobility here; it was strictly necessity due to there being no more time to be noble.

She looked me up and down, and then approached me. The countdown was running.

She had everything on, and I had nothing on. I stood before her, and she embraced me, fully, in a manner that I was unprepared for.

Megan Trapper was spunky, but there was a beauty there that I beheld perhaps for the first time. She removed her glasses and gazed deep into my eyes, staring into the well of my soul. There was no smile, no affirming words, just... understanding. And for the first time, I gazed into eyes that I had before found to be shielded; aloof. Now, this close, and this connected, I found them alluring. Tempting. Human. Gorgeous beyond words.

I smiled at her, and then took a deep breath, glancing back briefly at Nova, with its open door beckoning to me.

If I didn't come back, Trapper would have to spearhead this herself. But the reality was that she was nearly as good at coding as I was, and she knew *Courier 5.1* well enough, and the stars even better. PCb was, after all, her idea. If I didn't return, everything would be in competent hands. I had do this, and she knew it.

Trapper pulled me close, wrapping her hands around my naked back, holding me tightly. I reciprocated, wrapping my arms around her, smelling her hair, pulling her into me. It was the sweetest hug I think I had ever experienced.

"I have a note on my desktop to give to my mom and dad, should I, ya know…" I mumbled.

"Don't," she said, firmly. It was almost a plea, commanding yet breathy.

I stopped, exhaling, and finally nodding, steeling myself. "You're right. Don't think that way. I'm coming back. I know."

She crinkled her nose, and tilted her head at me. "No, you dummy. Don't *ruin the moment.*"

And then Megan Trapper reached up and pulled my face down toward her own. She kissed me deeply, and then buried her face into my chest, turning her cheek to my chest and resting softly against my own.

We both turned toward the laptop. Thirty-seven seconds. "Go," she said, pushing me away. "And come back, or I won't have anyone to call 'pudgy,' *Pudgy.*" She playfully slapped my left butt cheek.

I giggled through my nose, and then pulled away, walking briskly and resolutely toward Nova. My eyes went to Ava beside her. She was ready. Further, my eyes were drawn down the seventy-five foot line to the waiting Aurora.

Everything was set to go.

I stepped in.

The door whirred and then closed silently behind me and locked. The floor felt cold, but not frightfully so.

I remained standing, unapologetic and confident. This was it. All or nothing. Go time. All in, right here.

I closed my eyes. I didn't want to watch the countdown. I had done this before, and it would be fine, I told myself as I whispered a silent prayer to whomever might be listening. I felt Megan watching me through the glass.

My hands were at my sides. I craned my neck toward Nova's ceiling and fanned my arms out slightly, as I let the sequence break me down into a trillion particles under a complex DNA profile, reducing me to a data stream in the most peaceful moment I have ever experienced… just like Isaac had.

Images flashed through my mind. Dreams. I saw the Earth, old and new, I saw my parents, myself as a baby, our planet ripping apart in a horrendous crumpling show of force by Norma. I witnessed friends and family wishing me well and sending me off, and then they were burnt to smoldering ash in the heat of a supernova. One remained whole and well. I knew him. It was Isaac. He was in there only as a residual memory, I realized, but it felt so tangibly and hauntingly real, as if his spirit had left some imprint on the SSD's partition.

And then all was silent and still, as I was breathlessly whisked into a vortex of peace, riding me on the soft sails of ships steered by stars, gliding me through the galaxy. I heard laughter and tears, joy and pain, sobbing and cheering, all fused into a funnel of sentience, tingling my flesh and coursing through my arteries. Life and death merged into a single stream as I filled a partition on a drive…

…and slept.

Don't know until ya go.

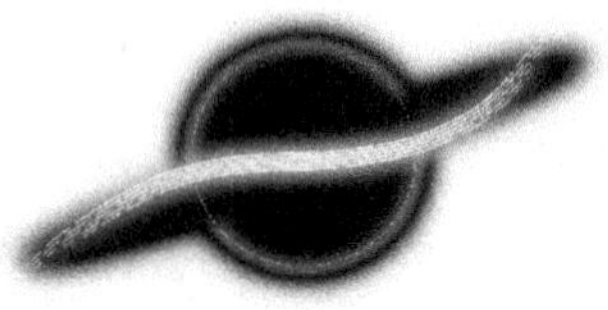

December 9th, 2025

"Well, you're still pudgy," a voice said, and then someone hugged me in unbridled laughter, bolting toward me and leaping into my arms as my eyes blearily came to, struggling in the bright light. If I didn't know any better, there were tears forming in those eyes as I strained to see them.

Megan Trapper stared longingly into my eyes and kissed me deeply. A faint whimper emitted from her as she continued to kiss me. *I could get used to this kind of wakeup call*, I thought, and realized that the thought was my own, the inherent body heat I felt inside me was mine, my consciousness remembered leaving *and* returning, and the familiar sights of the lab coalesced into clarity around me, revealing my memory to be intact.

My heartbeat was strong, and it was mine.

Trapper looked at me. I didn't know or care how much time had elapsed since I had gone; she would tell me. The look on her face revealed everything had gone just as planned, and I took her in and kissed her in return as the swirling fog enveloped us and streamed out of Aurora.

It was then that I realized that a few other techs had gathered around in the background, aware of our tests and wanting to celebrate this victory. It meant something to them as well.

"I'm suddenly acutely aware that I'm still naked," I grunted to Trapper.

She just stared at me, sighing through a smile. "Some things never change. I told you not to ruin the moment!"

She kissed me deeply, and she held me.

Hungry and weary, I had returned.

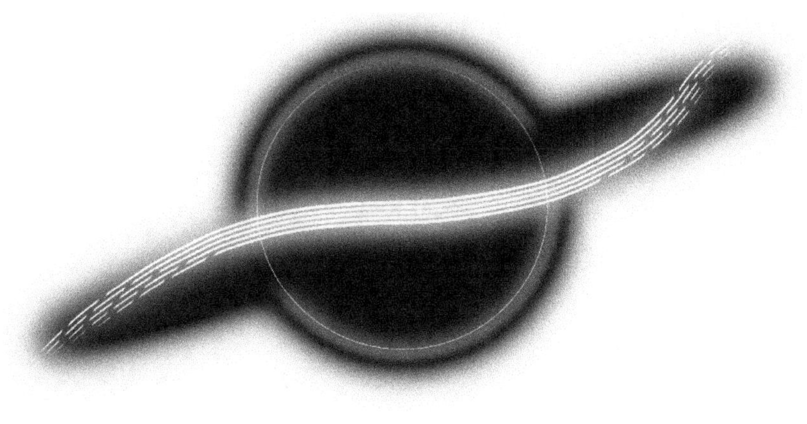

16 | Breakdown
December 12th, 2025

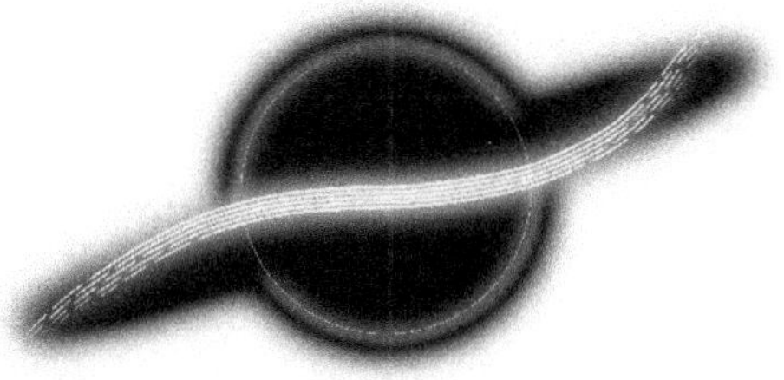

We had done it.

I had gone through, after having been in stasis for a whole week.

Dina was at first angry beyond words that she had not been allowed to be part of my teleportation, but she ultimately relented, realizing that had something gone wrong yet again, she couldn't take it. I shared with her my dream of Isaac, and she sobbed. Trapper and I embraced her and held her for what felt like a solid ten minutes as she rode that wave of longing and loss. It was precious and necessary.

I had been checked out by medical, and given the all clear. I truly didn't feel any different. For a while I thought that Dina might be resenting my wholeness; the fact that I was relatively unaffected by the teleportation relay. After all, a whole week had gone by, and I was in stasis, and I was fine…

…and her would-be boyfriend was dead.

For the first day or so, admittedly, I felt as though I was walking on eggshells around her, hypersensitive; not sure if she was judging me, stewing in silent resentment. I thought I knew Dina better than that, and she remained her usual self, so I had to press on despite my suspicions.

A lot had happened while I was away.

The biggest news was, of course, that Trapper had also gone through a day after I had, almost as though she sought to check on me while I was in stasis. As if she even could. That news blew me away. Dina had set her up for the relay jump, and programmed her to be in a partition right next to mine. However, she only wanted to be gone for a day. That was all the risk she was willing to take at this time. Dina seconded it, and sent her through.

Trapper said that all readouts were clear and lights were green, so she felt much safer knowing that I was in there, alive and well. I felt there was something more, however, and told her as much. My *Just couldn't stand to live without me, huh?* resulted in her sporting a mocking tone and contorting her face with a *nnh, yeah, nnnh, that's it, yeah.*

I chuckled through my nervous fear *and* amazement that she had gone through before even receiving any assurance that I had successfully returned. She was brave *and* foolhardy. However, all three of us had now gone through, and all three had returned. But only Trapper and I had made the relay jump. Dina was still holding out, and we couldn't blame her.

They filled me in on the week I had missed, and nearly all of it was bleak.

Jupiter, that massive 43,440-mile radius gas giant, 11 times wider than Earth and on a far orbit close to Norma, was reluctantly answering Norma's nefarious call, sliding across the galaxy into the black void, never to return. It was not there yet, but its trajectory was being mapped, and it was on its way. Neptune was unfortunately close to Pluto on their apogee orbit, and it was now gone as well, a silent death of a planet we had never visited, and never would.

Australia had split in two. So had the Arctic and Antarctic poles. There had been seventeen deadly tsunamis in the past week alone, caused by glacier collapse. Indonesia was wiped out. Greenland was flooded. If global warming was an issue before, nothing could have prepared us for what was happening now. Norma, as it approached, was causing unpredictable gravitational disruptions. Its very presence warped gravity, causing catastrophic quakes and atmospheric collapse. The radiation levels were growing at an alarming rate, and the number of earthquakes now occurring were taking on a frightening exponential curve.

The Genesis craft was nearly ready. The nuclear propulsion component was being tested in a separate bunker deep underground at the launch site, shielded from public view and keeping us safe on the surface.

The Stock market had tanked and bottomed out, and would probably never recover, not that anyone cared. What blew me away was that Wall Street was still actually open, and there were reports of traders eagerly conducting business should Norma 'pass us by.' Ridiculous. You can't beat idealistic hubris. Humans are unquenchably hopeful.

That wasn't all of it. A collective fever was afflicting those of us who were still here on this planet, awaiting the inevitable. It was dark, and it was rampant.

President Trump had slid. 'The slide' was definitely real, and he was not immune. The slide was indiscriminate, touching everyone differently. The funny thing was, I felt fine, better than ever, in fact. As with my first teleportation using only Nova and Ava, I felt improved. Was I now immune to the slide? Time would tell.

But for the President: he had been reduced to a babbling idiot, like so many had been: a strange phenomenon seemed to just rob them of their soul, absconding with their personality, their mind, and everything that made them *them,* as they silently drifted into dementia. Exposure to Norma's event horizon – drawing nearer though still distant – was causing ego dissolution. The slide was no joke, and it grasped at us with silent invisible tentacles, gently and violently ripping our identities from us as we meandered here still.

Norma's influence had triggered a collective existential crisis. Religion was surging anew, and my mom was sharing her newfound faith with me over the phone and pelting me with faith-based messages daily. There were no messages from dad. He had killed himself while I was away. They had called my cell while I was gone, and couldn't reach me. I had told them where I was going, so they called the mainline for Chantilly and discovered that I was not here. Dad's mental acuity had been going anyway, and he jumped to the conclusion that I had died. He couldn't take it. Norma was coming *and* his son was dead? He went down to the basement where he kept his liquor and his shotgun, and that was that. I was always closer to my mom, but now I had lost him to despair, and was losing her to religion.

It was bizarre and sad, and it was all I could do to close myself off to my emotions and just *focus*.

The VP was also sliding, and thus, the Speaker of the House, Mike Johnson, was in charge of the national address. He would be on in a few moments today to announce our plans, as well as the creation of a lottery to allow those lucky six thousand souls to teleport off this rock into an uncertain future of colonizing PCb.

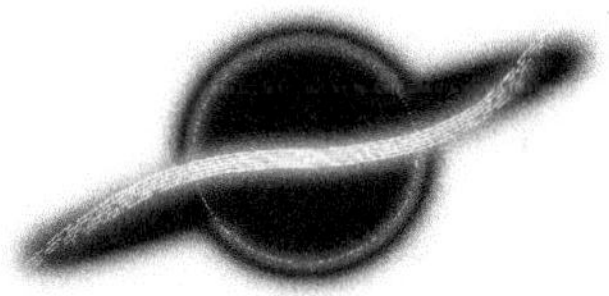

"Forgive me," Speaker Johnson uttered, dabbing his forehead. It was hot, but that wasn't the only thing affecting him. Johnson was also sliding.

"What I meant to say, my fellow Americans, is that we may have found a way to revive, sorry, *survive*, I mean. Through diligent work by fellow scientists, ah, excuse me, *technicians* at the University of Washington, part of the original team that had discovered the comet… I'm sorry, the *black hole*, forgive me, they have devised a method by which we may be able to leave Planet Earth and find shelter nearby. Well, not exactly nearby, but somewhere in a neighboring system. It isn't guaranteed, but it's the best chance we have to escape Farrow-," he stumbled, "Ferrisgut… I'm sorry. *Farragut*. The black hole. The one that is on its way to us here and that you've heard about."

I think we know which one you're talking about, pal, I thought judgmentally, though my heart went to him in pity, wondering if this is what my dad had gone through.

He dabbed his forehead again while we watched, cringing. This was not Mike Johnson's finest hour.

"In fairness to American citizens and to fellow world leaders, we have instituting, uh, *instituted,* rather, a lottery system. For the drawing. I mean, excuse me…," -here he shook his head quickly and then squinted to focus- "for those souls who will be chosen to board a special vehicle for passage to the system in question. You will receive an automated mailer from the Social Security Administration in the next week if you are chosen to go. If you do not receive one, I'm sorry, but we've had to accommodate a limited number of people only. Please await word and instructions, and thank you for your attention. May God bless everyone, including all of you. Ev- everyone," he said again, smiling weakly and signing off.

I turned to Dina and Trapper, eyes ringed with amazement. "Well that wasn't awkward at all. How are *you* guys feeling?"

"Fine," Dina said.

"Annoyed," Trapper said at the same time.

"Yeah, me too," I agreed. "This thing, this, *slide*, as they're calling it, I wonder if we're immune to it somehow, because we went through Nova. We've been improved, right? All of us. I had those sulfur burps. They're completely gone. Do you guys have anything that had been plaguing you that's now gone?"

Both of them thought, with their eyes roaming off into space. Eventually, Trapper spoke up.

"Oh! I had this guy who was bugging me who I actually kind of like now. He's not such a pudgy dork anymore."

"Flattering. Thanks." She nodded and gave me a thumbs up and a hearty smile. "No! I mean, I appreciate it, but I'm officially offended, just for the record. But think! Anything?" I probed.

"Well," Dina said, "I've always had some lower back pain from a lumbar injury a decade ago. Come to think of it, I don't recall… thinking of it?" She ended it with a question, verifying her own certainty.

"Yeah, well, you said my complexion was clearer the other day, Dina, remember that?" Trapper asked. "That could be something. That and the improved pudgy dork guy."

I grimaced again. "Seriously though, you know what I mean? Ever since we went through Nova, we've been 'improved' somehow. I wonder if we're immune to whatever 'the slide' is." I held out my hands, waiting for agreement.

Trapper nodded with a clenched lip, as if considering the possibilities of it. Her eyebrows flicked up. "Sure."

I turned to Dina. Her countenance had fallen, and her face wore a wry, thousand-yard stare.

"Dina?"

"We've been improved. Hmm," she finished.

She didn't need to say it. I knew then she was thinking about, and mourning, Isaac. *Ever since we went through Nova, we've been improved somehow,* I had said. Her expression resounded something else.

Except for Isaac.

I gazed at Dina with pity, and took her into my arms. Trapper rubbed her back sympathetically.

"I think with Isaac," I said to her, "there was nothing to improve. He was already perfect, Dina."

Dina sighed softly, yet heavily, into my chest. Trapper clenched her lip and studied me, approving of my sentiment. Memories of the first time Isaac went through, and his subsequent exhilaration, flowed through my mind, bringing a grin to my face. Isaac Farragut was a good man and a good friend.

"So," I said, trying to lighten the load a bit. "Lottery, huh? Sounds serious. I wonder if we'll make it."

Trapper laughed. "Relax. We're on it. Donze stacked the deck after Isaac. But I think we were already at the top of the list anyway, Dane. There was no way we were going to get left behind. Not after all we've done."

"How do you know?" I asked, a bit incredulous.

She shrugged, pulling out three government return address envelopes out of her pocket. They said, clearly, in the top left corner, *Social Security Administration.* They had our names on them.

I smiled, feeling a bit relieved, although I was never really worried that we wouldn't be chosen. The deck had been stacked indeed. I was okay with it.

PCb was calling our names, and it was only a matter of time before all three of us were reduced to data streams once more, and launched 4.24 light years into space.

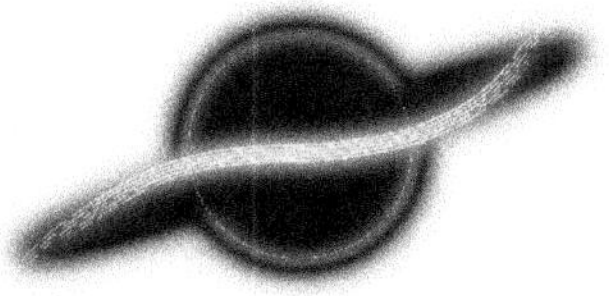

December 12th, 2025

Christmas was fast approaching, and with it, you might expect a feeling of festive Yuletide.

Not so.

Jupiter was no more, crushed to fragments.

Venus was on the same trajectory and was not expected to last the month.

Time itself seems to warp in localized pockets. Sunset was irregular, as was the occasional sunrise, changing times with increasing frequency.

New, powerful winds were rushing over our planet, and they were increasing in speed, whipping up detritus and soot in the air. Deserts were being reformed as the sand was redistributed across the globe. Most of humanity kept to themselves, locked indoors now. The three of us were no exception, but that was out of necessity while we worked feverishly. However, air travel was expected to become perilous by mid-January, and we had to get the chambers down to the launch site before then.

As governments failed and people fell prey to the slide, cults emerged right and left. Looting and violence replaced calm, stoic determination to face our demise. Those who were already reduced to a mental fraction of themselves were easy pickings for these new predators. Desperate to latch onto anything that felt more solid than their own failing hope, they were sucked right into the cultists' vortex, as we all would be into Norma soon. They preached enlightenment and peace, with a healthy sprinkling of government uprising and revolt. Many of them actually worshipped the black hole as some kind of divine entity: righteous judgment for our numerous failures as man.

Various religions amplified their messages with a fervor that they had never employed, and megaphones blared night and day from street corners proclaiming that Jesus was coming… or Brahman… or Joseph Smith… or Allah… or Taylor Swift. No one cared who was 'coming': none of the listeners regarded anyone 'coming' stronger than Norma. That was the one who was inevitably coming for them, and their fear could not be assuaged.

But even stranger – and sadder – than all of that, a new, dark phenomenon emerged. It was wholly terrifying.

People who were in the throes of the slide began to report seeing alternate versions of themselves in reflective surfaces, each version representing a life they could have lived. These versions drove some to madness, others to obsession, as they lost themselves chasing these impossible realities.

Humanity was slipping into oblivion long before Norma even touched Earth's orbit.

Hysteria abounded. Mass suicides were taking hold. People were selling off possessions to people who were *actually* buying them, as if storing up goods against some kind of nuclear winter. Looting abounded. Stores and businesses closed by the hundreds each day.

Civil unrest prevailed. Violence multiplied. Discontent blanketed everyone.

Everyone, that is, except for the three of us, and others like us. If there was any hope of saving mankind, we needed to get the lottery-chosen passengers into stasis as soon as humanly possible, in order to preserve what was left of their humanity and give us a fighting chance on a new planet with people who were at least halfway sane.

Thankfully, many still remained so here, in fact. A chaplain was stationed at Chantilly with us, and, boy, was she ever busy. Her name was Rosalita... Campion, I think. Odd last name. It meant *champion*, and that seemed a bizarre name for a person of faith. She attended to all of us here with a holy determined fervor, with her diminutive stature, peeking over thick-rimmed glasses at us and speaking in a thick Mexican accent.

Trapper knew I was still bugged by Isaac and heartbroken over my failure that caused his death, so she encouraged me to go see the chaplain. And so, reluctantly, I was on my way to see her now. Why, I didn't know exactly, but I guess everyone can use a shot in the arm of faith now and then.

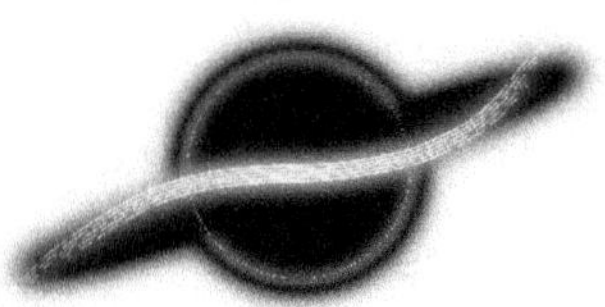

"Yes, Mr. Currier, come in! So nice to meet you," the tiny Latino woman greeted me heartily, jumping up from behind her desk and shaking my hand warmly. "If I am not mistaken, you are the head of the team that discovered the phenomenon, yes?"

"I am. I didn't discover it myself, that was my colleague Isaac Farragut, actually. Sadly, he passed away last month after testing our new system," I said, glumly.

"Yes, I had heard about Isaac. I'm so sorry, Mr. Currier. May I call you Dane?"

"Sure."

"I'm Rosie," she said, motioning me to a seat, and retreating once again behind her desk. "I think what you're doing is truly remarkable, Dane. The Lord bless you, and your team, for all you're doing and have done."

"Well, we'll see if it will be enough," I said, and I couldn't hide a slight roll of my eyes.

Rosie noticed it, sure enough. "Well, that depends on your definition of 'enough.' Is trying and doing our best 'enough?'"

I made an attempt to answer, but before I knew it, I had simply furrowed my brows and made a noisome exhale.

Rosie paused, and then snickered. "It's hard, isn't it?"

"What is hard?"

"Being forced to go see a chaplain when you're a man of science."

"I wasn't forced."

She looked at me over the rim of her glasses. "Are you sure?"

I raised my hands helplessly, but I wondered if she was somehow a fly on the wall when Trapper encouraged me to go see her. "Do you always start off your sessions by antagonizing your clients?" I asked, chuckling.

"Sometimes," she replied. "It calls them out. Brings them forth. It all depends on what you think is antagonizing."

"I guess," I responded. Pause. "Okay, ha! Fine, you got me. My girlfr-, well, my friend, Megan, she encouraged me to come see you."

"Oh? And why did your girlfriend-slash-friend do that, exactly?"

I chuckled. Rosie smiled knowingly as I did so.

"Well, because of Isaac. We've designed this really incredible thing, right? And he went through it. He *was* fine. But then, I don't know what happened, he just…"

I drifted off, staring past her and wondering what to land my eyes on.

"Passed away?" she finished for me.

I nodded, slowly. "Yep."

"And, as the person in charge, you've probably been beating yourself up because of that, most likely, yes?"

I chuckled and then shook my head. "You're good, Rosie."

She shrugged, tilting her head. "Eh. You could say I've been around the block. I've felt bad about a thing or two in my lifetime, of course. It was always making peace with it that brought me through."

My smile faded. "How do you make peace with getting someone killed?"

The chaplain just stared at me. "Is that what you think you did?"

I gritted my teeth. In all honesty, *no*, I didn't think I did that. Based on what I knew about Isaac, on his overall health, on the fact that he had already gone through the basic teleportation as I had, on the fact that we had tested it with other lifeforms, *no,* I didn't think I had gotten him killed. Logic told me that was a lie. But my feelings said otherwise. Isaac *had* died following a teleportation that incorporated a faulty procedure I had programmed; there was no way around that. I swallowed hard and inhaled slowly.

"Honestly, Rosie, no. But he did die because of my failure to see everything clearly," I mustered.

She stared at me, piercingly, her chin resting on her fist. "When do we ever get to see everything clearly though?

As a pastor, I know that the answer is 'never,' because only God can ever see everything clearly. All we can do is *try* to look with clear eyes in this murky world. It sounds to me as though you've been carrying this shame for a bit because you haven't been seeing the truth clearly enough."

"And what truth is that?"

"Well, if I told you," Rosie laughed, "I wouldn't be a very good chaplain, right? Your journey on the road to truth is your own to make." She smiled at me gently.

"The only truth I know lately, Rosie, is that our planet is on a collision course with a deadly supermassive black hole. If God can see everything clearly, I kind of wish that he would, I don't know, help us out a little more. Give us a way out. I don't know. I wish he would have saved Isaac," I finished quietly, but it felt a little like I was throwing down a challenge. "A lot of sad shit – sorry, crap – is going down, and is about to go down. You'd think he'd be interested in providing us less murky eyes in all of this. Me included."

"I understand," she said, and that was all she said. She waited and just watched me until I started to fidget. "I wonder, Dane, if all of this 'sad shit' will make sense someday in a way you didn't expect."

"I thought pastors weren't supposed to swear."

"Stay focused."

"Sorry. How will it make sense someday?"

"As a pastor, I have to believe that God is in control. That everything happens for a reason, and that everything is either God-caused, or God-allowed. That's what makes Him sovereign. Maybe one day, if He allows us to reach this

Proxima Centauri b planet your team is shooting for, we'll have our answers there. Maybe we won't see clearly until we get there. With new eyes." She looked at me over the rim of her glasses and grinned.

"But why would he do that?

"Do what?"

"You know, uh, wait so long. Give us eyes to see only once we get there, instead of helping us find our way through this mess now."

"Do you not think you've found your way?"

I didn't know what to make of that question. Thankfully, she answered this one for me.

"As I just said, God is sovereign. Everything is caused or allowed by Him, remember?" she asked rather pointedly. "Do you not think that you were brought to this very moment, with that phenomenon out there barreling toward us, with eyes that see? The black hole is allowed by God, yes. But without your eyes, Dane, *every one of us* would have died here. Because of your eyes, six thousand of us might actually be saved. I have to think that because of what you've invented, God has already caused you to have eyes that see."

I didn't see that coming.

"You're talking about balance."

"Yes, I am. Cause, meet effect. Action, meet reaction. That's scientific, yes?"

I nodded. "Well, there are certainly laws that govern the natural world and bring a sense of equilibrium. Every action has an equal or an opposite reaction. Things always equalize or normalize, no matter how loud or quiet they get-"

"And where does your shame fit in that?" she asked me, interrupting.

"My shame?"

"Over Isaac."

I looked around. "I guess I'd have to say that one day it will be replaced by *no* shame."

"When you have less murky eyes to see it," Rosie said, almost before I had finished.

"So you're saying I have to accept it for it to be true."

She nodded. "Always."

"But isn't that counterintuitive to faith? Doesn't faith in something make that something more real?"

Rosie shook her head. "Nothing is more or less real just because we place faith in it. Is a chair more real because we've successfully sat on it? No. It is a chair. It's designed to hold you. You just need to *accept* that it's designed to hold you, and then you can sit on it. It's your faith that allows you to sit on it."

"So, if I understand you correctly, once I realize that everything is either caused or allowed by him, I'll have more faith?"

"Perhaps. But I think the more important thing for you right now is realizing that you *do* have the eyes. You've had them all along. So did Isaac. You both have eyes that saw our fate clearly; as such, you took what you could give to find a way through what you saw coming. You didn't have to invent or use your chambers for this purpose. Isaac didn't have to go through. But you all saw clearly, and you simply followed that vision clearly and are using them for a good purpose. There is no shame in that in God's book."

I watched her closely. I allowed the gracious words falling from her lips to fall on me and provide some much-needed warmth to the coldness of my faith, and as I did so, I could feel a weight lifted.

"Alright, Rosie. I appreciate it," I said. "I'm getting there. I appreciate it. One day I'll know it in my heart for sure, but this has… helped."

"Has it?" she asked me skeptically.

"Yes. I mean it."

"Well, you know what they say," she stood, shaking my hand and smiling endearingly at me. "You don't know until you go."

Don't know until ya go.

My jaw fell open and I squinted my eyes at her, shaking her hand. My heart warmed further at either the great, strange, mystical coincidence of her words, or the God-caused truth that reverberated all around us, and that I was only just becoming aware of.

"That's true," I said hesitatingly, studying her. "You don't. Thank you, Rosie."

"My pleasure, Dane."

It couldn't have been coincidence that she uttered Isaac's words to me just then. She had to have been given them by the God that she served.

Whatever the reason, it had worked.

That did it.

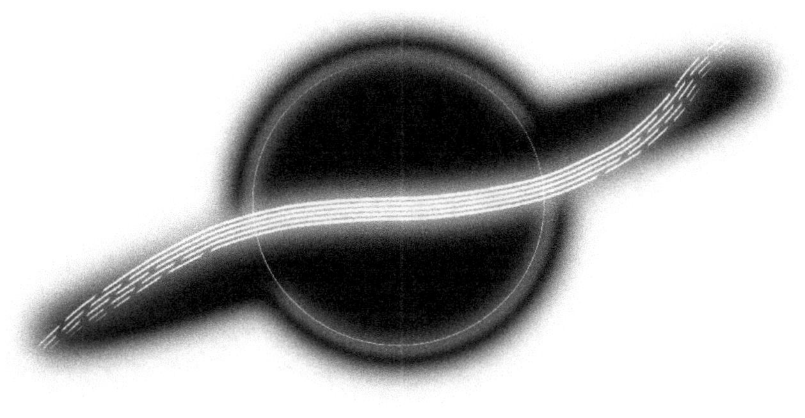

17 | Collapse
December 23rd, 2025

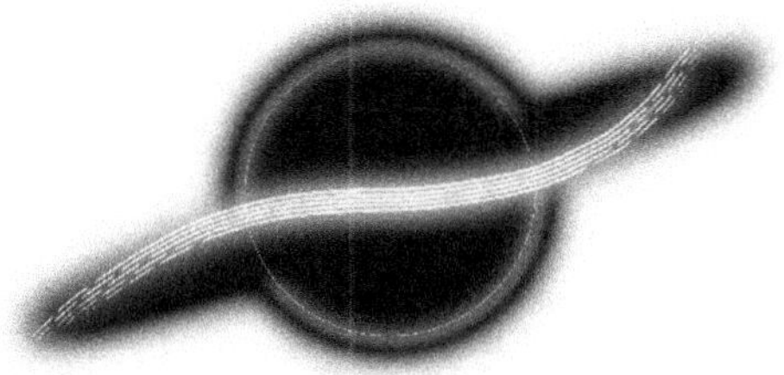

People were sliding, and we were losing them.

They were forgetting what it meant to be human. The very nuances and idiosyncrasies of what made us so special were being lost in the face of annihilation. They were losing themselves not just mentally, but physically as well. A strange 'droop' took over some individuals' visages, to the point where some simply became unrecognizable.

But recently, we all became aware of a new terror. Something horrifying had happened. Some individuals were actually *fading* as the magnetism of the supermassive irradiated them and wrestled their pigmentation away from them. Not like vitiligo; no: they were becoming transparent, and abhorrent to behold. Society labeled them *ghosts*, and they were cast out, left to die in abandon; invisible to others in more ways than one. Some of them used their invisibility to strike back, and horror stories abounded of these frightening apparitions stalking others and taking their revenge. It was utterly frightening to consider. I hoped I would never meet one.

As for those who were diminishing in their capacity, the cultists still preyed on them, feasting on their weakness, their faith, their money. It was abhorrent. Police had little power to do anything about it, much less crack down on them; they were warping just as much as those they were assigned to protect and serve.

Employees still active at DSN and other agencies discovered something unique about Norma: a tremendous amount of radiation was at its core, higher than anything previously catalogued. It was literally altering human consciousness, causing memories and identities to fragment. I know because I called my mom – she didn't even know who I was. That was a difficult call, and one that I will, sadly, never forget. I told her I loved her, and then hung up forever.

Indiscriminately, yet in large pockets of society, humanity was indeed forgetting what it means to be human. Dementia fused with Alzheimer's combined with amnesia to degenerate humans on a scale never before seen. Many were simply left to die; there was no saving them, and it was too hot outside to do so.

For the Earth was moving: slowly, as we were, mercifully, still on the far side of the sun, but surely nonetheless. We were following our star straight into Norma, powerless to do anything about it. Eventually, our small planet with its limited gravity would be pulled right into the fragmented entrails of the sun, splintering and cracking even more than it already was. The temperature outside was sweltering, heating up even more now as a result of drawing near to Sol, and our star was at risk of a supernova, that risk rising with every day Norma drew nearer. Today, in the thick of the winter season, it was a balmy 89 degrees, and even hotter down in Florida where we would launch from.

The problems the slide posed for the lottery were that some people, having already been chosen, were completely ignorant of what was happening around them, and oblivious to the need for them to escape and survive. Letters went unanswered, and lottery selections went disregarded.

That would mean only one thing: filling up the corners with those who were still sentient. Arguments and opportunistic abuse broke out; those who were not chosen insisted that they be so, *or else.* They didn't realize that it would be a difficult chore to get anyone to listen.

In the end, we knew they would simply show up, go through last after all those chosen had done so, and then they'd have to turn away the rest when our SSDs were at capacity.

Space and time became warped; stretched at times, as if the continuum was destabilized and there was no more consistent chronology.

Venus had been destroyed. In a surprise, Uranus was sucked into Norma and actually collided with the other planet on its way in. A massive burst could be seen low on the horizon late at night last night as both planets met their doom, and then were easier prey for Norma to swallow in fragments.

For the three of us, we were still okay, at least for now. But we would certainly have to remain that way. A time was drawing near where we would have to begin the cataloguing and teleportation en masse, or those poor people – and us – would never leave this planet. A long line of naked people was about to form outside our lab, and it was set for January 1st. In a mad hope that we would actually have a new year – let alone *any* more years – some felt the date was fitting and ideal. Those chosen by the lottery were instructed to make their way to the Washington, DC area as soon as possible, where they would be provided accommodations at one of a few local hotels that had been cleared of occupants. They were provided detailed instructions and scheduling for their teleportation.

In this Christmas season, no one even realized that it was Christmas Eve eve. We just didn't care anymore.

Five days ago, our other overgrown third chamber, Aurora, had been disassembled once more and transported to Florida at Launch Complex 39. Genesis was on its way down there as well under massive security escort, surrounded by tanks and covered by fighter patrols.

Aurora was then reassembled with care according to our detailed schematics, and finally welded to the inside of the Genesis spacecraft in prep for launch. It was online, and *Courier 5.1* was reading it in the green, five by five and ready to receive human signals.

As a last test, we sent Macy through, and they sent us a selfie with her a few minutes later. She was smiling and happy as usual. It was clear from the selfie that her tail was blurry from continuous wagging. I would see her once I got down there. Nova and Ava would also be shipped down to Florida for the crew down there to join in storage once all the passengers up here had all been teleported.

Donze was still okay as well, but he was the last survivor of the three that we had talked with. The President and Vice President were no more. Speaker Johnson was no more. The slide struck young and old, elite and common. *Many* world leaders were no more. In the scorching heat, some decided not to wait for Norma to take everything from them; it was their last act of defiance, to control their own fate and take their own lives. The President and Vice President did as many did.

The Secretary of Defense was feeling ill from overwork, but holding steady. He called me up and asked me to meet with him, and I was on my way there now.

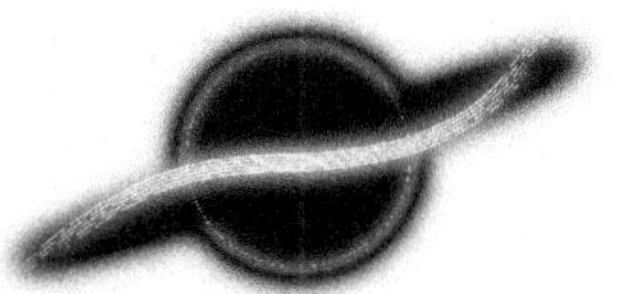

When I knocked on his door, Donze looked disheveled yet determined. His desk was littered with all kinds of file folders and paperwork, and his office reeked of BO like onions.

"Currier, come on in. Sit down, if you can find a seat anywhere." Indeed, I looked around and there were piles of files and paperwork everywhere. I glanced back at him and smiled meekly.

"I'm OK to stand, sir."

He shrugged. "Everything a go for January 1st?"

"Yessir," I replied.

"Good," he said, nodding and sliding aside a mountain of file folders. "Everyone's arriving in DC at either the Waldorf Astoria, Embassy Suites or the Hilton. They're filling up. We're gonna have to make sure everything's ready to herd them in here."

"A question about that, sir," I asked, "have they all been fully briefed as far as the process? How exactly they'll be getting to Proxima Centauri b, I mean."

He shook his head and frowned.

"The mailer should have had all that. It's the same one you got," he said. "Honestly, every time I reread that letter I'm surprised anyone took it seriously. But the hotels show they're checking in in droves, so, here we go."

Actually, I had never read my letter. Dina had read hers, and Trapper and I assumed ours said the same. "I… haven't actually read mine," I apologized. "I naturally just assumed we had been chosen, and-"

'You didn't even open it? Currier, there was specific information in there for you! Yeah, you're definitely going! This is your baby! You're the *Courier,* remember?" he sneered, playing off my name. "Of course you're going. You've got the caboose, mister. You'll be going in last and coming out first. Your other team members will go in before you at the front and the middle. But we need you to take up the rear. You and your team will populate first."

Populate wasn't exactly the right term, but whatever. My mouth fell open and I wasn't sure what to say. "Ah! OK, got it. Sorry, I should have read it. My apologies."

"Fine. Just need somebody who understands all your equipment and lingo and can spearhead the unloading of the herd. All of us naked humans on our new rock in space will need help with the initial organization."

"All of us…?"

"Well, you can bet your ass I'm not sticking around here."

"Of course not, sir," I replied, but I wondered if the deck had been stacked for Donze, or if he had stacked it himself in light of Trump, Vance, Johnson and others no longer making the journey.

"Yeah, my ex-wife is still here. So's her lawyer. They can have this rock. I'll take Proxima Centauri," he joked, lighting up a cigarette. "Sure hope we can bring these things with us," he said, shaking his head and pointing at his own smoke.

"Yessir. Well, we'll be ready."

"Good. Take this and look it over," he said, throwing me a file folder. "We'll have them coming in blocks of twenty at a time, with breaks in between to check and make sure that everyone's been demat-, disint-, broken down into data, or *whatever* it is that you wanna call it. I still think it's crazy, but what do I know? Anyway, those people will be under your care as you operate your system. It's gonna be busy, but we'll try to ferry them through as quickly as possible, Mr. *Courier*," he joked again.

"I get it, sir," I said, grinning. "Thank you. We'll be ready."

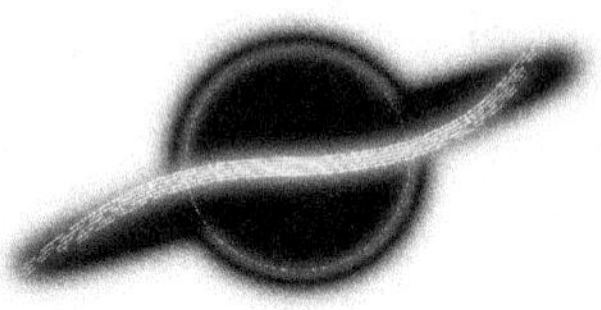

January 1st, 2026

"Hello, Chaplain Rosie," I greeted her. "Good to see you. These are my colleagues. This is Dina Jensen, part of the original team responsible for discovering Norma. That's what we're still calling the supermassive. And this is my friend and undergrad student Megan Trapper who helped me build and code the *Courier* system. Ready to go places?"

"Oh, heavens, no! I'm not leaving," Rosie said quickly. "I'm just here to encourage and bring support to any who need it. I know this will be a difficult day for some."

I tilted my head and squinted my eyes. "You're… not… leaving. May I ask why?"

"Dane, I have complete confidence I'll be taken care of, and that my God will cause or allow me to end where I should, just as He had me begin where I should," she replied. "I'll be fine."

I studied her inquisitively. She had clearly made up her mind, but I couldn't recall one person I had met who actually wanted to stay here.

"You really aren't coming," I said. I didn't intend it as a question. I couldn't believe it.

Rosie smiled and said nothing in response, just looked at me over the rim of her glasses again with that *God is in control* expression.

I took a quick look at Megan and Dina, then returned my gaze to Rosie. "Well, alright then, Rosie. Saddle up. The passengers are coming, and this could get hairy."

"Hairy is exactly what The Father is good at handling," she said.

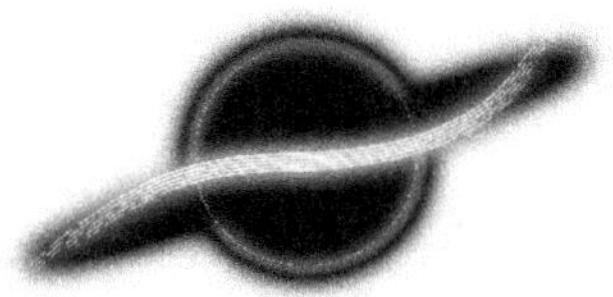

"My name is Dane Currier, and I'm the head of the *Courier* project here, in coordination with the United States government and the SSA. These are my colleagues Dina Jensen and Megan Trapper. To our right here is Pastor Rosalita-"

"Rosie," she butted in, a warm smile across her face.

"Sorry, Pastor *Rosie*, should any of you like to pray or seek counsel before going through. And to my left here is the Secretary of Defense, Mr. Erick Donze." Donze nodded to them.

They were all gathered around us. Whatever protocol SecDef Donze said he had setup regarding 'twenty at a time' was completely disregarded. There had to be at least seventy-five passengers here, all awaiting our instruction, all, presumably, nervous as hell.

Donze spoke up. "Uh, okay, has everyone read their letter thoroughly? You all understand the process of what we'll be doing?"

Various nods and *yes's.*

"Are there any questions?" he asked them.

One boy, who looked to be about six, stood in the front row, raising his hand shyly. He was missing his bottom two teeth. Donze called upon him. "What will happen when we get to Proxima Centauri b?"

"Great question! What's your name?"

"Asher."

"Great question, Asher," Donze answered. "I'm going to let Mr. Currier field questions such as those. Dane?" He turned to me.

I cleared my throat. "Thanks Asher, great question. Yes. Today, we'll be teleported into storage, and down in Florida they'll receive our signals there and get us ready for our flight. It will take about eighty-five years, plus or minus. That sounds like a long time, but when we get there, we won't be any older. We'll be exactly the same age, but in some cases, we'll be even better. If you have a hangnail, it will probably be fixed. If you have stomach problems, those should be cured. If you have back problems, you shouldn't experience those any further," I ended.

A disgruntled-looking man who looked like his father stood behind him and interjected. "Thanks, Mr. Currier. I'm Levi, Asher's daddy. We're naturally a bit confused because he and I were drawn, yet his mother and sister weren't. Do you have any explanation for that?"

Donze shifted to my left. "Uh, I'll handle that one, Dane, thank you. Levi, I understand your concern and frustration with that. This process has undoubtedly caused rifts and irritation across the world. The system had to be indiscriminate so as to not show favoritism. The lottery drew names from young and old, rich and poor, single citizens and family members, with a 2/3 ratio of males to females in order to repopulate our species on our new home world. There was no way to draw a whole family as it would undoubtedly imply favoritism and/or nepotism."

Levi cut in. "I understand that, but with the thing that's been happening to people, the slide I mean, have people dropped out or died off? What happens to their spot? Is there any room for replacements?" I didn't get a good sense of where this was going, and we watched Donze volley with him. It was an impossible question as there was no logistical or fair way to pacify all those seeking to keep their nuclear families together.

Levi burned holes through the Secretary from under his brows as he waited.

"With all due respect, Levi, that's something that we're still working on. 'The slide,' as you call it, is an unexpected phenomenon that has caused all kinds of readjustments and shifting of our plans so that-"

"So why can't you shift your plans to accommodate all members of a family?" Levi interrupted angrily, unable to suppress his frustration. He looked around briefly, as if rallying people to his cause. Those around him nodded.

The crowd began to murmur, and there was a palpable angst building. This was not something we expected or were prepared to deal with.

Various outcries erupted.

My dad wasn't chosen, but my mom was, what's up with that?

How come all the important government people were chosen? Were you chosen, Donze, huh?

Sure seems like a lot of rich people were chosen!

Donze looked around and tried desperately to keep from rolling his eyes. Rosie just stood there, her hands clasped and head bowed, presumably in prayer for peace.

Suddenly, from the rear of the lab emerged several armed guards in fatigues, brandishing M16s. They walked briskly up to encircle us in a wide arc. The crowd perceived that this was not a political forum in which to air grievances, and they began to quiet down.

Donze waited for relative silence.

"Folks, let's keep this thing focused, please," Donze said. "As I mentioned, we are working on that, and we do have some time, but I'm going to have to ask for your patience. Today is all about getting those who were initially chosen to safety. That thing out there is not slowing down," Donze said, pointing out west through the windows at the sky, "and neither should we." He turned his attention back to

Levi. "I promise you that we want to do the right thing in our final hours."

Levi clenched his lips and nodded slightly, his eyes smoldering and his lip quivering. Asher was quiet as he stood with his father's hands on his shoulders.

Donze inhaled deeply and motioned back to me without looking at me.

"Yes, uh, thank you, Mr. Secretary." I felt conflicted, because I empathized with Levi and Asher. I did. But I also understood the rock-and-a-hard-place position we were all in. We couldn't save everyone. Surely, Levi understood that. "Anyone else have any questions?" I asked at last. A middle-aged woman raised her hand. "Yes, ma'am?"

"Hi, Mr. Currier. My name's Janine, and I'm curious what exactly the teleportation is like? Is there any pain?" she asked timidly. "I'm not big on pain," she giggled sheepishly. Several others giggled in response. That eased the preceding tension.

"Neither am I," laughed Dina. "I'll take this one, Dane, if that's okay." I gestured for her to take the helm. "Janine, I *totally* know what you mean. The *Courier* system is designed to teleport you quickly, painlessly, and completely, to your new location. It actually improves you somewhat, believe it or not. It's like the computer takes your DNA profile and idealizes it upon transfer. I used to have lumbar pain for years, but now that I've gone through, it's gone. Dane here used to struggle with GI issues. Those are gone," she said.

Megan shifted next to her.

"Yeah. My complexion improved, so, ya know, ready for my first date on Proxima," Megan said with a fist pump. The crowd seemed to appreciate that. I was just glad that she looked at me as she said it, thinking back to those hugs and kisses after I had gone through.

A college-age man raised his hand to my right, punctuating the laughter. "Mr. Currier and team, have you ever lost someone in teleportation?"

Oh, crap.

"Lost someone?" I asked him. Cue the knot in my stomach.

"Has anyone died from it?"

Talk about the wrong place at the wrong time. My mind raced as Isaac swarmed through it. I didn't want to lie, but I also didn't want to tell the truth. "Thank you. What's your name?" I asked him, stalling.

"Parker. Or, just 'Park.'"

That helped. "Well, Parker just Park, I appreciate you asking." I gathered air into my lungs and tried to sweep away the knot I was feeling. "I'm not going to lie. We had one accident early on, before the code was perfected. We lost our colleague, Isaac, the man who first discovered the black hole."

The crowd murmured silently. Feet shifted uneasily.

"It was…," I faltered, and my eyes fell to the floor momentarily. "It was my mistake, and I take full responsibility for it. He was my friend. I had failed to incorporate some crucial code for after he had been reintegrated. He came through, rest assured, but it was… difficult." I swallowed. I could feel Dina shifting uneasily along with the rest of them. "He had to be resuscitated, and we *did* bring him back, but then we lost him the following day. Some sort of congenital complication interfered…" -here I faltered, realizing that I was starting to actually blame Isaac's own health for his demise and how improper that was- "but the truth of the matter is that I made a mistake. I hadn't seen clearly," I said, turning to Rosie. She was watching me, and she clenched her lip in empathy. "I see clearly now. I fixed it, and we've had no issues since. You have my word. I went through after the correction, and here I stand."

"He did. I was there," Trapper instantly supported. "And I went through right after him."

Parker stared at me lengthily, studying me. I wasn't sure if my answer appeased him, but the lull in the conversation seemed to eventually satisfy the crowd. After all, it was 'take the silent plunge now of your *own* will,' or 'forever be silenced by Norma *against* your will.'

"How long will we be asleep?" an elderly voice asked next. "I'm not getting any younger," the old man jested. "Worried that I'll be meeting God before I get to the new system."

That question was twofold. I answered the first part and gave him the straightforward 'approximately eighty-five years' response. "But," I added, "your question has bearings on life and faith, and so, I think that for that, I'd like to defer to Pastor Rosie here." I turned to her.

Rosie glanced up at me, beaming. "Thank you, Dane. And thank you sir, what is your name?"

"Hudson Stigall," he answered gravelly.

"Mr. Stigall. Pleased to meet you," Rosie replied, hands clasped and addressing him directly. "As an aging person myself, I think I understand the root of your question. From what I understand of Mr. Currier's system here, you won't get any older, and you will not die, unless something goes catastrophically wrong with their system. But I have faith," she said, turning and smiling at me sidelong, "in the gift that the Father has given us in their system for such a time as this. I'd like to see another day as well. I assure you that you'll outlast the ride to the new world." Rosie winked at him, which made me smile heartily.

The old man smiled back.

I looked around, waiting for any more hands.

"Well, if there are no further questions, shall we proceed?" I asked. Various nods. "I'm sorry that we couldn't be more accommodating in terms of the teleportation, but we could not afford to mix inanimate signals with animate ones, or we'd risk fusion. Put more plainly, you'll need to all remove your clothes and go naked. We have rooms at the back where you can deposit your clothes, and you can keep your undergarments on until just before you go through, if you'd like. We'll have to leave modesty on Earth in our move to Proxima Centauri b, but I promise you I'll be among the first to welcome you to the new galactic nudist colony." I smiled, and hoped that it was disarming enough.

It worked. Big laughter, even from Levi. Asher covered his mouth in comical surprise.

Here we go.

In another thirty minutes, people were lined up, nude and semi-nude, standing in a long line scrolling toward the door, where two more sentries stood, preparing to allow in the next group when called for. A sudden chill went through me, and I sighed, realizing we might have to field these questions all over again.

Dina took the blood samples. Rosie took the prayers. Trapper took the names and checked them off a list. And then, one by one, they were sent into Nova, never to be seen on this Earth again.

Quietly, they slipped in. Some cried. Some were rooted to the ground outside Nova, desperate to will themselves to enter, reluctant to abandon everything they knew. Rosie stood beside them and prayed beside their trembling forms. A few changed their minds and ran out. There was nothing we could do to stop them, nor should we. It was their own choice to make. The hardest part was soldiers barking that they could not be readmitted.

But here, in this lab, it was finally happening, and Aurora was waiting.

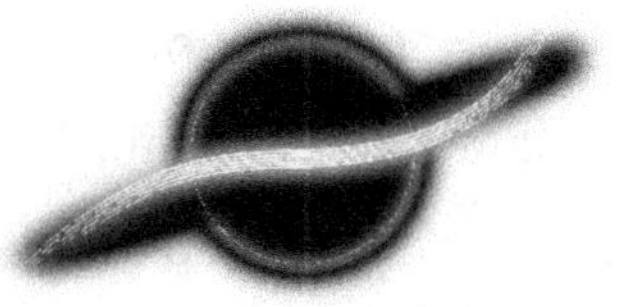

January 8th, 2026

The ghosts came last night.

Before we were really aware of what was happening, strange forms swaddled all in thick clothes, donning shades and hats, somehow overpowered the guards at the gate and forced their way onto the base. They killed the guards and stole their DBIDS cards, gaining access to the Chantilly lab. Dina was sleeping, dead tired from all the finger pricks and cataloguing all the DNA profiles of our passengers.

It was just Trapper and I in there, still transporting people and getting them catalogued as quickly as possible.

Their leader burst into the lab, brandishing the guard's M16. He trained it on me. Another few armed ghosts accompanied him, forcing the rightful lottery appointees back. Everyone screamed in revulsion.

How did we know they were ghosts? The leader removed all of his clothes, all the while yelling and insisting that he and his companions be let through. One kept his gun on Trapper while the leader marched up to her, organs and bones on full display, jostling and shifting within him as he yelled. His mournful, deathly white eyes glared at her.

If I thought he was disassembled in his ghostly form, I had never seen Megan Trapper so disassembled. She came undone, covering her eyes and shrieking. The overall cost exacted by a constant teleportation stream, long hours and exertion, fear of Norma drawing nearer, and now this, was too much for her. She screamed and dropped to the ground. The ghost grabbed her, yanking her up and forcing her to take his sample, create his DNA profile and send him through.

Someone in the crowd lunged at the leader, angered at being supplanted and echoing the urgency that we all felt. "You filthy son of a bitch beast!" he growled at him, leaping haphazardly at the leader. Another ghost whirled and gunned him down. He fell heavily and slid in his own blood.

The ghost who mowed him down turned his gun on the crowd, flanked by another who did the same. "Don't try anything! Stay the hell back! We get let through and nobody gets hurt!'

There was nothing I could do, or I would have been shot as well. I gritted my teeth and glared angrily at the translucent degenerate swaddled up in front of me, his muzzle pointed at my face.

We couldn't let them through; these apparitions would appear on PCb just as frightening as they had here, and that was no way to start a new world, with terror.

Trapper pleaded with her assailant, her hands raised in the air. "Okay, okay! Please don't shoot me!" she feebly whimpered as the pale, translucent man continued to bark orders at her. His shape shimmered as he moved, his outline flickering through decrepit patches of pigment desperate to still frame his once-human form.

Trapper pricked his unseen flesh, and then backed away, ready to initiate the teleportation relay sequence.

Alarms suddenly screeched throughout the lab, and every passenger covered their ears, many of them screaming.

The ghosts reeled, inadvertently pointing their guns at the flashing lights dotting the ceiling.

From every external door suddenly burst in squads of security personnel, brandishing their own weapons and advancing, shouting commands. A few of the ghosts whirled around, lacking the presence of mind to put their hands in the air and drop their weapons. They engaged, and were shot on sight.

Their leader, weaponless and naked, eyes bulging through translucent sinews and bone, made for his gun, but a few of the passengers, enraged at the death of their fallen compatriot, were on him before he knew what hit him.

It was all over in a matter of minutes, but we were left to pick up the pieces of man against man, grudge against trust, and abomination set fiercely against hope. This was a setback none of us needed, and it made us all the more eager to leave this place. Not only did we have to contend with Norma out there, but chilling specters here as well.

Loud curses echoed angrily throughout the lab, but eventually, order was restored. Medical personnel came in, bearing away the ghostlike figures who still breathed. As for their leader, he was choked to death by a large, lumbering man with a wrestler's build. He never stood a chance.

Megan ran into my arms, sobbing, utterly spent.

Before too long, after an extended break in which we were all reassured and provided protection, we calmly collected our breath and dutifully resumed our posts. The line of passengers resumed.

Rosie, roused from sleep, re-emerged into the lab and consoled or prayed with those traumatized by the whole ghost ordeal.

And once again, *Courier* did its job. These people were not taken captive in a place of hysteria. They were sent to a place free of madmen and death.

People were teleporting, and we were saving them.

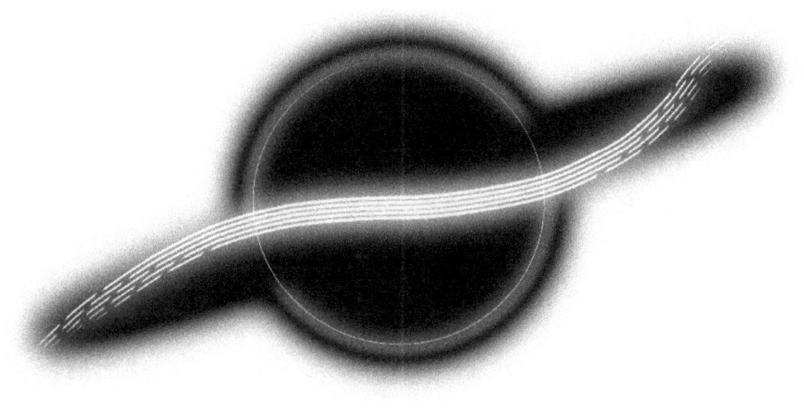

18 | Downhill
January 13th, 2026

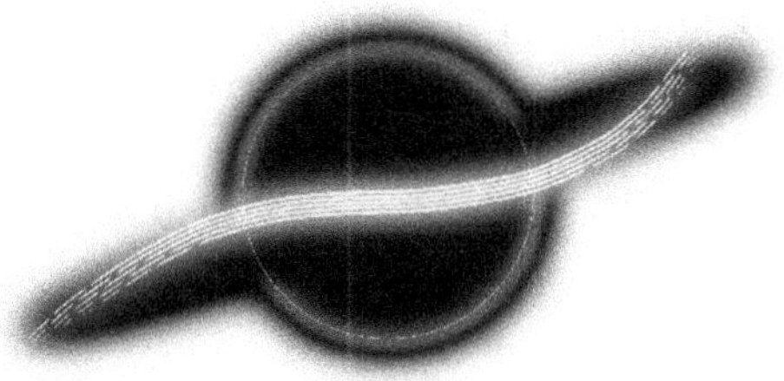

It was the most frightening thing I ever saw.

Someone came running into the lab screaming at the top of their lungs at 10:31 pm on the 10th. We didn't know what all the hubbub was about, and we were, frankly, still reeling from the ghosts of a few nights ago. Eventually, however, we determined from her frantic ramblings that something tragic was happening outside.

We raced out and looked up.

A white orb, much closer than it had ever been, now suddenly pulled away from us, and we could literally trace its movement across the sky. Norma was drawing nearer and nearer, and our moon held no strength to repel its irresistible pull. It slid over the horizon, and with it, celestial lights swirled across the dark canopy above. It wouldn't be long before the tides would respond with fury. In a singular tragedy, *one small step for man, one giant leap for mankind* became utter fiction. It eventually combusted, hurtling closer and closer to our sun like a celestial fireball, and was gone.

More people were ghosting. The radiation levels were sky-high. On this winter day in January, we were at 113 degrees. The sun was enormous in the sky, growing larger every single day. Norma was pulling in the sun, and pulling us into *it*, and pulling us toward the *sun*. Soon, all of us would be but a flicker in time; a faded memory of life and civilization. The winds that now rushed over the earth were a combination of natural and solar winds, but they were hotter than the ambient temperature at times.

The teleportations were still going. Aside from a brief flicker of Internet outage two days ago, which saw the subjects reintegrated back in Nova where they started, everything had gone according to plan. Five thousand two hundred and twenty-nine souls were now digitized and currently resided on SSD partitions in Florida. All of the livestock had been brought in and teleported as well. It was much harder than we imagined. All of them had to be domesticated to some degree, or it wouldn't work. Thankfully, their caretakers had worked hard to ensure that they were compliant, though agitated.

Megan, Dina and I would be flying to Kennedy Space Center tomorrow, and the door would be shut for any new interested parties in Washington, DC. The last to go through would come from Florida, and then the door to Aurora would be shut forever.

If people missed their opportunities or were unable to make it to Washington, DC, there was simply nothing we could do for them or anyone else.

Except for Levi and Asher. Taking a cue from Rosie, I exercised my right to make a singular event both Dane-caused and Dane-allowed.

I had the mother and sister flown here and sent through. Maybe I was seeing clearly after all.

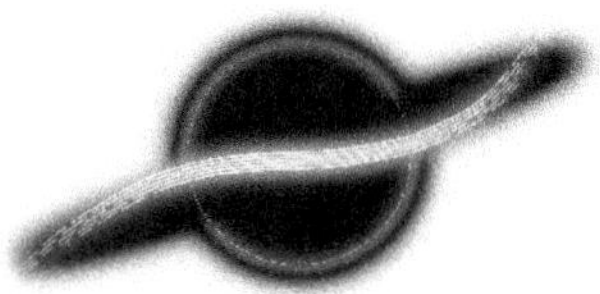

January 14th, 2026

The ground fell away below us as we soared into the clouds. All three of us were in first class. I had never in my life flown first class, so this was much appreciated. Hey, when you're working with the government, they have big pockets; first class upgrades create as little noise to them as a ceiling fan.

But speaking of wind, the flight was already choppy, and would be all the way down. The solar winds were creating havoc for pilots, and it was near time to ground all air flights before they were simply thrown out of the sky.

We were now bound for our final destination on planet Earth: Kennedy Space Center in Florida, at Launch Complex 39. That is where they would setup Nova and Ava one last time, and we would be the last ones in. I *myself* would be the very last one in.

At last count, they had five hundred seventy-nine personnel at KSC that were awaiting us and ready to go through. They were government or military, or in close cooperation with them, so they had already been briefed and their questions answered. So, we were spared that part.

Rosie remained behind. I found myself ruing that. She was a good woman, and she had imparted some invaluable wisdom to me which I would take with me to the new world. Wisdom about life, about God, about faith. Furthermore, she had helped me leave behind the shame over Isaac that had been eating me up inside. I tried to use 'Don't know until ya go' with her, but she wouldn't have it.

"My place is here," she said proudly, with a warm and contented smile. "You'll be free of this place. So will I, just in a different way."

That was the last time I saw her. But I still had the woman beside me that I was interested in, and I was really looking forward to seeing my other woman again: my Macy-girl. I smiled as I thought of the wags in arrears that she would doubtless be providing me upon my arrival. Megan held hands with me on the plane flight to Florida, but for Dina's sake, we didn't flaunt it.

The Genesis space shuttle had arrived in Florida a week ago, and she was mounted up. Aurora was securely fitted inside her. The plan was for her to close off and stop receiving signals just before launch, to protect the precious cargo of her drives, and minimize any risk of electromagnetic interference. *Burn the ships*, we said. *Don't look back.* That was the plan.

Once Genesis reached PCb, the shuttle would land, and then, Aurora would begin the reintegration process on an automated schedule. I would be first out, followed by Trapper and Dina. The rest would follow.

At this stage, we couldn't afford to wait any longer. Various safety and compliance tests were performed on the nuclear pulse propulsion. As far as everyone could tell, it was ready to go. 'As far as everyone could tell,' though, was the extent of confidence they could muster, because it had truly never been deployed commercially or privately. It would be risky. However, as we were all going to die anyway, we were all willing to engage a little risk.

Out there in the uncaring void of space, Norma was coming. Her outer reaches were now only three trillion miles from earth, and the sun was increasing in speed toward it. Norma's event horizon was approaching fast, and the tidal forces were growing in enormity, pulling and stretching our planet, tugging at its seams. Someone reported that a large land mass in central Asia had begun to fracture and bend skyward, tugging at the earth's crust and peeling it up toward Norma, pulling more and more as the earth rotated.

Soon, our planet would fracture and spaghettify, and that would be that. We were being pulled right behind the sun, increasing in speed toward it. Either we would fly right into the sun, or both the sun and the Earth would fall into a parabolic arc and fly side by side into Norma, cracking and dismembering in its flight, and then explode under strain.

More continents had split, and the new tidal patterns had inundated coastal cities, killing off poor unwitting civilians before their time. The slide took all the others.

There was no cure.

If it wasn't natural calamity, then it was the slide, and if it wasn't the slide, it was the scorching heat and the fires. And if it wasn't the scorching heat and the fires, it was the ghosts, looters and scavengers.

Earth was almost at its end, and so were its people.

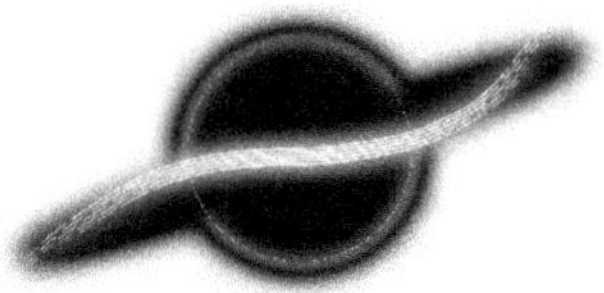

January 18th, 2026

Macy did not disappoint.

She leapt into my arms as I crouched there after having disembarked the plane, and in the scorching heat, she was panting frenetically, but her love was not lessened or inconvenienced in any way. I had missed her so much, and it made me so overjoyed to know that she would be coming with us. She was now digitized aboard Aurora, a belly full of treats and a tongue chock full of the scent of my face, along with many other domesticated pets.

Launch Day was tomorrow. It was upon us. Genesis had been transported to the launch pad using a crawler-transporter, and then mounted to the rocket assembly.

Before that, we would initiate the autopilot, teleport ourselves into Aurora, and prepare to leave this planet forever. Nova and Ava would be left behind. That was a melancholy realization to me, as they had served such a glorious purpose, and yet they would be destroyed within a few weeks, while we would be marooned on PCb forever, never to see them again.

But it would be harder for those left behind. Crews entrusted to our launch and automation – as well as overseeing the nuclear pulse propulsion – would remain here, nobly sacrificing themselves in the process.

Hopefully, Rosie would be side by side with them as they all hurtled toward their deaths, comforting them.

The last of the personnel from Florida had been disintegrated and loaded onto Aurora. She was holding steady, and cyclical checks confirmed drive and data integrity every ten-minutes on an uninterruptible refresh. Her solar power would see to that, as long as the sun lasted.

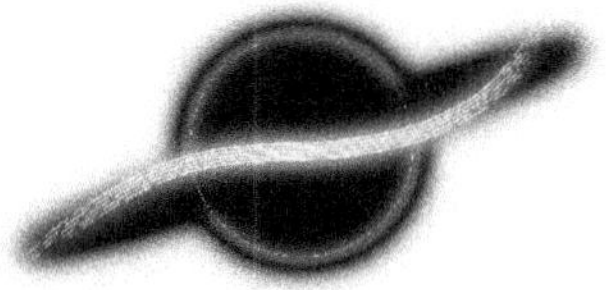

It was late. In anticipation of such a seminal event tomorrow, I couldn't sleep, and it was 11:13 pm.

You wouldn't know it, however, as it was unnaturally amber out through my curtains, as if the morning sun was already climbing up the sky. With all the space-time disruptions, it might actually *be* morning, and we wouldn't even know it.

The noise was near deafening outside my window; an unnatural byproduct of the new winds racing over our world. The A/C units were working overtime to keep us cool, but those hot winds brought with them a precarious environment which was turning our planet into an ashen wasteland.

Fires raged all across the globe now, enveloping every forest everywhere. Mount Rainier in Washington had erupted under pressure, and a quarter of the conical top blew and slid down its own crest much like Mount St. Helens in 1980 before it. The sonic boom was reportedly causing electromagnetic interference on the west coast.

Under enormous strain, other volcanoes followed suit. Hawaii had been evacuated a few weeks ago; Mauna Loa had devastated most of the islands in its blast zone, raining down hot ash that only served to accentuate the existing heat beyond human tolerance. The lava flowed nonstop, as if Earth was desperate to empty its own core. The island was buried under either burning magma or scalding hot ocean water. Drone footage revealed floating marine life dotting the waves. Dolphin, shark, whale carcasses and more littered the oceans.

My A/C was struggling to keep up in the heat, and it was muggy. It would be a long night of little sleep. I think I was *finally* starting to fitfully drift off, when there came a soft knock on my door. I turned to look toward it, and heard a quiet voice calling.

"Dane?"

Megan Trapper.

My eyes went wide with incredulity. Megan Trapper and I had already said our goodbyes earlier in the evening, and she was scheduled to go through a few hours ago. What was she still doing here?

I got up and bolted to the door. "Megan! What – how are you still here? You okay?" I looked her up and down.

"Yeah, uh-huh," she said, seemingly somewhat urgently. "Can I come in?"

"Yeah, uh, yeah, come in. It's a bit messy but, definitely, come in. Kinda lonely without Macy-girl." I plopped down on the couch facing a big plush recliner opposite it beyond a slim cherry-wood coffee table.

"I'm glad she got in there okay. You'll see her again soon, Dane. Just like Dina."

Dina had already gone through and was safely aboard Aurora as ones and zeros along with the rest of our passengers.

However, there was a strange tone in Megan's voice, and in the dim light I could see her hair was pulled back tightly into a pony tail. She glistened with sweat in the increasing heat. I looked her up and down again. "What's up? Why didn't you go through?"

She plopped down, slapping her hands on the arms of the chair in my new Florida digs. "I will. I just needed to see you one last time. Whoo! This heat, man. I know it'll be better in space. Just hope it's still better on PCb. You ready for our 25.44 trillion-mile trip?"

I chuckled. "Yeah. I have snacks. Never-ending Gobstoppers. They should last."

She gave me a confused look as if to say *you dork,* and then burst into a snide laugh. "Sure. You know, the Parker Solar Probe can go 394,736 miles per hour. That would take us 7,229 years. I'm glad this one's under a century. We won't be any older, but I have a feeling for that longer trip we *would* be. The speed of light is 11,176,920 miles per hour. Our fastest craft, before Genesis that is, can only go up to 429,988.86 miles per hour. Isn't that crazy? Yep," she nodded to herself awkwardly.

I watched her rattle off statistics. For some reason, I couldn't shake a supposition that she wasn't really here to share metrics and travel stats.

"What's up, Meg? You okay? I mean, as much as I love discussing the speed of light at close to midnight when we've got interstellar travel scheduled the next day…"

She rolled her eyes and sighed. "Fine." And before I knew it, she hopped over to the couch and sat by me, leaning against me. I could practically feel her heartbeat through her shirt. She looked up at me seductively.

"You've always been great at stating what you want," I affirmed her.

She shrugged. "Something I learned as the youngest child. Always had to fight my way through with the older brothers."

"Got it. I don't know anything about your family."

"And you don't really need to. They're all boring anyway," she said dismissively, as she stared at my lips. If she wanted to remain a closed book, she was going about it the right way.

"You really wanna do this with someone so pudgy?"

"You're not so pudgy," she said nearly instantly, and then grabbed my chin and wrenched me to herself, kissing me with wholehearted abandon.

I didn't resist. Why would I? This was our last night on Earth, as they say, and it was just the two of us.

There, in my little Florida apartment, on our last night on Earth, Megan Trapper and I made love.

Our bodies nearly combusting with heat, baking in the inescapable simmer of an ever-approaching sun, we drank deeply of life, nearly choking on the nectar as our sweat merged.

We both knew full well that the two of us, along with Dina and all those other six thousand people could die in the next eighty-five years, but we didn't care.

We just didn't care about anything else right now.

Tonight, we were alive.

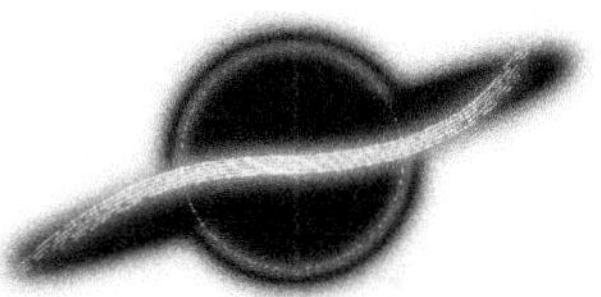

January 19th, 2026

The launch countdown had commenced! Four minutes remained from the nine-minute countdown.

Megan and I stared deeply into each other's eyes, remembering last night through our sleep deprivation. She was beautiful in ways I had never realized before, and she was mine. I thought back to our love, beaming as she stripped down, entered Nova, turned to face me, and was gone. I was the last human who would go through, assisted by the techs who remained here.

We couldn't accommodate any more, or we would risk overcrowding the drives and compromising the memory or paging file space on the drives. The remaining personnel were under strict orders to ensure the survival of the rest of our race. They seemed honorable enough to do so.

Two minutes until launch. Everything was warming up. The crews had performed meticulous inspections. The shuttle, the external tank and the solid rocket boosters all checked out. In the scorching heat, they had been further insulated to preserve their integrity.

Final assembly checks were complete. The external tank was loaded to the brim with liquid hydrogen and liquid oxygen just before the flight to minimize risk. And the risk was increasing. The crews also had to meticulously inspect and ensure the nuclear propulsion system integrity was verified.

All systems were tested including the orbiter's APUs, primary engines and all of the flight control surfaces. Pre-launch checks were done. There were no astronauts of course; it was all entirely automated: mankind's final feat of grandiosity, its final act of defiance in the face of annihilation.

The Ground Launch Sequencer was now in command, monitoring all of the flight vehicle's parameters and prepared to halt the countdown if any issues arose.

I stared out the observation window to behold Genesis as it prepared to lift off. It was treacherously difficult to try and behold it in the sweltering sun. Outside, it was blindingly bright. They say you shouldn't look straight into the sun, but looking into the sun was all we could do anymore; it dominated the horizon.

The orbiter's auxiliary power units kicked in.

I stripped down and paced slowly toward Nova. A tech acknowledged me. I myself verified *Courier 5.1* and hit *Commence Suspend,* turning to the tech and hugging him. He awkwardly leaned in and hugged the naked man who stood before him. I leaned over and kissed my laptop lovingly. And with that, I walked into Nova for the last time as Dane Currier on Earth.

10 seconds to disintegration…

The glass door closed behind me as I overheard an announcement that the GLS was handing off control to the shuttle's onboard computers and the automation kicked in.

9… 8… 7…

Nova lit up white beneath my feet. I kissed the walls and then stood still, keeping my eyes open and staring out at the brave souls who were remaining behind. I nodded to them, touched my chest over my heart, and extended it out to them. Those watching me did the same. It was so hot…

6… 5… 4…

An announcement blared that the solid rocket boosters were a go for ignition and the explosive bolts would release the boosters.

3... 2... 1...

I closed my eyes.

A flash; a blinding explosion of multicolor took me.

It was the most beautiful thing I ever saw.

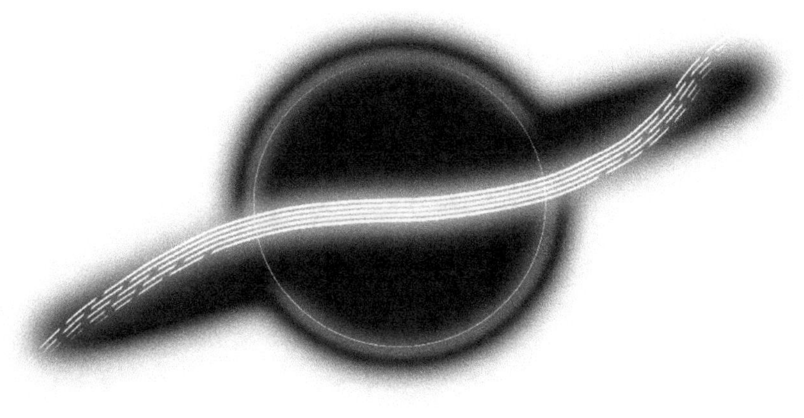

19 | *Space*
Date unknown

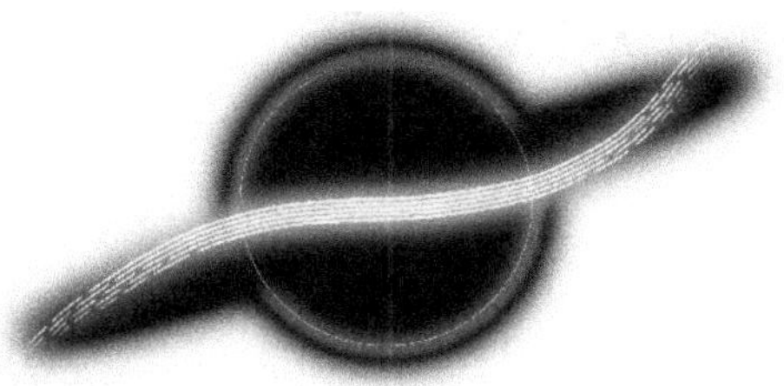

Where am I?

It was all consciousness, all awareness, all dreams, fused into one magical swirling vortex. It was enlightenment and bliss fused into a tranquil, indescribable serenity.

My body – it felt free. Floating on the wind… unrestricted… boundless. I couldn't see myself.

My mind – it saw everything. Rosie's words echoed through me as I reflected on my entire life and the whole history of all mankind. Memories I had never made echoed through me, ushered into my soul through an interconnected labyrinth of human experience.

My eyes – I think that's what they were – looked around and beheld the glory of space. Where I was, I didn't know. I panned around and could see Norma. All I could see was the supermassive, drifting there, silently. There were no planets. There was no sun.

Norma was all.

Was I still me? I felt like me, I knew me. I'm Dane Currier, I said to myself, but the sound was not there. My vocal cords seemed disembodied and intangible. Every expression was in my mind, and my mind was every expression. All around me was energy; all things were energy, and energy was all things: interconnected, tied together in harmony.

As when I stood before Nova the very first time I went through, I was aware of everything. My senses were heightened, unrestricted and free from the confines of this world, at peace with everything around me.

Suddenly, my eyes were drawn to a white speck, shooting across the stars, its stern illuminated with a deep blue-hot trail streaming behind it, heading speedily in a direction opposite from Norma.

I streamed toward it, spreading out imaginary arms in my flight. Our paths converged. It was a symmetrical shape, long and tubular, and wrapped to its frame was a familiar shape: geometric and aerodynamic.

The Genesis space craft.

Somewhere out there, in line with its current path, was a star called Proxima Centauri. And in that star's orbit was a small, habitable planet called Proxima Centauri b.

Our new home.

But where was everyone? How could I see the craft? It was almost as if I was weightless, free from the restrictions *of data, free from the confines of solid state drives and all manner of physical containment, ethereal and true.*

We were pinpricks of light, the craft and I, as we sped timelessly across the vastness of space. My curiosity at my own state was engulfed and absorbed by the beauty of it. Stars I saw, nebulas I beheld, gaseous clouds of luminescence I delighted in; all swirled around me in a silent reverence. Other galaxies beckoned to us as we passed, completely silent, yet their unmatched beauty was loud and breathtaking. The solar wind blew through my intangible hair.

Once more, in the midst of my spellbound state, my mind wondered back to Earth, and our recent departure. Was it recent? How far along were we on the journey from Earth? Had something gone wrong? By all rights I should be inside *Genesis, fast asleep in stasis for the flight to our new star. So why was I out here, dreamlike and whole, riding the streams and wisps of outer space?*

My confusion was swallowed up in delight as up ahead, suddenly, there loomed a bright red orb… a star, shining brilliantly, lit from within with an unextinguishable and indomitable fire.

Proxima Centauri. There it was.

Out here, time was a non-issue, and time was not time. The roughly eighty-five year flight was nearly complete, and our new home lay ahead of us.

We flew past it, the craft and I, almost in parallel symmetry, as we slowed in our approach. The blue light trail still emanated from the stern of the ship, aboard which slept six thousand souls in cryogenic dreamlike stasis.

I watched, hovering and floating on a multicolored gaseous stream, as the Genesis craft decelerated, its forward thrusters slowing its nuclear pulse-propelled forward momentum. Before long, it achieved a stationary orbit.

I watched as the solid nuclear pulse rocket detached and floated off silently into space. The Genesis craft slowly and silently rolled over in a calm rotation, engaging its stern thrusters as it slowly began its descent. I followed it.

It was beautiful and intrepid, placid and enthralling to watch, knowing our craft was touching down on its new soil for the very first time, and soon, all of our beloved fellow pilgrims would disembark and begin their new life.

The thick atmosphere felt stuffy… and yet not stuffy. Wisps of strata slid by me as I accompanied Genesis down to the surface. Following its programming, it gently banked, and its Harrier Jet engines rotated vertically and clicked on, firing a steady stream of thrust to slow its descent down to PCb. As silent as a drone, I followed it down in parallel, sending good thoughts its way for a successful landing.

The Genesis craft touched down. I looked around this new alien world. It was reported to be hot and cold, depending on which side of the terminator you were on. I felt neither as I slowly revolved around to take in the sights, floating in a dreamlike ether.

All was silent around me.

Eventually, a slight mechanical whining emerged from behind me, and I turned back to face the Genesis craft. Air escaped it in hissing whispers through the opening aperture at its stern. I could hear it. The cargo bay doors opened, and there, on the precipice of the ship, stood a beautiful human woman.

I knew her instantly.

Megan Trapper.

She looked around, and I hovered closer to her. I tried to give voice to her name, but it wouldn't come. I could feel it in my stream of consciousness: myself calling for her, but she couldn't hear me and didn't acknowledge my call. My ethereal brow furrowed in ethereal confusion. Why couldn't she hear me?

Megan Trapper stood there nude, whole, healthy, reintegrated, new, and breathing new air.

Beside her stood Macy, wagging and panting. Behind Macy stood Dina Jensen. They had survived. They had made it. Their hair blew lightly in the breeze in our new Garden of Eden.

But they were crying. Why were they crying?

Dina approached Megan and put her hand around her shoulder. Megan turned and embraced her as Macy scurried off to sniff out the new rock. Every step they took seemed somewhat slowed, as if gravity wasn't the same here. Far more dreamlike, it was like floating.

But, again, why were they crying?

I drew nearer to them, approaching the craft.

One by one, people reintegrated in sequence from Aurora, naked as jaybirds, some of them getting right to work on setting up equipment and handing out water. Many filed out of the Genesis craft and drunk in the sight of their brave new world and its red dwarf star. There were Levi and his *son Asher. There were Levi's wife and Asher's sister. Macy ran to them and sniffed them.*

But I only had eyes for Megan. She nodded to Dina, voicing something inaudible, and then heaved her chest in a belabored sigh. I watched as she turned around to the monitors. Scrolling down the screens were status reports and all kinds of data: feedback from the teleportations and the trek across the stars.

Megan appeared to fixate only on one screen. I drew near to her. She didn't acknowledge me. She couldn't hear me. Why hadn't I been reintegrated? Where was I? Who was I?

I drew close to the screen she was watching, and I read it as clearly as she did:

Currier, Dane, 28, M. Subject failed to relay. Reason: Catastrophic system failure due to ambient heat overload. Unable to return to Nova.

My intangible eyes stared with horror as the weightless truth descended me upon with all the inescapable gravity of a thousand alien worlds:

I had never made it through Nova. Or… perhaps I had made it through Nova to Ava, but the relay had failed? Clearly, one of them had overheated or exploded.

The slide had taken me: just, a different kind.

I turned to gaze upon Megan. Naked and captivating she stood there before me now, and I was unable to connect with her, or say anything to her where she'd hear me.

I scanned her beautiful form in pity and longing, and for a moment was captivated, struck by something new. Her midsection radiated a special warmth, an increased light, a luminescent presence exceeding the rest of her body heat, almost as if I was beholding two lives.

Two *lives.*

My formless mouth beamed, realizing the truth as my eyes and mind beheld it clearly for the first time, knowing my child was growing within her. Waterless tears filled my shapeless eyes as I silently whispered to her, "I love you," with indistinct lips that gave no voice to my thoughts.

A slight flinch. A momentary flicker of her eyes. Had she perceived my disembodied form? Had she heard me in the wells of her soul?

No.

I was a ghost on an alien world, doomed to roam forever. Megan Trapper and my child would live out their lives on this new world, without me at their side, without her 'pudgy' graduate student partner, without the love we had shared just the night before… or, more actually, a few decades ago. The only memory would be a tiny human formed from our mysterious bond of flesh and signal.

I was no longer Dane Currier. Like those poor souls back on earth deprived of their flesh, I had become a ghost. Deprived of substance, I had been reduced to a data stream, a wireless signal cursed to haunt Megan Trapper amongst the stars… for all eternity. The concrete had become abstract, and there I would remain, never more to be reintegrated. After all, Aurora had been cut off, and could no longer receive signals. Nova and Ava and everything else had been swallowed up by a supermassive black hole.

I stared once more at her abdomen, and I perceived the life growing within. Sure enough, it was there.

'That, Rosie,' I thought to myself, 'I can see clearly.'

I turned to watch Dina roam out and investigate the new landscape. I wondered if she silently wished to herself that Isaac was here with her in her new Garden of Eden. I wondered if her reintegrated self would yearn for him to the same degree that her previous self had. I wondered if Rosie passed in peace. I wondered if the Earth slammed into the sun, or into Norma, or neither… or both.

I wondered so many countless things as I yearned here, alone and disconnected. I was a free spirit… and yet I was a prisoner. Esoteric and ethereal oneness and bliss separated, and the intangible tear scrolled down my shapeless cheek as I drifted formless in the void.

Only one question remained, and would remain forevermore, out here among the stars on a world not my own.

Who am I?

THE END

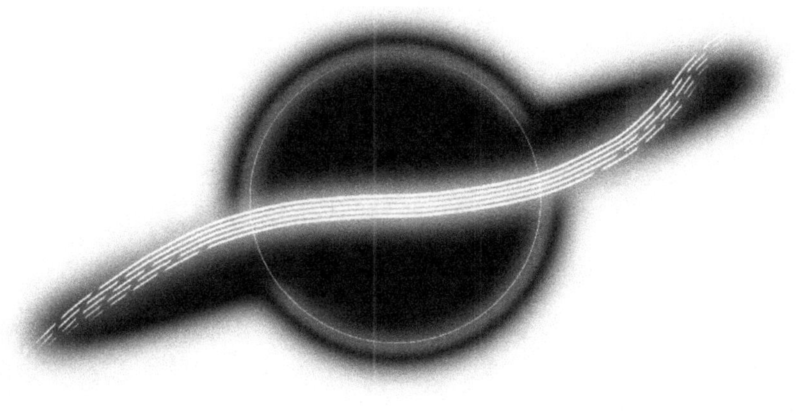

Afterword

When I wrote *Dissonance Volume IV: Relentless*, I fell in love with the hard science of it all, in the same way that I fell in love with watching *Contact* with Jodie Foster, and the scientific mumbo-jumbo that they would spit out in rat-a-tat fashion, expecting us simple mundane Cro-Magnon monosyllabic readers to arbitrarily swallow whole and pretend we knew just what the heck they were talking about.

I loved the ease with which the techies spoke it, and I wanted to mirror that understanding of their own technology in the written word for that book.

When I was finished with my Christian dystopian saga *The End*, I strove to return to this novel and figure out just what so attracted me to the intrinsically complicated tech-speak which those characters wielded so fluidly. This novel is a testament to that, envisioning what it must be like to be "in the know": watching something scientifically destructive heading our way, knowing just what to call it and just how to refer to its attributes, whilst leaving the rest of us mortals floundering for a meager scrap of understanding in the process and beholding the societal collapse in the process. I love hard sci-fi grounded in reality, and *The Slide* is my tip of the hat to that.

One other element I remain fascinated with is the finality of death from the first-person narrative. If a novel is narrated first-person, and the protagonist dies, the novel is effectively over. I had already done that with *Dissonance Volume Zero: Revelation,* so, for *The Slide*, I wanted to explore an ending filled with doom and longing; unresolved and inescapable limbo filled with yearning. That fascinated me as well, and I think I've accomplished that with *The Slide.*

Some novels come easier than others, and this one proved to be an enormous challenge. In some respects, given that I knew I was writing only a singular novel, my heart wasn't in it as much as it might be for a trilogy or a saga. There were elements of it that were new to me, for example the PREapocalyptic nature of it. Ultimately, it turned out well, and, as with *Forecast*, it took some work, but in retrospect I'm grateful I took on the challenge, as I'm pleased with the final result. I'm not finished writing post-apocalyptic or dystopian content; nothing could be further from the truth. Those just come more naturally for me. However, I *did* want to venture into the *pre*-apocalyptic disaster realm, and see just what the emotions, the life, the environment was like before all fell apart. *The Slide* scratches that itch.

I'm excited to offer this book to you, and I hope it was just as exciting a read as perhaps *Dissonance*, *The End*, or *Forecast* were.

I want to utterly thank my ARC readers Victoria Richmond and Jeannine Dryden. Thank you for reviewing my work so ardently pre-publishing, and giving it the attention it deserves. Thank you to my beautiful wife Janine for editing so many of my works so well, so carefully, and so attentively. I hope I've done this one justice since you were busy with my other novel and other clients! 😊 Thank you to my audiobook reviewers Vance Pease, Victoria Richmond and Rhonda Davis. I so appreciate you!

And finally, as always, a HUGE **thank you** to all my readers who continue to pick up Aaron Ryan books and go "Hmm, I wonder what this one is about!" (As opposed to *Oh, no, here we go again. Honey! Ryan's put out another load of tripe, should we buy it???*) I really prefer the former over the latter.

I love creative writing. I love storytelling. I love holding it in my hands when it's done, and thanking my God in Heaven that I got the story, that I was given the premise, that I was given the characters and the narrative in order to craft something special. Thank you, dear reader, for continuing to believe in me and support me with your purchases and your reads. I can't tell you what it means to me: it's one of the most indescribable gifts I've ever received, and you all keep on giving it, allowing me to keep on receiving it.

Thank you so much for supporting *The Slide*, and I hope and pray that it blesses your library with repeat reads. May there never be a Norma, and may we as a civilization stay the course and not slide.

With love,

Aaron Ryan

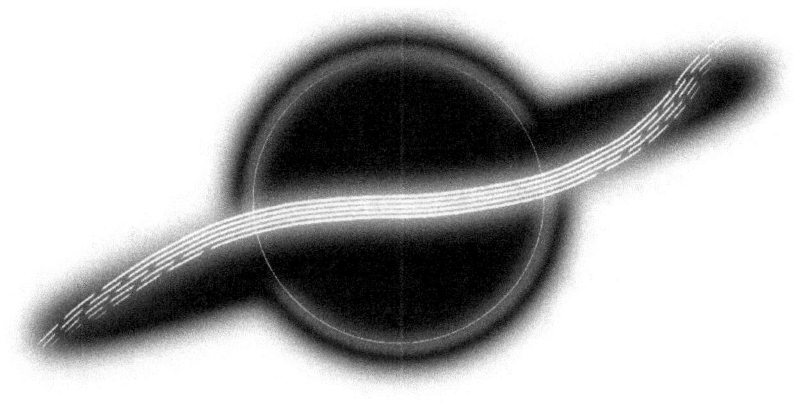

About The Author

Award-winning and bestselling author Aaron Ryan lives in Washington with his wife and two sons, along with Macy the dog, Winston the cat, and the finches Inky, Pinky, Blinky & Clyde.

He is the author of the bestselling *Dissonance* 6-book alien invasion saga, the dystopian Christian fiction saga *The End*, the sci-fi thrillers *Forecast*, *The Phoenix Experiment* and *The*

Slide, *God Is Not Santa*, *Examining The Lord of the Rings*, the children's picture books *The Ring of Truth*, *The Sword of Joy* and *The Book of Power*, the business reference books *How to Successfully Self-Publish & Promote Your Self-Published Book* and *The Superhero Anomaly*, 6 business books on voiceovers penned under his former stage name (Joshua Alexander), as well as a previous fictional novel, *The Omega Room.*

When he was in second grade, he was tasked with writing a creative assignment: a fictional book. And thus, *The Electric Boy* was born: a simple novella full of intrigue, fantasy, and 7-year-old wits that electrified Aaron's desire to write. From that point forward, Aaron evolved into a creative soul that desired to create.

He enjoys the arts, media, music, performing, poetry, and being a daddy. In his lifetime he has been an author, voiceover artist, wedding videographer, stage performer, musician, producer, rock/pop artist, executive assistant, service manager, paperboy, CSR, poet, tech support, worship leader, and more. The diversity of his life experiences gives him a unique approach to business, life, ministry, faith, and entertainment.

Aaron's favorite author by far is J.R.R. Tolkien, but he also enjoys Suzanne Collins, James S.A. Corey, Michael Crichton, Marie Lu, Madeleine L'Engle, John Grisham, Tom Clancy, C.S. Lewis, Stephen King and Dave Barry.

Aaron has always had a passion for storytelling. Visit his author website at https://www.authoraaronryan.com, the Dissonance post-apocalyptic alien invasion website at https://www.dissonancetheseries.com, or *The End* dystopian saga website at https://thisisnottheend.com.

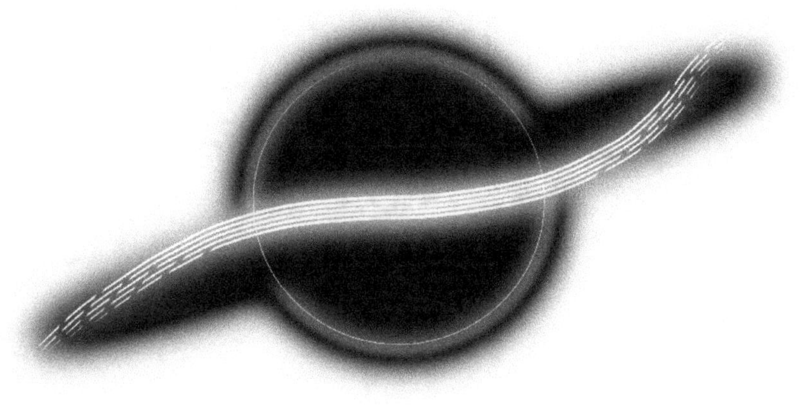

Reviews

If you liked this or any of Aaron's books, please visit the Amazon and Goodreads pages for the specific book(s) and leave a positive review. Once it shows up, please email the screenshot of it to me@authoraaronryan.com for a discount on your next book purchase from him! Thank you so much. Reviews really do help a ton!

Visit Aaron's website and sign up at the Blog:

Subscribe to Author Aaron Ryan

Follow Aaron and connect on Social Media:

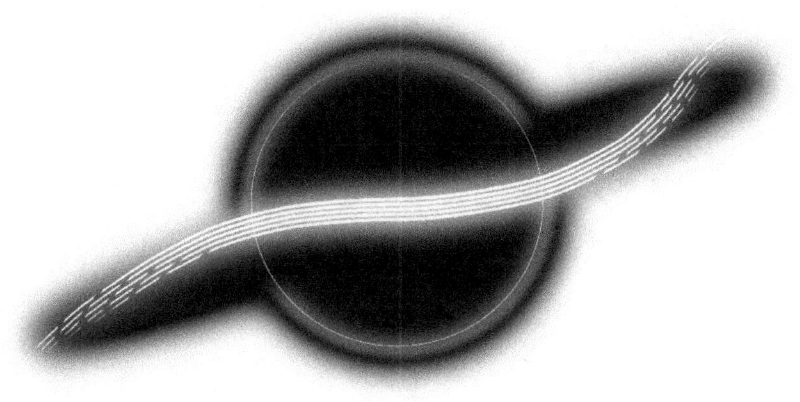

Connect with Aaron

Feel free to check out the following links for further information on Aaron:

Subscribe to Aaron's blog for free giveaways, news and new releases at **https://authoraaronryan.com/blog**

Join the Author Aaron Ryan Facebook community at
https://facebook.com/groups/authoraaronryan

Subscribe to Aaron's YouTube channel at
https://youtube.com/@authoraaronryan

Visit Aaron's social media links to connect with him at
https://dot.cards/authoraaronryan

Visit https://thisisnottheend.com/ for information on the
entire epic "The End" saga, or Aaron's website at
https://authoraaronryan.com

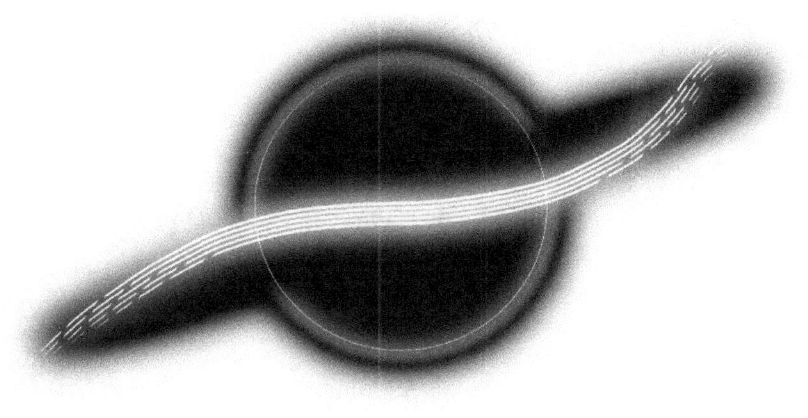

Also by the Author

As Aaron Ryan:

Dissonance Volume I: Reality

Dissonance Volume II: Reckoning

Dissonance Volume III: Renegade

Dissonance Volume IV: Relentless

Dissonance Volume Zero: Revelation

Dissonance Volume Up: Rising

The Complete Dissonance Alien Invasion Saga

The End: Alpha

The End: Omicron

The End: Omega

The Complete "The End" Christian Dystopian Saga

Forecast

The Slide

The Phoenix Experiment

The Ring of Truth

The Sword of Joy

The Book of Power

The Christian Kids Values, Identity & Affirmation Series

God Is Not Santa

Examining The Lord of the Rings: An independent critique by Aaron Ryan

The Superhero Anomaly

How to Successfully Self-Publish & Promote Your Independent Book: A Self-Publishing & Business Marketing Guide For The Independent Author

Reflections: A Compilation of Journals and Poetry

The Omega Room (abandoned in the early 90's)

Autobiography (no longer available)

Glimmerings – works of poetry

As his former stage name, Josh Alexander:

Voiceovers: A Super Business, A Super Life

Voiceovers: A Super Fun Pursuit

Voiceovers: A Super Responsibility

Running a Successful Voiceover Business

How do I get started in Voiceovers?

Five T's to Triumph: The Secrets to Getting Cast in Voiceovers